Tempting
DEMONS

Rena Marks

ELLORA'S CAVE
ROMANTICA PUBLISHING

What the critics are saying...

ഇ

5 Dark Angels "I have to start of with AWESOME! DEMONIC PASSIONS by Rena Marks is just so cool. I loved every single thing about this book. I couldn't get enough of Keara and Caleb. This book has a group of unforgettable characters, amazing action, and some totally, hot, erotic scenes. [...] Ms. Marks knows how to deliver an incredible erotic scene. There is never a dull moment in this story. [...] The ending is just to die for. I would say Ms. Marks has another hit." ~ *Dark Angel Reviews*

4.5 Rating *"Demonic Passions* is an entertaining, erotic, emotional and romantic tale about Keara's self-discovery and the man who doesn't give up on the woman he loves. [...] The sex scenes were quite deliciously scrumptious with oral stimulation, m/m love scenes and voyeurism, which will have you reaching for your own partner. [...] I look forward to reading future stories from Ms. Marks. Thanks for the adventure!" ~ *Just Erotic Romance Reviews*

An Ellora's Cave Romantica Publication

www.ellorascave.com

Tempting Demons

ISBN 9781419958625
ALL RIGHTS RESERVED.
Demonic Passions Copyright © 2008 Rena Marks
Demonic Pleasures Copyright © 2008 Rena Marks
Edited by Helen Woodall.
Cover art by Philip Fuller.

This book printed in the U.S.A. by Jasmine-Jade Enterprises, LLC.

Trade paperback Publication February 2009

TEMPTING DEMONS

ၹ

DEMONIC PASSIONS
~11~

DEMONIC PLEASURES
~185~

DEMONIC PASSIONS

ဢ

Acknowledgements

℘

Thank you, Dr. Shawn-Patrick, for never cringing during my searching questions and appalling nosiness. More importantly, thank you for continuing with the help.

Glossary

Luciefyiore (Loosh fyoree) — The demon dimension.

Luciekynokus (Loosh Kyin ah kiss) — A prestigious all-girl demon school.

Yanka (yanka) — Title of respect for a teacher used before their actual name.

Horntreau (horn troe) — A demon race. Jenesi is the last of the line and she's diluted with human blood.

Prologue

ॐ

One final push and a bloodcurdling scream.

It was over in a gush of bloody fluids, a relief so long overdue that Elizabeth sobbed.

Demitris looked at his young wife tenderly. She was absolutely stunning, this gorgeous human woman with skin so soft and hair the color of wheat. He'd used his incredible powers to force her to fall in love with him, to look upon him and see what he was not.

"Does it look human, Demi?" she asked, her voice exhausted.

"Yes, my love," he whispered, his non-human voice so deep it would normally have hurt the ears. Yet, because she loved him, she was able to hear it. "A girl. Human in every way, she looks exactly like you. Except for her hair color. That's mine."

The texture of her hair was human, though. The unusual purity of the black hair, in these days of mixed human races, pure ebony so shiny it seemed unnatural, was not only a rarity but a dead giveaway. To certain beings.

The infant never bothered to cry. She looked up at her father with trusting eyes as he swaddled her tiny body to hand to her mother.

Although exhausted, Elizabeth reached out with shaking, tired arms.

"Human babies are not born with waist-length hair, sweetheart."

Chapter One
The Need Begins

෫ා

Keara nursed her drink at the bar. There was no sense in drinking quickly enough to catch a buzz, as alcohol had no effect on her. While it was an expense she didn't need, appearances must be kept.

She eyed the cocky young man sitting a few barstools away. The friend he had brought with him disappeared, probably playing pool. He, on the other hand, stayed behind and was definitely giving her the look.

He wasn't bad. Not her type, but when the need arose she could feed from him. When she was hungry enough, anything with a penis could be her type.

She sensed rather than saw his approach. She inhaled slightly, smelling for the pheromones that rose from his heated flesh and approximated his age. Mid thirties. Good.

"Hey, beautiful."

Although his voice was deep and sexy enough, she kept herself from grimacing at the corny pickup line. Of course she was, her mirror told her that. She didn't need his affirmation.

And on the inside, she wasn't beautiful. No demon could be. Lucky for her, she was merely half.

She turned her head slowly to give him the full effect of her inherited beauty. Glossy black hair hung in sultry waves around her heart-shaped face. Her eyes were the same sky blue as those of her blonde mother but seemed more pronounced with her frame of ebony surrounding them.

Her skin was peaches and cream. Absolute perfection. High round breasts, a tiny waist and rounded hips—she could have been a model had she wanted to be in the public eye. But with a father like hers she learned to keep as much out of the spotlight as possible.

"Hi." Her voice was compelling, comforting. Sexy and alluring, but at the same time meek and non-threatening. Just the way guys liked it.

"My name's Mike."

She swirled a delicate fingertip over the rim of her glass, a flirtation move she knew well. "Come here often, Mike?"

"Not usually as a customer. I'm a cop so I come in here from time to time to make sure everything's okay."

She nearly groaned at his egotistical way of introducing his occupation. As if the uniform made the man. As if she herself couldn't choose to be a cop if she desired.

Still, one had to play the game.

"Cop, huh?" She widened her eyes, hoping she looked properly impressed. And nearly giggled as she wondered if she should ask to see his badge. He was so predictable he was already boring.

"You here all alone? That's not safe."

"I'm not looking for safe."

"What are you looking for?"

"Excitement. Hot and passionate."

"Looks like we need to talk," he said, thinking he was in charge as he sat on the stool next to her. Not realizing he was already trapped. He signaled at the bartender, holding up two fingers for more drinks.

Keara smiled as she downed the drink she already had. His ploy to get her drunk was so obvious it was pathetic.

"So, you single?" he asked.

"Yep. Just looking for a man to keep up with me."

"I can be that man," he said, deliberately looking her up and down. "What do you like?"

"Someone who wants a good time and then goes his own way."

The bartender dropped off the drinks and Mike the Cop reached for his and slid hers closer to her hand, as if to encourage her to reach for it.

She drank from the second, noticing his smug smile of satisfaction.

"Not into relationships?" he asked.

Keara finished the drink in one swallow, looked him square in the eye and said bluntly, "Just steamy sex."

Mike gulped and this time Keara slid his glass gently toward him. Taking her example, he downed the drink.

The bartender, watching all, carried two more over. Keara smiled at him and he nodded. He'd become an unknowing ally.

"Wow. A woman who just wants sex? How do you like it?" Mike asked.

"Any way I can get it."

"Most women don't admit to actually liking it. My ex-wife didn't."

"What's not to like? Sensuous kisses, lots of tongue. Lots of oral. I'd be willing to try a ménage a trois."

His interest was piqued, she could see the visions of two females together running through his tiny brain. "Oh, yeah? You got a friend?" he asked, unable to control the excitement.

Stupid man.

"*You* came with one."

"Roderick Malet?" His voice wasn't quite as deep now as it was when the conversation started. Instead it had a horrified squeak to it. He sounded like an overgrown sissy, someone who would pick a fight on the playground and then go get his big sister to save him.

"Um-hmm."

"I thought you were talking about me and two women."

"Why would I find that sexy? I much prefer the thought of me with two men."

"No way. He's not even a friend, he's just my attorney."

At last. We are getting somewhere. "What do you need an attorney for?"

"Just going through a divorce." And by the smirk on his face, it was definitely his idea. The casual way he was picking her up suggested the reason. Probably the sort of man who had an affair and when caught, told his wife she was just a good friend who offered support during a difficult time.

"So what's your name?" he asked.

Why not? "Keara."

"Umm. I like that."

"It means Dark One, 'cause I can be bad."

"How bad?"

She deliberately licked at her lip. "Very naughty."

"Were you going to give me your number?"

Keara barely glanced at the handsome young man. "I don't need a relationship right now. I just need to get fucked. Think you can help out?"

She could almost feel his cock rise.

"Hell, yeah."

"Let's go."

She downed her drink in one swallow, then rose. Knowing it would never get that far.

* * * * *

From the second floor of the bar, Caleb watched through the one-way security glass. She was leaving with yet another loser. She sure knew how to pick them. Mike Goudy, the crooked cop. Known as MG, to some. Always brash and on an ego trip.

She'd been coming here for three weeks now. She paid cash and never ran up a tab. Tonight he had his bartender eavesdropping.

He reached for his phone, pressing the button to reach Jesse.

"Boss?"

"What'd you find out?"

"Still no number or address. She did mention her first name this time, though whether it's fake we'd have no idea. Keara."

Keara. No, it was real all right. He felt it in his gut.

It used to be Jenesi. A form of Genesis. *The coming into being of something; the origin.*

"Good job, Jess. If she returns, same situation. Keep an eye and ear open."

"You got it."

Caleb hung up the phone and stared down through the window thoughtfully. There was no reason for such a gorgeous woman to hit on losers, no matter how good each one looked.

He'd watched her for a while, almost stalking her. He smiled grimly to himself. Yes, you could consider it stalking since he had his employees spying on her in addition to his watching her from the one-way glass.

She had no idea he was coming. And that someday, he would save her.

* * * * *

Keara allowed Mike to take her to his place. She didn't have to fear for her safety and pitied the women who did.

He tried to insert his key into the lock but had a little drunken difficulty. She gave a deliberate giggle that could be interpreted as nervous or tipsy. Finally the door swung open and he let her pass first.

His place looked exactly like she'd imagined. Bare white walls for a cold, unfeeling man.

She turned and he stepped immediately toward her, invading her space. She fought a sigh for his brash technique. No wonder the ex never enjoyed it.

"Show me to your room," she whispered in her most sultry voice.

He opened the bedroom door with a crash. Once there, he tried to grab her breast.

"Um. Hold on," she said with a smile plastered to her face to mask the grimace. "Get undressed."

He began pulling off his clothing while Keara felt around in her handbag for her silk scarf. She pulled the cool material out and watched while he stripped down to his dark blue t-shirt and matching dark socks.

When he pulled those off as well, she led him forcefully to the bed and pushed him onto it. She then crawled on top of him, knees on either side of his arms.

"Hey, aren't you taking your clothes off?" he complained.

"In a sec. Trust me, you'll like this." She smiled. They always did.

She tied the scarf around his wrists and fastened one end to the bed post.

"Hey, what gives? Let me go," he said, pulling against the ties.

"Shh. It'll make you come harder. I promise."

Slowly, she dragged her glossy waves of hair over his chest, pausing for a moment to kiss each nipple.

"Oh, fuck," he whispered, struggles forgotten.

She allowed herself to appreciate his broad chest and muscular biceps. Too bad his soul was so rotted. He was a beautiful male specimen despite the ugliness within that exuded from his pores in a permanent stench.

She lowered herself to the area she was most concerned with. Average in size, which was normally okay with her. In this case with his bulging muscles, however, it appeared smaller. Which was probably why the pea-brain worked out so much, trying to compensate and never realizing he defeated his own purpose by bulking up. Still, his penis was as beautiful as the rest of him. For a petite woman.

Which she wasn't.

She loved the male organ. Jutting hardness covered with silky soft skin. Sweet and powerful. Just like her.

She fed off that power. The power to make the owner groan and explode, while he didn't have a clue of what was really happening.

Keara slid her tongue up the shaft to the tiny ridge that connected the smooth head. She licked the seam of skin, thrusting her tongue into the triangle shape that was so familiar.

"Oh, baby," he groaned. "Damn, you're good."

She almost smiled. He had no earthly idea.

Keara sucked reams of power through the head of his cock. He was so far gone, he likened the feelings to a massive orgasm. But the power filled her every pore and she could see deep inside his soul.

She'd made the right choice.

He was crooked through and through. He'd cheated constantly on his wife and left her with small children so he could take up with the girlfriend. Already, he was cheating on that one too, discovering the grass wasn't greener on the other side.

The wife refused to take him back so he and his attorney put her through hell. They lied under oath to gain parenting time with the children. Parenting time meant no child support. Maintenance was wiped out with a simple call to the judge to have imaginary income imputed to the stunned woman.

She lived on antidepressants now but her life would get better really soon.

Keara smiled up at the panting Mike. "Feel good?"

"Oh, you wiped me out," he apologized. "I'm not used to finishing that fast."

She smiled. "I know what I'm doing. Let's talk about that threesome."

"Oh, no. I told you, never with another guy."

Keara rolled her head, loosening her tense neck muscles. She exerted the tiniest bit of power.

"Try again."

Mike blinked. "Is next weekend good?"

Chapter Two
In the Beginning

છ૭

She'd always known her father was different from most daddies. When she hit twenty, she found out she wasn't like the other girls either.

She always understood what her father was, of course. But she wasn't allowed to spend much of her childhood with her parents until fourteen years of age when she was banished to Earth along with them.

Six years later when she turned twenty, she was sick and no one knew why. Her parents watched her suffer for two days before they explained matters to her. What could possibly be happening? What could make her well?

They told her that mommy was human, but she was only half.

Daddy was a demon.

She was also half.

Most demons had the power to alter their appearance to humans. Her father had the additional ability to make humans fall in love with him. Not that her mother minded, it was true love as far as she was concerned.

Keara found it appalling that her father had taken her mother's will from her. She often thought, what if it were me? What if someone made me love him? How could anyone be that evil?

Not that her father was evil. He'd obviously done this once, but he truly treated Elizabeth like a goddess. But the "what if" scared Keara more than anything.

What if the demon lord had that power?

What if that was the reason why she'd fallen in love with a human male?

That hidden ability was also the main reason why her parents kept her away from teenage boys in school. Especially after the first incident with Johnny Dakin. She'd had a girlish crush on Johnny when she was fourteen, after she had hit her human puberty. Johnny was a senior in high school dating the head cheerleader.

Until Keara wanted him. Imagined herself in love with him. Imagined him loving her back. No one could understand why Johnny broke up with Rebecca and began to stalk Keara.

His attraction became an obsession. Even after Keara's crush ended and turned to stark, plain fear. The honor student and quarterback of the football team just went crazy. Literally. He was still in a mental institution to this day.

She continued to feel guilty over it.

She hadn't felt guilty over the men she'd driven insane since then.

Not that there'd been many. She certainly made sure they were deserving of the fate before doling out the punishment.

The wife beater. And the serial killer who only got off on necrophilia.

And now it appeared the snake cop and his slimy attorney were making a decent woman's life into a living hell. The wife would never know it but paybacks were a bitch. Like the old saying: *What goes around, comes around.* Especially when Keara was involved.

It was almost an obsession with her. She'd gotten a taste of the power and was reluctant to let go. At first she'd only visited the bar a couple times a month, lately it was once a week, and now this would be her second visit three days later. She'd have to get a handle on things.

But in spite of that, she was visiting again tonight. First though, a stop at her parents' house. Her father had called her earlier and wanted to talk. It would be a serious issue since he called tonight, her mother's Bunko night. Obviously he didn't want Mom to overhear.

She rapped lightly on the door before pushing it open and calling out.

"Dad?"

No answer. She shut the door behind her and wandered through the house. She found her father where he usually was, apron clad in the kitchen simmering various sauces and stews.

"Daddy."

He leaned down to hug her, giving a little squeeze. "I'm glad you're here."

"Cooking for the Bunkos tonight?" She teased, referring to the neighborhood women who met monthly for food, gossip and games.

He grinned back. "I told them I'd take stuff over when it was done. Sit, babisna. We need to talk."

"Sounds serious."

"It is."

She sat, contemplating the gravity of his deep voice.

"Enishka has risen."

"And found that you've married mom?"

Her father nodded, deeply solemn. "Now he wants her daughter. You."

Keara was silent and her father continued on. "Don't worry. He'll take you over my dead body."

She grimaced. "Exactly what I don't want, Dad."

Enishka, or the demon lord, had his eye on her mother all those years ago. Had actually raised the human infant to be his bride. Demitris hid his ability to make others fall in love with him and used it on her mother, easily stealing her away from the demon lord.

Enishka was banished from his dimension for twenty-five years. For how could a demon underling exert more power than he? It appeared his time was up.

"I don't want you to do anything silly," Demitris warned.

"Of course not. But I am stocking up on power."

Her father agreed. "You need to protect yourself as best you can. Just remember everything I've taught you and be careful with the power sucking."

"Oh, I do, petreno. I'm a big girl."

"You'll always be my little girl."

She smiled and leaned toward her father for a kiss. His natural skin was hard and cold, more of a reptilian texture than the soft, warm feel of a human.

"Where's your human face?" she chided. "Anyone could have walked through that door."

His eyes glowed with demonic mischief. "Wouldn't it be great if it was that crazy old bat across the street?"

"Nope," Keara laughed. "You drive her any crazier and mom will catch on. Isabel's her friend," she reminded.

Her father sighed. "I've given your mother everything she wants for too many years."

"You love it," Keara laughed again. He was insanely fanatical about Elizabeth Knight, enough to happily give up his own dimension and hide among humans. "And I love you. I'll see you later," she said with another kiss to his roughened cheek.

* * * * *

Keara entered the bar as usual. She headed to her favorite spot and the bartender nodded, sliding her a drink without bothering to ask what she'd like.

She hoped Mike would be in tonight. She was ready for round two. Knew which direction she'd take next for an even bigger power explosive.

Instead of the anticipation of Mike however, instant need filled her midsection, melting her insides with liquid heat. She inhaled deeply, smelling the pheromones she'd smelled so frequently here. The enigma she hadn't yet met. The whole reason why she was drawn to this spot.

She never bothered to turn her head. "You've been watching me."

"Yeah." The voice held promise. It rolled over her fevered body like rumbling silk, cooling and soothing at once.

"Why?"

"Wondering why you could keep picking the wrong type."

"Are you so sure I am?"

"You can't reach satisfaction with any of those losers."

"I'm not looking for love."

"No one looks for it."

Finally. A comment worth her full attention. Keara slowly turned in her seat to face the stranger who had approached. And to see the owner of that incredibly sexy, deep voice.

He was gorgeous, although with her own looks such a hindrance, she never really cared about anyone else's beauty as being a desirable trait. With her father's appearance, she learned to love past the skin. But the look that met her first glance was impressive, blond hair with darker blond eyebrows set over contrasting chocolate brown eyes. Narrow nose. A sexy cut of jaw covered lightly in darker stubble. Stern, masculine features. A Greek god come to life.

She'd forgotten what she was thinking. Geez, his eyes were gorgeous and she'd been told that often enough about her own. Entranced, she used her gifts to look deeper.

Into the windows of his soul.

Ruthless. Powerful. Determined. Sensuous. Raw sexuality.

Familiarity.

She froze as shock hit her midsection at the recognition.

Caleb watched her reaction. It definitely was Keara, though he'd known her as Jenesi. Finally. She stared into his eyes, stunned. How would she react to seeing him in the flesh for the first time?

About as expected. She clammed up. He could almost see the shutters that veiled her gorgeous eyes with a sweep of the long ledge of black lace that hid the sultry blue light long enough to mask her emotions.

So she'd pretend ignorance. He held out a hand.

"Caleb Van Trump."

"Nice to meet you, Caleb."

"Are we meeting, Keara?"

Like he expected, she didn't respond to the odd question, choosing instead to ignore it.

"Mind if I sit?"

She shrugged and he sat in the seat next to her.

"Why are you here?"

"I'm just meeting people. No crime there."

"No crime," he agreed. "Unless someone's getting hurt."

She almost snorted. "Please. We're all consenting adults. There's no pain involved."

"Then you'd like a normal relationship. With someone who knows the game you're playing."

"You offering?"

"Don't I always?"

Once again, there was no response. Then a hesitant, "I don't understand what you mean."

"Don't you?"

As if tired of playing a game in which she didn't know the rules, she tossed a twenty onto the bar and grabbed her purse.

"Wait," he said, reaching out and wrapping long fingers around her bare arm. "I'm sorry. We got off on the wrong foot. And I think we can help each other out."

The touch of his bare skin to hers was so warm and sensuous, it felt magnetically charged. How could she not want it? Temptation was so sweet she could almost taste it.

"How?" she murmured.

"You're looking for guys. And I can help you find them." He pointed to a mirrored window high in the bar. "My office. From where I see lots of interesting things."

"I'll think about it," she hedged. "What would you want in return?"

"Nothing."

"There's always something." Her voice was harsh as she walked away without a backward glance.

Caleb watched her walk and cursed himself mentally. Dammit, he'd come on too strong. She refused to believe in their connection and wanted to pretend nothing out of the ordinary existed. He could let her pretend for a while but he was so excited to find her, it was unacceptable that she'd deny their attraction.

And he'd missed her. Worried over her. Craved her, like a man craves the very air in his lungs.

Still she denied him.

How could he care for someone who refused to be protected? How could he love someone who refused to be cherished?

He knew she believed her psychic abilities had contacted him all those years ago. She would turn tail and run if she thought it was a remote possibility that he'd searched for her instead. Keara, the most sought after woman on the planet was tired of being chased. She'd changed her name and was learning to fight back. And he didn't blame her.

Okay, so he'd slow down. He'd let her take the reins. For now.

Caleb glanced at Jesse and the other man gave an almost imperceptible nod. She'd be back.

When Keara did return later in the week, to the bartender's frustration she sat at a more secluded table. Jesse couldn't see or hear a thing from his spot behind the bar.

Mike waved at her from two tables down and she gave him an encouraging smile. He grinned broadly and whispered to his attorney. Both looked her way and she gave a slight finger wave.

It didn't take long for the men to approach.

She twirled a lock of glossy hair around her finger. "Who's your friend, Mike?"

"A good friend. Roderick," he said, using the words she put into his mind.

Roderick looked slightly taken aback at being called a good friend, then pleasantly pleased. She guessed he didn't have too many. When she looked into his soul tonight, she'd know for sure.

She held her hand out and gave a slow, sexy smile to the attorney. "What are you boys doing here tonight?" She directed the question to Roderick, trying to pull him in.

"Just discussing Mike's case, someplace where we won't be overheard. We both work for the city and can't use an office there. Too many ears."

"Ever think of using Mike's apartment? It's nearby," she said, casually letting it slip that she'd been there.

Roderick looked intrigued. "The drinks and the company are much better here though."

She laughed, a light tinkling sound meant to titillate a man's senses. Slowly she uncrossed, then re-crossed her shapely long legs for his enjoyment.

He stared unwaveringly. He'd be easy. Still too macho for the power conduit of a threesome however, so she'd have to tread lightly.

"Mike," she purred. "How about another drink?"

"Sure, Keara. Anything." He practically begged to fetch for her and walked quickly to the bar.

Unfortunately, Roderick noticed.

"Got him whipped, do you?"

She shrugged. "He's sweet."

Roderick raised his brows.

"Okay, then. He's not quite as experienced as I would have liked."

She could see by his face that the reasoning was much more plausible.

"What are you after?"

"A man who may want to inflict a little bit of pain on his, umm… Oh. So. Willing. Partner," she said deliberately and watched his expression.

Bingo.

"Yeah," Jesse answered the phone on just one short burst of a ring.

"What the hell's she doing at a table?"

"Don't know, boss. Can't hear a thing."

"Dammit to hell. Think she's onto you?"

"I can't see how. It doesn't seem to be, she hasn't glanced this way once. I think maybe she sat at a table to separate the two guys, to send one over here for the drinks."

"I should have the damn place wired," Caleb muttered.

Jesse was silent for a moment. "Going a little overboard with this chick, ain't you, boss?"

Caleb sighed. "Don't worry about it. Go back to bartending. I'm coming down."

He probably did look neurotic over Keara. If only they knew.

Mike returned with the drinks, carrying her usual martini rather sloppily because his eyes were focused on her. Looking past him, Keara caught the bartender's wave. She raised her glass to him and returned her attention to the staring attorney and besotted cop.

She slipped another mental push into Mike's Neanderthal brain to start the ball rolling.

"Keara," he asked suddenly. "Doing anything special tonight?"

"Nope. Just here killing time," she smiled.

"Want to stop by my place?"

What the hell for, idiot? Do I have to put every single thought into your head?

"I would but I've interrupted your business discussion. You two probably would like to finish it up."

"We can finish," Mike said. "Then you can come over. We'll have a party."

"Keara."

She looked up and tried not to groan at the deep, sexy voice she knew so well. "Caleb," she said, her voice on a whisper. What was he doing here? He'd ruin everything.

"What are you up to?" he nearly growled.

"Just talking."

Caleb narrowed his eyes at Mike. "Goudy."

Mike's personality returned without Keara's influence. He gave a hostile glare before muttering, "Van Trump."

Keara watched the display curiously. Caleb and Mike obviously had dealings in the past.

Caleb turned his sexy eyes back to her. "I thought I'd hear from you?"

She shrugged.

"You ready for that tour now?"

"I'm, um, busy tonight."

"Not with these losers. It's not safe."

"Hey," Goudy protested as he rose.

"Wait a minute!" Roderick joined in.

The glare Caleb gave had both men returning to their seats. And had Keara rising from hers.

"I need to talk to you," she said shortly. She whispered a mental command to Goudy. *"Stay."*

She walked quickly over to the phone area where things were a little quieter. Caleb followed, eyes narrowed.

"What is going on?" she demanded.

"It's not safe. You know those two somehow. What are you up to? Trying to get yourself killed?"

"I know what I'm doing, dammit."

"Then what is it?" he drawled.

She almost slipped up but caught herself just in time. "I'm a big girl. I can take care of myself."

He looked down at her long enough to make her feel petite compared to him. Her chin rose just a fraction of an inch higher.

Determined. Stubborn.

He tried a new tactic. "I'm just worried about you. There's two of them and I know all about them. They hurt women."

She tried not to soften but felt her reserve slip. "Look, Caleb, if you and I are going to be friends and I'm going to continue dropping in here, then you need to back off. I have my own life and I don't need anyone's protection."

"Why do I look familiar to you?"

"I don't know," she said after a brief hesitation.

"You've needed me throughout the years. I dreamed about you while you dreamed about me. There's something between us."

"That's ridiculous," she scoffed.

"You deny dreaming of me?"

A version of the truth would probably be best. "I dreamed of someone who resembled you. Maybe you dreamed of someone who resembled me too, but they're dreams, Caleb. They're in no way connected."

Poor Caleb was human. He was probably baffled as to why so long ago she'd obviously called out to him psychically. He'd never believe such things as demons existed and that she exerted power as a child when she didn't even know what powers she had. He looked stubborn for a moment before his face smoothed over.

"Maybe you're right. It does seem a little silly," he conceded.

She slung her handbag over her shoulder. "Look, I'm heading out of here. I'll talk to you later."

"How?"

"Excuse me?"

"Shall I call you?"

"Um, sure."

"I'll need your number."

Keara rattled it off without a pause or slowing down in any way. Then she smiled prettily and swayed away, knowing without a doubt that his eyes were on her ass as she returned to Mike and Roderick.

"I'm ready to leave," she said to Mike.

Roderick was the one to speak. "You sure you want to come with us after all that?"

"I do what I want when I want. Especially when someone tells me I can't," she said, looking him square in the eye.

It didn't take long to get to Mike's apartment. After they walked into the front door, she gave a mental push to Mike to "remember" an errand at work.

"I won't be long," he promised Keara.

"Take your time," she said, while Roderick said nothing at all.

The door had barely closed when he turned to her and said, "So. What shall we do while we wait?"

Keara stood. "Let's see what you got."

There was a gleam in his eye and a smirk on his face. He unbuttoned his shirt. His movements strutted, a typical cocky male, as though he was sure she'd appreciate what she saw.

And she did. Especially what was inside. For there was no guilt at taking what he offered.

Utter, vile corruption. The perfect match to Mike Goudy. And he'd been sweet when she drank him down.

Keara inhaled deeply as she unlatched his belt and stared into his eyes. She could see his thoughts as clearly as though they were her own.

I'll enjoy the leather of my belt ripping across her white ass.

Not a chance, Mr. Malet.

His fat, short penis burst free as she tugged on his pants.

I hope she's got a virgin ass. I'd love to rip through it, to pound into it 'til I come.

Keara merely smiled at his thoughts.

"Take it into your mouth," he demanded when his erection was freed.

They were so cocky when she didn't tie them first. Oh, well, it was different.

"If I choose to," she told him.

"You must like pain."

"Oh, I lied. I don't care for my own, thanks." She kept her voice deliberately sweet.

"You're way too uppity. You need to be taught your place."

"What is my place?"

"Tied up and naked. Taught to serve a man. I'll enjoy teaching you."

Keara smiled. "Not before you're taught your own lesson."

"Excuse me, bitch?"

He wound his fist in the back of her lush locks. And yanked her face up to him.

But only because she let him.

Keara rolled her eyes up to look at him. Let him see the glow of her inner demon. He opened his mouth to scream and she caught it with her lips.

His dark power was rich. He was quite the evil soul, Keara thought as she sucked it up to store in her reserves.

* * * * *

The ringing of the telephone woke her. Was it morning already? She was groggy and needed sleep. Her heat phase was high, the amount of power she'd inhaled wouldn't settle for a few days.

"H'lo?" she mumbled.

"How'd it go last night?"

Caleb. She'd know the sexiness of that voice anywhere. He'd obviously paid attention when she'd rattled off her number.

She smiled grimly. A version of the truth would suffice. "Another loser. You were right. I am so done picking up guys in bars. I'm done dating. I'm done everything."

"Why don't you try waiting for a guy to pick up on you?"

"I do. It's not like I approach *them* in bars. I just sit and have a drink."

He laughed. "Yeah, I can see that. So you coming in tonight?"

"No. I told you. I'm done with it."

"You don't have to come in to pick up a guy. Come in to see me."

"Why? I'm talking to you now."

"You can't remember how good I look when you just talk to me," he retorted.

There was a pause on her end of the phone. "Are you flirting with me, Caleb?"

"Maybe. Depends on if you'll take me up on it."

She wasn't quite sure how she felt about that. A good guy. A good human guy. But then she'd thought that about the last one she had.

No way.

He laughed, a deep rich baritone. "Come hang out and quit thinking about so much, baby. I'll have some food brought up and you can help me watch through the security window. You'll see how I first noticed you."

Her curiosity piqued and she was lost. It wouldn't be long before she had to find another bar, anyway. Caleb was becoming too curious about her.

Chapter Three
The Need is Satiated

શ

She entered the bar she'd visited so frequently and the bouncer at the door took her directly up a back flight of stairs.

"The boss is expecting you."

"Caleb owns the bar?"

The muscle-bound man appeared surprised by her question, as if she was the only person that didn't know. "Yeah."

They'd arrived at the top of the stairs and he rapped on the heavy door with his knuckles. The door was buzzed unlocked and the bouncer opened it.

Caleb sat at a desk on the phone. He motioned for her to come in and the door closed softly behind her with a click.

She walked across the room, watching his facial expressions as he spoke. He was harder somehow and she knew by the conversation it was focused on business.

He reached out and stroked her shoulder as he spoke. Casual, almost as if he thought nothing of it. She, on the other hand, nearly went through the roof with her rising heat phase. She'd gorged on a load of power last night and it hadn't settled. She'd have to take a step back if she wasn't going to jump him.

Her nipples peaked and she inhaled deeply, fighting the urge at the last moment to arch her back and thrust her breasts outward. She was pleasure-drunk and he didn't even know it, as busy as he was with his business call.

She wanted to writhe beneath him naked. She wanted to whimper as he tugged and pulled on her hardened nipples.

Moisture slickened her cleft and her labia swelled. She could actually feel them, swollen between her thighs. If she walked right now, they'd rub together erotically, the smoothly shaven skin at its most sensitive.

Good thing he was human or he'd smell her liquid sweetness and know how turned on she was by the slightest touch of his hand.

She had to get away. But why was it she craved the pheromones that rose from his skin? Was attracted to him like a bee to nectar?

He hung up the phone and turned to her. The smile that crossed his face lit his eyes. "Thanks for coming," he said, pulling her toward him for a casual kiss to the cheek.

She didn't mean to but she remained slightly stiff. Trying so hard to control her raging hormones.

"What's wrong?" he asked.

"Nothing." She smiled. How could she explain that it was best not to touch her?

"Hungry?"

Not for food. "No, I'm not. Not right now."

"Okay." He walked her to the security window, keeping his hand on her elbow where she could feel the heat from his body. She could smell his aftershave wafting up, mixing with those tempting pheromones. It tantalized her senses and made her want to throw caution to the wind and obtain a release, just once. To enjoy herself instead of stealing power. To appreciate real sex without a purpose.

"Geez, you have cameras and windows? Peeping Tom much?" she joked.

He shrugged. "Voyeurism does something for me."

Dammit. Another curl of heat just slammed the walls of her vagina with his words. She'd ignore them the best she could.

"So this is where I first noticed you. Seeking out whichever losers you could find."

It was her turn to shrug. "I don't want a relationship."

"People come to bars to find relationships."

"Men come to bars to find relationships. Women come for other reasons."

"Like?"

"Relaxation. Drinks. Dancing."

"Yeah? So if that's what most women come for, why are *you* here?"

She paused. Then decided on honesty. To a point. "A one-night stand."

"Excuse me?"

"Look, I'm hornier than most women. I need sex." It was the easiest way to explain her supernatural heat drive.

"You don't have to use losers."

"You think a nice, normal man will want to be with me for one thing only?" she mocked.

"Why just that? Why not have a real relationship with someone?"

Because how do you explain to a new boyfriend that you're half demon? And that men, no matter if they're demon or human, just use you? I'm the epitome of a biracial relationship, sweetheart.

"I'm not interested in having a relationship. I just want the sex."

Caleb stepped closer to her. Close enough to give her a whiff of that aftershave that lurked on the edge of the magnetic pheromones. "Try it, baby. You might," he leaned in to hover above her sexy lips, "like the two together."

He stayed poised there above her mouth, waiting for her move. As if he knew she was uncontrollably insatiable.

Need arose and slammed into full force. Moisture gathered between her legs as her heat spiked again and she literally felt like purring.

It was just an inch to raise and meet him. One tiny inch and a horny little demon could have heaven.

She rose onto her toes and pressed her lips to his.

The rush of heat was instantaneous. She gasped as together they opened their mouths to melt into one another.

He pulled her into him with one muscled arm while the other gripped the back of her head and kept her pressed tightly to him. He searched her mouth, exploring and tasting, while she thought she'd die from the sheer pleasure. Who would think a plain mortal could raise her heat this high?

Not even *he* had done so. But she refused to think about *him*. Not while another had his hands on her.

Caleb's hand left the back of her head and trailed down to below her shirt. She felt him casually brush the skin of her abdomen before his fingers slid slowly upward. They skimmed under her bra until he reached her nipple.

The tight bud ached so badly, it nearly reached out for his touch. He rolled it between his thumb and forefinger, giving her pleasure so intense she cried out.

Gently he plucked at it and at her gasp of satisfaction, reached for her left nipple with his other hand and tweaked them both at the same time.

She was used to *giving* pleasure this intense, not receiving it. She drove men insane with need and when they wanted her so desperately, they were receptive to her mental push for falling completely, utterly in love. For the first time in her life, she could understand how and why.

"Caleb." She moaned his name.

"Mmm?"

"I need you."

"I know, sweetie."

Somehow, his hand delved into her jeans without her being aware of becoming unsnapped and unzipped. But there was his finger, inserted deeply and stroking her inner passage so deliciously.

Way too much temptation. She'd never be able to stop, not until her need was sated.

She found herself pressing into his hand, melting, her juices flowing over his finger. Slowly she rolled her hips, masturbating herself uninhibitedly.

"Come for me, baby," he whispered. She could hear how turned on he was in his voice.

She was so close, with his warm hand cupping her sex and his middle finger stroking her deep inside. She wanted to squirm and twist around his hand, to press against it as hard as she could.

Then, with his middle finger inside her, massaging the lip of her cervix, his thumb reached out and pressed against her clitoris.

Her body rang out and she arched her back. One deep inhalation and she exploded, liquid heat pouring from her passage as she readied for his cock.

Her body quivered around his hand, her arms and legs tingling with the force of her climax.

She expected him to throw her on the desk and fuck her now. To take his turn. Instead, he held her close.

"Feel better?" he asked.

"Umm." Although curious, she didn't want to ask how he knew.

"You need me, Keara," he whispered against her forehead. "Like I need you. But not today. I'll wait. You'll trust me first."

"If you're waiting for trust, you'll lose out," she warned. "Take what you need now while you have the chance. It won't come again."

"We'll see."

Fire sparked in her eyes at the challenge. She needed to be careful or they'd glow.

A knock sounded at his office door and he adjusted her clothing for her before buzzing it open.

"Delivery, boss."

Still watching Keara, Caleb motioned his head toward a side table in his office where the employee left the bag. When the door closed behind him, he kissed her gently on the forehead and retrieved the bag.

"Come on, baby. Let's sit here and watch people while we eat."

She was wary still, untrusting that he'd let her go without obtaining his own satisfaction. But she came toward him anyway, sitting primly in a stuffed chair and peering down through the window with him. He handed her a box and fork before taking his own.

They began to eat in silence. Eventually, curiosity overcame her as he knew it would.

"What do you watch for?"

How could he tell her he'd watched all his life for her?

"Anything. Any trouble that might arise."

"Like?"

"Fights. Guys dropping something into women's drinks. Crooked cops with their attorneys," he finished pointedly.

She rolled her eyes in response.

"Gorgeous women hitting on losers."

"How do you know if they're losers?"

"I see them. I know them."

"But I don't."

"Yes, you do."

"How would I know if someone is a loser before getting to know him?"

"We both know you're not the average woman, Keara. Just like we both know there's something unexplainable between us."

For once, she didn't argue. She didn't acknowledge his statement at all and it was a challenge to him.

He moved closer to her. Close enough to smell the flowers of her faint perfume. Close enough to sense the satiny softness of her skin. Close enough to taste her, if she'd let him. If she'd trust him.

"There's something very unusual between us," he whispered, his lips close to hers.

"Maybe," she hedged. Finally.

He leaned in and tasted her ripe bottom lip. Nipped it ever so gently and then kissed it better. Sucked it until she inhaled with pleasure. Until her tongue searched for his and the kiss deepened. Until she gasped and he knew he had her.

"Deny it," he challenged.

She kissed him back, finally. Lost. Out of control. "I can't," she admitted.

"Then come home with me."

"No."

"Why not?"

He knew the answer. Because he was dangerous and he forced her to face her fears.

"I don't know you."

"You don't know half the losers you leave with. You don't even know enough to admit they're losers."

He was right and they both knew it.

"What if I go home with you and you're a loser?"

"Then you'll know tomorrow, won't you?" he asked. "No different from with anyone else."

And then he slipped his hand into her bra and hardened her nipple again.

Need slammed into her. Again. He knew how to raise her temperature, call her heat. Was it instinct?

She knew without a doubt she had to finish this. For once, she had to have complete fulfillment. A cock to fill her void. To rock her to completion.

Just once.

Then she'd be fine. She'd go on her way and find a new bar to search out creeps.

She curled her fingers into his hair as she brought his mouth to hers. She searched his mouth aggressively as if seeking something.

And found what she wanted when she nodded.

"Let's go."

His eyebrows raised in surprise. She could tell he was prepared for a lot more cajoling. But he didn't seem as if he was going to argue when he took her hand to pull her to her feet.

"Where are we going?" she asked.

"Just upstairs to my loft."

"Another upstairs?"

He nodded. "My apartment."

It was reached through a tiny staircase in his office. The apartment itself barely registered in her heated brain, she was so intent on getting him naked.

Their lips meshed together in panted, heated breaths. She sucked his lower lip, nipping it gently. His biceps were hard steel beneath her curled fingers.

He pulled her roughly to him so there was only the thin layer of clothing between them. Pressed her against him to feel his stiff erection so there was no doubt as to how eager he was for her.

His neck was so tempting, heady with a pulse throbbing. She kissed the throb and sucked the warm skin beneath her lips. He was delicious.

What else would taste good? She wanted to taste him from head to toe, inch by inch.

He was maneuvering her into his bedroom slowly, hard muscled thighs pressing against hers to walk her backward.

He peeled her clothing from her body, her blouse, her bra, and then she kicked off her shoes at the same time she yanked off her jeans, leaving her clad in bikini underpants and nothing else.

She was soaked. Her panties were no barrier against the slickness that creamed from her passage.

He paid repeated attention to her breasts, massaging the pale globes and sucking the hard pink tips. Licking them, refusing to allow her nipples to lose their erection.

She didn't think she could stand it.

She removed her own underwear, hoping to encourage him to touch her, to finger her. To pleasure her.

He just licked her breasts. Wet them fully, every delightful inch.

She was on fire. She wanted to throw him down and ride him until she came in fierce waves, then continue riding him until she orgasmed again.

She wanted to suck him hard and swallow his ejaculation. She wanted him to be so weak with pleasure that they'd crash afterward, wrapped in each other's arms.

Where did that come from?

The thought made her angry. Could it be she who was so needy she'd crave being wrapped in his arms?

Her movements became choppy and aggressive. In turn, he became gentle and loving. The perfect balance.

But she'd thought that about the last one she was with.

This was just sex, dammit. Not power stealing, just good old fashioned orgasms.

He lay her on the bed. "Move up some more," he whispered.

She was already at the side of the bed and looked at him, puzzled.

"Exactly," he whispered again. "Drop your head over the edge."

He stood over her and spread his legs over her face, his enormous cock primed and ready before her mouth.

So tempting. She kissed it, then opened wide and took it into the warmth of her mouth.

He groaned at the sucking. Before she knew it he had leaned over her body and spread her vaginal lips with one hand.

Then his warm wet tongue was there, licking and tasting and giving pleasure unimaginable. How could she possibly concentrate on bringing him satisfaction when he distracted her with his own ministrations?

She sucked harder, loving his groans.

But then he attacked her clit in return. He nibbled it gently and French-kissed the whole area. She was so distracted and just wanted her release, quickly. They could go slower next time.

What next time?

She released his cock so he could lie down next to her on the bed. He reached for a condom and rolled it on in one smooth move. She straddled him and took that luscious, stiff rod into her body.

He fitted perfectly.

As if made for her. For her exact dimensions. He filled her up in both length and girth.

She rode hard. Uninhibitedly.

"Slow down, baby. I only have so much control."

She smiled at him, and he reached down and pulled one leg straight so he could flip her onto her back.

And then he thrust. She wrapped long legs around his waist and hung on as he bucked into her.

Her sheath gripped him, trying to pull him deeper into her as it reached for something on just the other side of this reality.

It grabbed her and she curled her body as the waves washed over her. Her body shuddered with internal contractions that went on and on, her organs quivering uncontrollably.

She had no idea it could be like this.

She looked up at him. He'd watched her face while she came. Saw the emotions that stole across her soul. But now it was his turn.

But she wasn't prepared for what happened then.

He delved into her, harder and faster and she could literally feel his heart race, almost as demonic as she. He stiffened and pressed his face into her neck.

"Fuck," he groaned as he came.

She gripped his cock with her internal muscles as he shuddered into her body.

She seized again, fireworks exploding throughout her system. A second orgasm, blossoming from the first.

Never before had that happened.

He turned to his side, pulling her thigh over his hip while they were still connected. He ran a finger down the side of her cheek.

"Thank you," he whispered.

She smiled lazily at him. "No, thank you."

"My pleasure," he said before touching soft lips to hers. His lids were heavy. "Ready for a relationship in addition to the great sex?"

"Nope."

He smiled against her lips.

"It really was great sex, though," she conceded.

"You could have it whenever you want."

"Why?" she asked.

"So suspicious. Just because we both enjoy it. It's good for us."

"What's the catch?"

"Does there have to be one?"

"There always is."

"It's small enough. Sex together, but no one else."

"I told you. I don't want or need a relationship."

He sighed, a long exuberant breath. "So stubborn. Suspicious and stubborn and... sexy as hell. You'll drive me insane."

He slowly pulled from her body and reached for a tissue to dispose of the condom in a nearby wastebasket. Then he laid flat on his back, curling her head onto his shoulder. His breathing was slowing down and his eyes were shut.

"Tired?" she asked, curious. It must be a human trait to relax afterward, instead of feeling energized. But how would she know? Technically she wasn't human and hadn't had real sex. Not like this. Not with satisfaction. Although once, she'd convinced herself it was satisfying. Now she knew otherwise. That relationship had been lukewarm at best.

"Mmm," he muttered.

She decided to close her eyes and enjoy the feel of his skin under her cheek for just the briefest moment.

Because it felt so right. So different from before.

He held her tightly and she curled her face into the side of his neck where she smiled softly. When she was sure he couldn't see her. Her body was soft and languid, for once satiated.

This was real sex.

How amazing. So unlike the power stealing, soul sucking. It was so hard to break from that. And that was addictive, no doubt about it. Hard to break from, because the more men you possessed, the more you craved. She wondered if sex would be that way.

She was so relaxed. She could close her eyes for just a second and pretend there was nothing more to life but this moment in time. She was barely aware when the world faded to nothing.

She was surprised a couple hours later when she awakened. She hadn't meant to fall asleep. She'd never let her guard down that much before.

She'd never even slept with *him*.

This wasn't right. She had a battle that could break out at any time and she should be out stealing power, not enjoying herself.

Beside her, Caleb still slept. She'd sneak out before he woke. Silently, she slid from his bed, careful not to wake him.

Her body was relaxed from the force of her orgasm. Languid. She reached for her panties lying on the floor and felt the room spin.

She closed her eyes and the force of sudden wind dropped her to her knees.

When the whirlwind stopped, there was instant chatter all around her. Creatures, demons, all sorts of different species, conversing in any language and understanding all.

She knew where she was.

Hell.

Chapter Four
The Challenge of Temptation

&

She was on her hands and knees, stomach sucked in, breasts thrust out. Unashamed of her nakedness. She was beautiful and she knew it. As did the rest of the creatures that admired her, unlike the old days when they pretended humans were ugly. Shunned them, even the innocent children.

"Keara Knight," whispered the throaty, broken voice as if it had forgotten how to speak.

"Enishka," she responded.

A slap bounded across her face from the dark-robed demon nearest to her. Slime dripped from his arm as he lowered it and she realized his entire flesh was made from it, a Rot Demon. The worst creature imaginable. A demon who had dedicated his life to uncontrollable soul sucking.

"No one is allowed to call him by name," the Rot Demon snapped. "Refer to him only as the demon lord. Master."

She dropped her head to acquiesce.

"My lovely." The demon lord whined. "So beautiful. You were to have been my child."

She didn't answer for there seemed to be nothing to say.

"How is your mother?"

"She is fine. Beautiful. Happy."

"Still in love with your father?"

"Of course."

Now it was the demon lord's turn for silence and Keara knew what the problem was. He was jealous of her father's power and infuriated that it obviously had no time restraints.

That for over twenty-five years and a dimension later it was still in full force.

"You were raised amongst the humans," he hissed. "I'd like you to spend time in *my* dimension amid the rest of your kind."

Very untrue but she knew better than to call him a liar. He knew good and well that as Jenesi she'd spent her entire childhood trapped in his dimension. She chose her words carefully. "At this time, I'm not looking for change."

"Your mother and father owe me."

She shrugged. "I do not."

Her eyes glowed as brightly as his. They stared at each other, both at a standstill. The swamp was hushed as the twin red lights burned bright enough to fill the darkness. In response, hers burned blue to counter his. There was an undercurrent of excitement in the swamp, a nervous twitching energy that could be felt by everyone present. Never before had they seen anyone's eyes glow as brightly as the master's.

"After all I've done for you? Innocent offspring of two breeds? I allowed you to remain in Luciefyiore and attend the finest school. I kept you from being banished until my absence, in which it was out of my control."

Allowed? Forced was more like it. Her banishment to Earth had been a blessing.

She shrugged, still refusing to speak, but losing the eye contact. And was surprised that her glow had not only rivaled his, but may have actually exceeded it. Apparently truths and lies were intermingled here anyway so arguing wasn't going to get her far.

"That is your final choice?" he asked after long moments of waiting.

"It is."

The swamp was still silent. Everyone waited for his response. Would he erupt and throw a temper tantrum?

Would he beg? Did he have a trump card to play? Could he force her to his bidding?

"So be it. Do not ever ask for my help. I only help out my own," he spat hatefully.

She didn't bother to respond as the whirlwind sucked the air from her lungs and hurled her painfully into to her own dimension.

Keara was left gasping on Caleb's floor before she could recover enough to dress. Her fingers were shaking so badly she'd have to wait anyway. What did Enishka mean by his last statement? Would he be trying to reach his tentacles out to cause a problem for someone she loved? Surely he couldn't touch her parents, but was that in the banishment decree?

She pulled on her jeans and then paused when Caleb sat up in bed. "Keara? Baby, what are you doing out of bed?"

Think fast. "Nothing. Nightmare. It's fine."

"Why didn't you reach for me?"

"Excuse me?" Did he mean physically? Or was he talking about pulling him into her dreams, the way she used to when she was a child?

"Face it. You know I wasn't just a dream. I was more of your guardian angel. I counseled you all through Johnny Dakin and then Dean."

"Caleb, I didn't know I was able to contact anyone mentally. I'm sorry I pulled you into my strange life."

"I'm not complaining. I'd never complain. But I am used to helping you. Until you shut me out during Dean."

"I don't want to talk about him."

"Talking about it releases it."

"No. Dean was the most painful thing I've ever been through."

Caleb's eyes softened. "You did good, Keara. You walked away with dignity and grace. He was the one in the wrong but you didn't let it make you bitter."

"Are you sure?"

"Of course."

But she knew differently. If she hadn't been bitter enough to punish other men for Dean's mistakes, she wouldn't be in a testing phase right now. That was something she couldn't share with Caleb, however. He would never understand about demons and dimensions and half-breeds. He'd run for the hills if she tried to explain.

"Your only mistake was locking me out from that point on." He sat next to her and pressed a tiny, soft kiss onto her temple. Keara closed her eyes for the briefest second, allowing herself to experience bliss she didn't deserve.

"Let me help you, baby," he whispered, kissing her again.

When he kissed her like that, she did feel good and whole and pure. As if her inner demon melted away.

He had been her friend once. As a child. The only one she ever had. So what if in her innocent youth she thought she'd made him up? A product of her desperate mind?

He had years to hurt her and never had. She'd be careful, she'd be wary. But just once, she wanted him. Needed him.

Tomorrow she'd test his patience just to see how he'd react. Maybe one day she'd introduce him to her parents and see how he dealt with the oddity. If he ran scared, so be it. She'd be no worse off for wear.

But for tonight she just needed some escape.

"Caleb."

He turned to face her, his expression questioning. Parting her lips slightly, she leaned forward and tasted him.

His mouth opened beneath hers and his tongue met hers. Slowly, softly, letting her choose the pace.

She couldn't slow down if she wanted. Her kisses became more demanding as she tasted the human sweetness being offered freely to her.

He leaned her backward, still at a snail's pace in case she changed her mind. She laced her fingers through the back of his hair, pulling him close. God, how she wanted him. She couldn't get enough.

He continued kissing her as his hand reached up to casually brush against her breast. She arched her back, encouraging and needing him to reach for more.

She was on fire and he loosened the waistband of her jeans. She raised her hips, hoping he'd take the encouragement.

He did. One hand slipped into her jeans and brushed against her mound. His finger parted her already swollen cleft and delved inside to find warm, velvety juices.

She whimpered at the sweet invasion.

"Are you too sore?" he whispered.

"Never," she promised.

He inserted his finger fully, letting the silky sweet liquid flow over him.

"You feel so good," he whispered. "Hot and wet. Ready for me. I smell you and it makes me want to taste you. Spread you wide and lick you up."

His fingers left her to pull the jeans from her hips. His tongue moved slowly along her lower lip as he undressed her. When she was naked, he placed two pillows under her back to prop her up. Then he spoke gruffly.

"Spread your legs. Bend at the knees."

She did as requested and felt his hand skim over her inner thigh before she felt his lips kiss the same smooth skin.

He leaned back and with his hands on the curves of her buttocks, he used his thumbs on her labia to spread her open for his view.

"You're beautiful," he said, his voice thick.

Keara inhaled deeply when the tip of his tongue glided up her moist slit. There was something so erotic about watching his head delve between her thighs.

He nibbled at her clit, tingles shooting throughout her body. Before she knew it, she couldn't hold still, clenching and unclenching her sheath in rhythmic beats.

She'd expected to feel good. Who couldn't enjoy oral sex? What she didn't expect was complete, utter desire for Caleb alone. She couldn't imagine letting anyone else touch her this way, and she knew she wouldn't feel this same way with another's mouth on her most intimate body part.

He curled a finger into her passage to rub deliberately at her G-spot. With his other hand, he pressed on her mound so he could feel his finger rub.

Lust exploded within her. His lips pulling and sucking on her clit, his finger rubbing those inner bundles of nerves, his outer hand pushing those nerves into his finger…

Keara brought her knees to her chest, gripping her ankles with her hands. It brought her bottom up higher, and Caleb took advantage of the situation to suck delicate, swollen labia into his mouth.

He sucked one tender outer lip into his warmth and then the other. By the time he turned his careful attention to her inner lips she thought she'd scream, the pleasure was so intense.

"Caleb," she whispered desperately.

"Just enjoy, love," he said, delving back to her spread-open pussy.

Soft whimpering sounds escaped her throat, making her sound feminine and eager.

"That's it," he rasped. "I want you to come in my mouth. I want to watch your lips quiver as your body clenches."

He stopped speaking long enough to give her another deliciously wet lick. "Finger your nipples. I want to see you pull and stretch them. Harden them, make them long so they poke out at me."

He watched her slender hand cup her full breasts, the globes spilling up and over. Long fingers plucked at the pink peaks that tipped her white skin as she twisted delicately. Staring deeply into her eyes, Caleb ground his hips into the mattress. As he lowered his talented tongue back down, he made a show of thrusting his hips, knowing her eyes were on his muscular ass.

He attacked her stiff clit, quick teasing tongue flicks against her reddened skin.

"Caleb," she screamed, her legs uncontrollably straightening into the air as she thrust her sex up against his hair roughened face. He clamped onto her with a hardened suck as she exploded, his hands cupping her ass and bringing her tightly to him.

Long, delicious waves rolled over her body, her breasts softly quivering under her hands. Moans escaped her throat as she came and Caleb knew she was the most beautiful creature he'd ever seen.

He pulled away from her quivering flesh and grabbed a condom from the pocket of his jeans. Her head was tipped back and her eyes closed as if his mouth on her was the center of her world. The packet was torn open and the condom rolled on in one smooth movement.

He rose up and slid into her silky wet body in one long glide, gasping when he reached the top and she clenched him with her inner muscles to bring him in deeper. He looked down at her to find her eyes open and watching as he thrust his cock into her, slow and sure.

He pulled out and left the head of his organ at her opening. "You're so hot inside. On fire."

She smiled at him and rolled her hips to get the tip of him into her greedy vaginal lips. "I'm wet, too," she murmured. "Bet it won't put out the flames."

He groaned and plunged into her, pausing for just a moment before he fucked her intensely. A few strokes, a dozen at most. Just a taste, a sampling of what it could be if he had any self control at all. Regretfully, he pulled out and gripped her rounded hips. He pulled her up and onto his lap, his cock still imbedded in her and her legs on either side of his body.

Her sex wide open for his view.

His body buried deeply in hers.

He circled his finger around and around her sensitive clit, never touching it directly. She pulsed her inner muscles tightly on him and he began to give her small little thrusts, inch by inch.

He felt the tension banded tightly in her body. Sweat broke out on his forehead as he concentrated on not coming, but he could feel the swell of her impending orgasm all around him. Could smell the concentrated sex in the air.

Saw the swollen pleasure bared before him.

"Come for me, Keara. I need you to explode around my cock so I can lose control," he said, an edge in his voice.

With a feminine gasp, she did as he asked and milked his cock in sweet, rhythmic clenches. Finally, he could thrust as hard and fast and deep as he wanted into her feverishly erupting orgasm.

Pleasure exploded as hot slick flesh gripped each other, sliding wetly and furiously.

Half propping his body onto muscular forearms around her, he curled his head into her shoulder to catch his breath.

And she stroked the back of his head tenderly. As if she planned what to do next.

* * * * *

She was gone before he awoke the next morning.

And managed to avoid him for whole three days. There was something softening inside her, melting whenever she thought of him. But she didn't need that.

The guilt was horrible. She avoided his call the first day because she felt guilty at having to summon Mike and Roderick.

The second day she avoided it because she felt guilty at being with Mike and Roderick.

The third day she avoided him because of the guilt over avoiding his calls.

When had she become a guilt-ridden female? She was half-demon, there should be none of that. Just pride. She was a monster, after all. She could never forget that fact. She was dirty and tainted and…

She needed the power surge of a threesome before a battle with Enishka ensued.

She would not feel bad about it. It didn't matter about Caleb, she owed him nothing.

She would not. But that didn't mean she couldn't think back over the last couple days.

The threesome had been easy enough to set up. Mental images sent separately to Mike and Rod had both of her minions scrambling to call her.

Minions. The side effect of stealing dark power. The twisted human was subject to her every whim and desire. A powerful trait to have, especially if you were a demon lord. If Enishka ever found out what she inherited from her dad and how it had morphed with her…

Rod was sitting on Mike's front porch in a slight daze, as if he couldn't remember how he got there.

"Something is going on with me, but I can't figure out what. I'd never have considered this before. Not with another man involved."

Keara had shrugged. "There's a first time for everything. Maybe you're just going with the flow?"

Mike looked out his front door. "Don't worry about it. Who'll even know? Ever? You and I are just with a woman, not each other."

So they thought.

Because for the most powerful surge, all three had to be involved. They thought she'd be a willing threesome partner, that she'd be involved, and she would. Just not in the way they expected. She'd be on the sidelines, stealing power.

Chapter Five
The Consequences of Temptation

ဆ

What had happened to her? The surge wasn't as powerful as it should have been. She'd sucked the threesome power but she didn't have the extra stores in her reserves. Something was wrong and she didn't know if she should dare try again.

Because would that endanger the human part of her soul?

She already craved power sucks like a junkie sought drugs. Needed them with uncontrollable urges. Her father had warned her but she was too worried about protecting her parents from Enishka to heed his advice.

Now in addition to the crabbiness she'd been experiencing, she was panicked. What if she did try another threesome? What if she didn't?

On top of it all, her eyes kept glowing with her distress. Like a damn futuristic robot with a short circuited laser beam. Not very many demons had the problematic glow but apparently she was one of those lucky few.

A pounding at the door matched the pounding of her head. She rolled her neck muscles to loosen the tension just enough for her stress to drop and her horns to descend.

Then she swung the door open to find Caleb. Avoidance was over.

He stood on the front stoop wearing a chocolate brown t-shirt that matched his eyes while serving a dual purpose of hugging his luscious biceps. Tight jeans encased muscular legs that made her mouth water when she recalled what was underneath the denim.

He looked good enough to eat while she looked like Elvira.

Her skin was too pale from the lack of sleep, with dark bruises under her eyes that reminded her of runaway mascara. Her normally glossy black hair had nothing much done to it but a ponytail to keep it out of the way.

And she was tired. So tired. So disappointed in the wasted effort of the threesome. So damn short-tempered and not liking the guilt. More demon than human.

"You okay? I haven't talked to you in a while," he said.

"I'm fine. Just...busy."

"You don't look fine. Have you been sick?"

That would have been a great excuse had she thought of it. Unfortunately, one of the downfalls of the Horntreau demons was their inability to lie. Oh, they could allude to something, perhaps withhold important data, but an outright bald-faced lie? Impossible. Which was why her father had been Enishka's second in command.

It was amazing that he was clever and powerful enough to trick the demon lord.

"I'm... I'm not sick. Just tired, and... Oh, I don't know," she snapped.

Before she knew it, he was right there. Invading her space with the strength of that amazing chest before her. Melting her into him until her traitorous body felt like butter.

He released her hair from its band and slowly stroked the back of her head. Why did a simple human's touch feel so wondrous? Was it something her human side craved? Had she teased her human soul with Dean and now it demanded another?

Or was it only Caleb who made her crave him?

In any case, her quivering muscles began to lose tension. He sensed it and bent slightly to pick her up and carry her into the bedroom.

Once there, he deposited her on the bed and lay down with her. He pulled her back into the honeyed warmth of him. It felt so good. Her body involuntarily stiffened once more as her mind pondered the meaning of her feelings.

"Just let me hold you. Relax," he whispered with his arms around her. It was so easy to listen to the soothing tones in his voice. So easy to let go and fall asleep. As long as he would too.

And there it was, his breathing growing steady and deep, his heartbeat slowing.

She drifted between worlds. The only place where she truly fitted in.

But through the heady thickness of sleep, something pulled at her. She had a brief moment of dread before she involuntarily left the warmth of Caleb in her bed.

The whirlwind of air reached out for her, sucking the oxygen from her lungs, twisting her stomach and making her pant for clean, familiar air. It was foggy where she'd landed and she wasn't alone.

Not again.

"Keara."

One word. Her name. Pronounced with the ancient accent that sent chills racing down her spine. She remained kneeling on the smoky ground, the fog rising in curled mists around her.

Slowly she raised her head to face her nightmare. His face and body were deep red, the color of a cooked lobster. But from the waist down, he was a horse. In the Earth dimension, he would be known as a Centaur. Minus the hair and tail. Just red lobster skin.

Of course, Enishka could change his form at will.

"Will you call me 'master'?" His voice was gentle, sweet. Cajoling, lulling her into a false sense of trust.

She knew the tricks.

"I am half human." Her voice rang with conviction.

Hissing followed her refusal, subservient creatures that reclined in the swampy mists around her. She fought the urge to recoil when a slimy hand caressed her ankle and the creature cackled in laughter.

"You are half *demon*."

Silence ensued at the standoff.

"Have you wondered why I sent for you?" His low growl continued.

"I'll assume I'm in my testing phase."

"You are," he agreed. "And doing so well at it. I loved the way you drove the necrophiliac insane. He'll be such a riot when he returns to Hell. But my favorite is how you talked the crooked cop into a threesome with his attorney. Who'd have guessed it? Such macho, macho men." His voice mimicked the song. The swamp underlings twittered with hysterical laughter.

A small twinge of apprehension knotted her midsection. If he knew the extent of what powers existed within her half-bred body, he'd never give up.

Yet even now, she couldn't fully regret her actions. Maybe she *was* more demon than human. The temptation to ruin Dean's life was nearly overwhelming when she was at her weakest. She had to fight with herself not to contact his wife and compare notes on the man they had shared. Just to make sure his wife knew how much of a loser he was.

"What will you do to the ex-lover who left you and returned to his wife?" the demon lord asked slyly, as if he knew what she'd been thinking.

Had he known? The familiar pain of betrayal clenched her gut at the mention of the one human she'd loved.

"Nothing," she whispered. "I'm done with Dean. He made his choice and willingly returned to her."

Enishka's shriek was ear-splitting. "What! Nothing? No repercussions for the one who started you on this rampage? Who treated my future queen deplorably?"

The underground chattering and hissing instantly stopped. The swamp of Luciefyiore was eerily quiet as his words sunk in. Keara stayed just as silent as everyone else, refusing to acknowledge the statement and condemn herself.

But he continued. "That's correct, Keara," he said in his slow, breathy voice. "I have chosen you to be mine for eternity."

To refuse would be scandalous. To agree would commit her. Which way was out?

She whispered meekly, her voice intended to mollify his irrational behavior. "I am not yet through my testing."

It was a subtle reminder. He couldn't possibly have her if she was human. Not since the fiasco with her mother. Rules and regulations had been enacted to protect the other dimension since that time.

His voice was sweet in return. "No. But I have no doubts the results of your testing will be most positive. In fact, I'm willing to bet on it, my child."

His patience at an end, he gave a flick of his clawed hand, the nails wickedly curled, mimicking the smoky tendrils of fog floating about in this realm.

With the casual flick, Keara felt herself flung back into the material dimension. She gasped as oxygen slammed into her lungs, the burn echoing throughout her body, nerve endings tingling in her fingers and toes.

She sat up and glanced around her.

She was back in bed. And Caleb lay sleeping soundly right beside her.

She fought to release the burning pain that hissed through her as she settled quietly back down, trying not to awaken him. She seemed to be safe if his even breathing was any indication. She should try to get some more sleep herself.

After lying there for twenty minutes, she was ready to concede defeat. Sleep was lost to her.

Her mind raced with the words of Enishka. He must have watched her for quite a while for the demon underground to know about her last boyfriend, Dean.

She had loved the full-blooded human unconditionally, faults and all. Unfortunately, the bastard was married. He made all the right promises, he and his wife were mismatched, but he was such a loyal man he had remained with her all these years despite her cruel and abusive nature toward him. Their marriage wasn't even a real one according to him, his wife suggested on more than one occasion that he take a girlfriend if he desired, for they had no physical relationship and she didn't want to be bothered.

He was ready to break free, he'd claimed. For Keara. To be with her forever. She was his soul mate, the only one he loved. Had ever loved. She dropped her head into her hands, rubbing her temples tiredly. She could still remember his last comment. *Good morning, sexy girl. I am thinking that we honeymoon in Italy & Greece or Bora Bora! I am thinking that I propose to you in the Caribbean and we travel the world making love in as many countries as possible before we die of old age!*

Promises, promises. How had she been suckered? He seemed so sincere, so perfect for her. All carefully contrived lies that she bought hook, line and sinker.

And then he walked away without a backward glance. Returned to the wife he was so incompatible with…just like that. As if he'd never left. Possibly he hadn't.

Her heart smashed to pieces.

He should have been her testing phase. After all, she let him walk without exerting the power she knew she had to force his love. To destroy his life. That alone should have proved her humanity. Made her the better person.

She refused to think of her revenge on the other humans since then as proof of her demonality.

Next to her, Caleb feigned sleep as his own thoughts swirled. He'd heard her involuntarily mutter the name Dean and knew what she was rehashing.

He had been unable to do anything but watch as Keara's heart was slaughtered by Dean. As much as he wanted to help her, she'd stopped contact with him at that point and he had never been allowed to contact her.

The affair with that bastard changed her personality from a sweet, loving girl to a cynical, harder woman. A woman he still loved but felt helpless to protect. A woman who now battled the existence of her own inner demons.

He knew she blamed herself for what she termed her stupidity. But the truth of the matter was, Dean had sought her out during a weak period in her life. And Keara was stronger than she realized for not turning full demon immediately.

For nine out of ten half-breeds would never have been able to resist the temptation.

* * * * *

She awoke to his liquid brown eyes watching her.

"Good morning. What's on the agenda for today?" he asked.

She stretched and yawned, the sheet pulling tight and outlining lush, full breasts. He'd undressed her at some point during the night and tucked them both under the covers.

"I need to run by my parents' house. I'm picking up something from my father."

"Need company?" His tone was casual, as if waiting for her rebuff.

But this was her chance. She needed him to anchor her to this dimension. With all the soul sucking, she'd given Enishka the power to summon her at will. The visits drained her strength, but by drawing on Caleb's, she had finally been able to sleep and rest. Besides, she'd see how he'd react to knowing her parentage.

"I'd like that." She slid from the cool silk sheets and walked naked to the shower. To have him follow her.

The shower spray was warm as it softly trickled down her body. When a comfortable, naked form pressed against her, his chest to her back, he pushed her gently up to the cool tiles.

Her breasts tingled where her hard nipples touched the cold.

She felt the hard strength of his cock pressing against her backside before his finger snaked over her hip to find her stiff clit, where it poked from its hood eagerly.

He oiled his finger with a bottle of moisturizing oil she kept in the shower. He rubbed it erotically against her slit. Her folds were swollen as he explored with the ultimate tenderness.

"Feel good?" he muttered into her ear as he pressed tiny kisses to her temple.

"Umm," she moaned.

He began to trace circles around her clit, slowly masturbating her as she rocked her hips in time to his hand. He reached around and grabbed the handheld shower head.

"Oh, Caleb, baby..." she said, and had no idea what she was even going to mention.

He sat on the built-in shower seat and pulled her onto his lap, impaling her on his rock-hard erection, but never moving. Just filling her emptiness with him.

"I want you to spray the warm water over yourself," he said. "Make your nipples tingle, or heat your pussy while I play."

She took the massaging spray from him and his hand delved back between her tender folds of flesh, pulling on her thickened labia while she sat on his cock. Encircling her clit again, round and round.

"Spray your clit," he instructed, pressing with the barest movement upward so his embedded cock pressed into the lip of her uterus.

"Ahh," she gasped, lowering the spray there. "God, it's going to make me come," she warned.

"Know what'll really flip you over the edge?" he asked and didn't wait before continuing. "Spread your thighs wider and open your eyes. Watch yourself in the mirror through the clear glass door."

Curious, she lifted her head from his shoulder where it rested. The visual was so sexy, her legs spread wide enough to see the root of his cock where it connected into her body. Her nipples tingled, flushed pink and perky, and the hot spray of water had her clit hard and reddened.

He had been watching this same reflection the whole time she'd been masturbating with the warm water.

And then she just exploded. Waves of pressured release began to roll from her uterus. When she inhaled deeply, triggering her gasps of pleasure, Caleb moved his hips the tiniest movement upward, pressing into her budding orgasm.

She literally fell apart on his cock. She ground herself down onto it, forcing his head as deep as it would go as her vaginal walls tried to swallow it whole. Over and over, ripples rolled through her body, tingling spirals setting each other off in every nerve ending of her pussy.

When her waves began to subside, she set the spray aside and moved slowly upward, pulling his hands gently to keep him embedded. When they both stood, she turned and bent at the waist, legs wide, and rested her hands on the bench they'd sat on.

Ass up in the air, she snuggled her precious globes into his cock to make him fuck her wildly. He slammed into her, again and again, until he came with a ferocious roar.

They soaped each other wordlessly after that, glowing and satiated and pressing soft, soundless kisses to one another.

Until the warm water ran cold, and they used more kisses as they toweled each other dry.

As soon as they were dressed, they headed out to her car. She was nervous but refused to let it show. If she scared him away permanently, she just didn't know what she'd do. She was even more reserved than usual as she wondered about his reaction to meeting her family.

He'd be stunned quiet when he saw her mother. Most people were. She was truly the most beautiful woman Keara had ever seen, and for some reason she was made even more lovely by the purity that shone through like an inner light.

And what would his reaction be when he met her father? When he saw the two people who together made her with their combined genes? That she may have her mother's beauty on the outside, but on the inside she was her father's daughter?

It didn't matter, she tried to tell herself. In either case, she didn't need his reaction. She wouldn't be seeing him much longer. She would move on to another bar soon.

She just wished the thought of leaving him behind didn't hurt.

They entered the front door with a slight knock after a push on the door found it unlocked.

"Sweetheart," said her mother's voice.

"Momma."

Always affectionate, her mother leaned into her for a kiss. Keara turned to Caleb.

"This is my mother. Elizabeth Knight."

"It's good to meet you, Mrs. Knight." Caleb held out his hand.

Point for him. He wasn't struck to silence as many of her friends had been. But then again, he hadn't yet met her father.

Speaking of which, heavy footsteps sounded right around the corner.

"And, Caleb, this is my father. Demitris Knight."

Her father turned into the room from the kitchen in his original form, as she'd requested earlier, rather than using the image he presented to strangers.

"Nice to meet you, Mr. Knight," Caleb said without missing a beat. He strode directly to her father and shook a clawed hand.

"You're not surprised?" Keara asked when she could close her mouth.

"No."

"You know demons exist? Run among us?"

"Yes."

So he wasn't as surprised as she'd expected. Why? Apparently he knew more about her than she realized. Perhaps it was from linking with him as a child. Maybe he'd searched the caverns of her mind and knew about other dimensions? No matter, he would be shocked later when she explained the rest. If she explained the rest.

"Keara, you planned for your father to show himself to Caleb?" her mother asked.

Keara shrugged as if it didn't really matter.

"Maybe you expect more prejudice than you get, babisna," her father said.

Keara smiled at him. She loved her father unconditionally and he made her more agreeable. "Perhaps."

"Caleb, can I get you anything?" Elizabeth asked. Purity shone through her, an inner glow.

"I'm good, Mrs. Knight."

"Call me Elizabeth. Let's you and I wander off and get to know each other while Keara and Demi search his office, shall we?"

"Of course," Caleb said, holding out his arm for her to take.

They'd just wandered out to the garden when her father said, "I like him."

"He's okay," Keara said noncommittally.

"Just that?"

"We'll see."

"Forever testing. One day you'll have to just trust."

"Trust what, Daddy? I've been screwed over by demons and screwed over by humans. What's left?"

Her father sighed. "Oh, sweetie. I'm hoping one day you'll find love."

"Have that. You and Mom."

He rolled his eyes. "Not that kind. You know what I mean."

"I'm fine, silly." She leaned her head onto his shoulder for the walk to his office.

* * * * *

Mike Goudy had just stepped out of the shower when his doorbell rang. Hurriedly, he tossed a towel around his hips. Somehow, he knew who it was on the other side of the door even before he opened it.

He looked forward to the man who stood there with an excitement that curled his toes.

"Hey," he said softly, then stood aside.

Roderick walked awkwardly into Mike's apartment and sat stiffly on the sofa, as if he were afraid to be touched. Mike sat down also, calming and soothing. Not wanting to scare him off after he took the first step of getting here.

"Soda?" Mike asked.

"No," Roderick said. "I, uh, just wanted to talk to you about, you know."

"The threesome."

"Yeah."

"Go ahead."

Roderick took a deep breath. "I thought it was agreed we weren't going to touch."

"I know. I never dreamed we would have. But don't worry. I'll never tell anyone."

Roderick was silent for a moment. "I didn't think you would. But what the real question was…was, well. I don't know. I don't even know why the hell I'm here," he growled suddenly, looking down at the floor.

They both grew silent, each wondering what to do next. Then Roderick spoke again. "Did you like it?" he rushed out, as if he might lose his nerve.

Mike was staring down at the floor. "How could I not?" he asked. "We were caught up in the moment. The excitement, the lust. A gorgeous woman between us." A pause, then it was his turn to whisper, "Did you?"

"Yeah," Roderick admitted. "How could I not like my cock in your mouth?"

Both men were silent for a minute, Mike still looking down at the floor.

"And I was wondering…if…you, um, might like it too."

Mike looked up. "You'd want to suck my cock?"

Roderick looked into his eyes and said softly, "Yeah. I think I would."

Mike's cock hardened, the bulge pressing against the towel that he wore. "Feel like trying?" he asked.

Roderick nodded. "Why don't you drop the towel?"

Mike stood and unwrapped slowly, as if he was still unsure. But the hardness between his thighs said otherwise.

It was very sure, hard and full and ready for action. Mike then sat back on the sofa with Rod, his cock bulging between them. "This is too weird."

Roderick leaned toward him and wrapped his large hand around Mike's thick erection. His thumb brushed against the tip, finding wetness there. "I know," he said.

Mike gasped at the contact of another male hand on his stiff cock. It was different from a woman's touch. Harder, more forceful. Rod leaned in and pressed a small kiss to him. Right there, right on the mouth.

Suddenly, tongues entwined. Rod was pumping his cock, there on his couch, and smearing the tiny droplets of pre-cum into him with his thumb. And then he was kneeling on the floor between Mike's thighs. He bent his head and took the muscular cock into his lips.

Jeezus, it felt so good. Roderick knew how he wanted to be sucked and licked, and he used those procedures right there on Mike. He cupped his balls and squeezed lightly. He rolled the skin of his sac around to feel the testicles inside.

And when he took those testicles into his mouth, Mike froze as if he was afraid to move, less he'd come.

Roderick chuckled. "I know exactly," he shared.

"This is great," Mike confided, his voice husky and deep.

"I wonder what else would be great?"

"What else you got in mind?" Mike asked.

"Got any lube?"

If he got any harder, he'd pop. "We'll both try?"

"Why not?"

Roderick stood up and pulled his own pants down, and it was Mike's turn to watch as he stroked his own cock. Together they glanced toward the bedroom.

As they walked toward the bed, Mike slipped his hand into Roderick's. Entwined his fingers with his and watched his ass as they moved.

"You first?" Roderick asked.

Mike bent over onto all fours on the mattress, his ass pointed at Rod, while he delved into the nightstand for lube. Roderick couldn't help but reach out to caress the muscles in that smooth ass.

"Put your head down onto the mattress," he instructed when Mike handed him the lube.

Mike pressed his cheek to the mattress.

"Spread your legs wider," Roderick said, his voice thick and husky.

Mike did as requested and Roderick gave him a surprise. A sharp, pointed wet tongue, speared directly into the tight muscles of his anus.

"Oh, fuck," Mike groaned, gripping the sheets while Rod licked his asshole.

Ever so gently, a slippery finger slid into his rim of muscles, lubricating his passage, preparing it for the hard cock that was coming. That finger felt so good.

"I want you not to thrust, try not to come," Rod instructed. "After I come deep into your ass, I want you to use mine to come in then, okay?"

"Yeah," Mike said, his voice muffled by the mattress.

He felt the tip of Rod's cock head stretching his asshole. More pleasure than pain, but to hold off his orgasm he had to not focus on pain.

When Rod slid all the way in with a wet, squishy slap, he began bucking his hips. "Try not to come," he panted to Mike as he worked his ass. "Remember, I want you to come in my ass, too."

Mike was trying hard not to think of the cock pounding into him, trying hard not to reach down and stroke his own cock. Rod was so excited, it didn't take long for him to groan and begin yelling. "Fuck, I'm coming. Sweet ass you have, God, I have to spread your ass wide…"

Large hands gripped his cheeks and roughly pulled them apart. Mike held still as hot cum filled his ass and a quivering cock pulled out. Rod collapsed on the mattress face down next to him and Mike all but jumped up and reached for the lube.

"Spread 'em," he demanded and then got the visual that Rod had been watching. He squirted lube right onto the crack of Rod's ass and began sliding his fingers up and down the hot flesh, before poking a slippery one into his hole.

Slowly, he stuck the tip of his own cock into Rod's tight asshole and waited for the other man's muscles to adjust to the strange feelings.

Rod would have none of that. He shoved his hips backward, taking Mike's whole cock at once.

"Shit, that feels awesome," Rod groaned. "And I just came."

"It feels awesome from here, too," Mike panted. "So tight and hard, and…"

He pulled out and slid his cock again into the tight chamber, not even going slowly.

"Fuck," Rod yelled. "Yes, fuck me harder." Because it was pleasure merging with pain and the pain is what tipped him over the edge. Although usually, it was someone else's. Never had he imagined it could feel this fucking good for himself.

"Oh, son of a bitch, shove that thick cock up my ass faster," Rod groaned and reached for his own slippery, cum encased rod. He slid his palm up and down it as Mike fucked him.

"Harder?" Mike asked.

"Yeah," Rod panted.

Mike groaned long and low as his world erupted. Fireworks exploded behind his eyelids as his cock emptied deep inside Rod's tight ass.

He pulled out and they collapsed on the bed, breathing heavily. Eyelids heavy.

Neither man noticed the very slight shimmer of a light in the corner. The outline of an invisible shape. An unusual horned shape, silently watching.

Sleep hit fast. Roderick was on his stomach when Mike reached out with a warm palm and ran it over the muscular curve of buttocks. He slid his hand up over his back and then curled his body around Rod's before he closed his eyes.

"There's a glow in here," Rod murmured sleepily.

"Must be the clock," Mike replied, eyes still shut.

The deep twin glows disappeared as the demon dematerialized from the room. Rod turned over and hugged Mike to him. Slowly, Mike wrapped his own arms around Rod.

Chapter Six
The Bitterness of Reliving

ᔥ

Keara's bedroom was deliberately decorated black and white. Black curtains, black vases. A white bed with a white canopy. She pulled the soft comforter and climbed into the stark sheets.

To remind her of what she was inside. Black and white. Demon and human.

Someday she might be one or the other.

That was her last thought as she drifted to sleep.

She sat under the old tree facing the school she'd attended as a child. She knew she was dreaming, because she'd burned the original building down years and years ago.

She was in the midst of a nasty dream. Her heart raced, the beat thumping throughout her veins like galloping horses. Did she dare pull Caleb in? Like she used to? He was so sweet, the other day. Holding her while she slept, keeping her safe.

It gave her the strength to face Enishka, knowing she'd return to find Caleb in her bed.

So why not? It was the tiniest want, the smallest wish...and then he was magically there. Support during the night tremors.

"You've finally contacted me," the dream-Caleb said with a satisfied tone as he sat beside her.

She shrugged. "Oh, well, I think we both need to admit that I am...well, sort of a psychic who is able to dream of others. You saw my parents, you know I'm not fully human. And you were my friend while I was growing up and the best counselor I've ever had."

"I missed the power you gave me when we visited in dreams."

"Then welcome back to it, Caleb."

He reached out and took her small hand in his much larger one. "It's good to be back. Now, let's go visit a certain spot in your life, shall we?"

She protested to no avail. He controlled her dreams. She'd allowed it by giving him the power long ago as a child. To keep her from the nightmares and taunts of the other children in the prestigious all-girl school, Luciekynokus.

Immediately, Caleb's physical body shimmered until he was an invisible hue she could sense but not see. Her counseling force that she could relive memories with, even though she was alone the first time she'd experienced the trauma.

Had she known which memories her dream Caleb was going to pull from her subconscious, she would have woken herself immediately. Instead she walked with him, enjoying the comfortable warmth of his hand in hers, watching as her dream physically clouded and then cleared.

Slowly, her feet dragged her into the childhood boarding school where she used to live. She pushed open the heavy door.

And she stood in her living room with Dean.

"No," she said in a panicked voice. "Not this."

Caleb's voice was light as a whisper, his body immaterial. "Yes, baby. You need to face it and learn a valuable lesson."

"No?" Dean's voice responded in the dream as if she'd spoken to him. His smile was tender. "Are you sure you don't want to go with me?"

"Of course. I mean, oh, hell I don't know what I meant. Of course I'll come with you."

Dean had been heading out of town that weekend, away from his wife and small daughter. He'd just asked Keara to come along with him.

It wasn't unusual. He had no real relationship with his wife, just two virtual strangers who lived together for the sake of the legalities of a Chinese adoption. According to him, his wife was having a female mid-life crisis and to keep her happy, he'd agreed to the adoption of one-year old Carissa. Once the adoption was final they'd part as friends and he'd get visitation rights.

Carissa was a sweet baby that he frequently brought over to get to know his fiancée. After all, when he and Keara were married, she'd be Rissa's stepmother.

Caleb's voice was a whisper again. "What do you see this second time around, Keara?"

Keara stared hard at Dean, trying to physically see him through enlightened eyes. He was frozen, returning her gaze. Caleb must have paused the dream like some modern day movie being watched.

Dean was as handsome as he ever was. Blond hair and gorgeous blue eyes, twinkling happily, peered back at her. A sensuous bottom lip curled, begging for her kisses. Her match made in heaven. The perfect mate for her.

An angelic image to balance her demonic looks.

"I don't see anything negative in the situation."

"Think, Keara. Look to see his true selfishness."

"I don't see it. He was sincere at this point, wanting me to get to know Carissa so she wouldn't be traumatized by a new stepmother when he left Annie. That's not selfish."

"Okay, baby. Did he want you to get to know Carissa? Or was he stuck watching her while Annie was having spa days and he brought her over for visits so you could baby-sit instead? For him?"

"Oh, crap," Keara said aloud as realization dawned. How many times had he set Rissa down to wander off, leaving

Keara to chase after the toddler? Assuming it was more natural for a female to nurture his child?

"See?"

"Okay."

She conceded to his argument and the dream resumed. Dean leaned in to kiss her. Her heart clenched, thrust right back into the love that they'd shared for so long. As if it had never left.

"I love you, sexy girl," Dean whispered against her lips. He kissed her again. "My soul mate. My best friend."

God, she missed him. For this small moment in time she could pretend the love was still real. Back before reality had stepped in to awaken her harshly, like a newborn ripped from the womb and thrust into the cold world.

She smiled slowly, as she had back then during the reality of the situation. "I love you too, baby."

His lips descended and she tasted the sweet familiarity of the man she missed. Before the bitter hatred had consumed her senses. His tongue met hers in the perfect duel.

Her moan was soft and he pulled away to trail a loving smattering of kisses along her sensitive neck. The usual demon heat raged through her body like an ignition. Sensing her mood, Dean pulled her to him and kissed her deeply to inflame her desire rather than quench it. Odd that he could sense her non-human needs.

His kisses smoldered. They always did between the two of them. The chemistry had definitely been there.

She slipped her hands under his shirt, feeling the warm skin beneath. A ringing was faint in her ears, growing consistently louder with each passing second. Pulling at her and refusing to let go.

She awakened to the ruthless shrill of the phone.

"Hello?"

"I didn't feel like sitting around watching you make love to him." Caleb's voice was short.

She'd forgotten she was even in a dream. She was silent as she slowly processed the information of past and present, reality and dream. What was now and what was once then.

"So you woke me up?" Her voice was thick and she felt groggy.

"Yes."

"Okay, I'm awake already. Dream's done. I'm going back to sleep now. Go away." She set the phone down with a click. Too bad it wasn't just as easy to disconnect herself from the situation.

* * * * *

Caleb rang her doorbell later that evening. She answered the door but didn't look all that happy to see him.

Manners prevailed. She invited him in and sat next to him on the sofa. He plunged in with the reason he was there.

"You need more Dean therapy." He knew what would happen when he forced Keara to face her past. She would resent him for the pain she had to relive. She would fight tooth and nail to keep from going through it again, even if it meant cutting off things with him.

Pain clenched deep inside at the thought, but he had to persevere. If she hated him forever, it was worth losing her to avoid relinquishing her to hell.

"Dammit, Caleb," she snapped. "I'm sick of revisiting my relationship with Dean. What is the point?"

"The point is this relationship caused your bitterness. You need to be the one to realize that. The bitterness is what will turn you demon."

"You are making me bitter. I was fine until you came along."

"You weren't fine. You were constantly sucking power and never obtaining your own fulfillment."

"How do you know if I climaxed or not?"

"How can you even pretend otherwise? You've never reached for the stars with any of them." He leaned in to whisper in her ear. "I've presented you the stars on a platter. Reach out and take them, baby."

She almost shivered at the hot whispered breath. Heat swept through her body like ignited fuel. But he watched her ignore it and knew he'd have to fight even dirtier.

"If you won't be honest, I'll have to show you."

"If I allow you to show me," she said, as haughty as ever.

His smile was grim. Grabbing her arm, he pulled her roughly to him and threw her over his shoulder in a fireman's carry.

"Let me down," she demanded from the vicinity of his rear.

"When I'm ready."

"Dammit, Caleb. I mean it."

"So do I."

They'd reached her bedroom where he glanced around before heading to a dresser. Opening the smaller drawers on top, he found what he was looking for.

He dumped her on her bed where she glared up at him with eyes that glowed with fury. Demon eyes.

"How dare you?"

He didn't respond, but reached for her wrists, deftly binding them and then tying her to her own wrought iron headboard with the scarf he'd grabbed from her drawers.

"What the hell? Let me go, dammit. Now," she snarled as she jerked at the bars.

He was done talking to her. Towering above her from where he stood near the bed, he began to slowly undress.

His shirt came off first, whipped over and barely pulling without tearing over his muscular biceps. Exposing the tight musculature of his bared chest, he stood before her with his eyes watching her face.

Hers were glued to his chest and he fought not to smile at her dazed expression.

Slowly her small pink tongue wet her lips and gave him a mental image of that sexy little tool caressing his cock.

He unsnapped his jeans, exposing the silky trail of hair that disappeared down below. He was so fucking hard he wondered if he'd be able to pull his pants down over his swollen cock.

God, he wanted to be buried up to his balls in her sweet, juicy pussy.

He whipped his jeans and underwear over his long legs and groaned when his rock-hard erection was freed. On his knees, he leaned over her body. His cock throbbed and ached, and he decided to give himself a break.

He slowly pumped his hand up and down it, imagining her hand replacing his.

She was breathing hard as she watched him and she'd stopped straining against the scarf.

Her nipples were stiff and poked through the thin cotton of her t-shirt.

He wrapped his fingers around the base of his cock and brought it up to rub against her cheek. "Lick me," he demanded.

She did so much more than that. She was greedy, sucking the head of his cock as though she could squeeze more pre-cum from the tip.

He groaned and slowly pumped his hand up and down his organ while she sucked at the head. He knew he couldn't take much of this. She'd get a shot more than pre-cum, that was for sure.

"Stop, Keara."

For once, the naughty little demon obeyed. She pulled away and watched his face, waiting for his next instruction.

He took a deep breath, shuddering as he fought for control. The last thing he wanted to do was explode now when they'd just barely started.

When he was ready, he reached over and took the hem of her t-shirt, stretching it up over her breasts. He ran one finger over her tight nipple as he trailed that hand down to her skirt and tugged it lower.

It barely covered her pubic hair. He loved the way she shaved her lips bare and smooth while just a tiny patch of hair was left for decoration. He kissed the flat expanse of skin between her belly button and the skirt and licked a path up and around her navel. She squirmed, trying to spread her thighs open.

"Shhh, love," he crooned as he tugged the skirt further down and off her legs.

He looked down at her exposed body, her white shirt up over her breasts, baring them like an offering of a berry tipped dessert.

Her flat stomach and tiny waist. Rounded, sexy hips.

Shaved sex.

Swollen lips.

Creamy cunt.

"Beautiful," he muttered in a deep voice thick with desire. "Spread your legs."

Still his obedient little demon. She opened them without hesitation, unashamedly exposing herself to his view.

He reached down and spread her labia with two fingers, the thick liquid coating his fingers. She moaned when he stretched her apart.

"Feel good?"

"Ahh, yes," she squirmed against his hand.

"Know what would feel better?"

"What?"

"My tongue there, caressing every fold. Finding every crevice. Tasting every drop of you."

She shuddered and helplessly thrust her hips up at him.

"Want it?"

"Yes," she admitted, as though it were torn from her mouth.

"Yes, what?"

"Please."

He smiled at his sweet little demon, the one who once refused to be possessed by a man.

He inserted the middle finger of his right hand into her sheath and used his left hand to keep her lips spread apart. He delved in.

"Ohmigod," she gasped at the first pass of his tongue.

He licked slowly and deliberately, coating her with wet warmth and lapping up her juices in return. Up and down her slit, circling her clit, then wetly nibbling at it with his lips.

She lost control. She began to buck her hips wildly and he clamped onto the swollen little organ, sucking hard as an additional finger joined the first to scissor deep within her body.

Her orgasm swept through her like a liquid force, coating his hand and quivering her sex beneath his mouth as he attacked her sensitive flesh.

He loved the moans she made, the constant, "Oh, oh, oh…" before she screamed through her release. If he could only get her to moan his name. His, no one else's.

He pulled his fingers from her body and stretched up over her. "You're not done yet," he muttered before dropping his sex-sweetened mouth to hers. He let her taste herself on him as he twined her tongue with his.

"I'm putting on a condom so I can fuck you now," he said. She nodded and watched in a daze while he did so. One day, she'd open up and share with him that she couldn't have babies until her testing phase determined which race she could mate with, but right now she just nodded. He felt a slight disappointment that he couldn't have the intimacy of his hot semen flooding her body.

It was too dangerous. If she felt wary about him now, he didn't need to crave that final intimacy that would bond them together. His essence embedded within her womb.

And then, pulling her legs up over his shoulders, he watched her wrists strain against the scarf while he fucked her slowly and carefully. Deliberately, letting her feel every movement.

Her swollen pussy was heaven as it wrapped tightly around his cock. There was nothing like entering a just satisfied woman, a warm, wet velvet glove wrapped around your hardness, snug and tight and moist.

His thrusts were hard and deep and rhythmic. She began to make tiny little sounds, little gasps of pleasure when each thrust was at its deepest.

Her gasps were making him plunge harder, to fuck her fully while beads of sweat broke out on his forehead as he tried to control his own orgasm.

Her snow white breasts jiggled as he pumped into her. Soft and womanly globes with hard pink tips. He reached out to pinch a nipple lightly and she clenched her eyes shut as another forceful orgasm rolled through her body, milking his cock until he couldn't stand it. His balls tightened and he exploded into the condom, like hot lava erupting from an angry volcano.

He collapsed onto her after loosening her wrists from the ties which bound her. Felt her arms slowly snake around him to hold him close.

It wasn't long before he felt her hands massaging his back. Feeling each indent of muscle. Indents that he'd made for her, long ago, in anticipation of their meeting.

They lay in silence, recovering, while he pressed tiny little kisses to her collarbone.

"Those are the stars, baby. You and me."

She continued to caress the muscles in his back. Silent as though pondering the bizarre feelings that were snaking through her.

He should have let his semen flood her womb.

* * * * *

The fog was thick today, swirled in mists higher than usual in the swamp. The demon sitting on his throne was in a foul mood. Tension crackled in the air like static electricity in a dry cotton blanket.

"I'm losing her," Enishka muttered to no one in particular.

"Master," twittered the twisted little creature at his feet.

"Someone needs to intervene. A female, maybe. To make her jealous over the new boyfriend. Maybe we can get Keara to punish him. And perhaps we can get the mortal to seek her out again. Dean."

"Who sssshall it be?" asked the demon. Its tongue was split down the middle and poked from its mouth in two pieces, making it difficult to speak.

"Fetch Natalya."

Natalya Hershkle was enjoying herself when Enishka's errand boy in training entered her dwelling.

She was propped up on pillows, thighs spread wide, moaning loudly as a head between her legs pleasured her. A blond head, hair as golden as hers but missing horns. A human. Poor pathetic creature, doomed to serve her for the rest of his pitiful life.

The errand boy felt a flush steal over his face. He'd heard rumors about Natalya, but had never been exposed to her before. He looked away, pondering what to do. She was the highest ranked female now that Keara was in the human dimension, although Keara never understood what her ranking would become or she might have fought harder to sway her ruling when she was banished.

"Don't stand in the doorway all indecisive. Get in or get out," Natalya's husky voice rang.

As she spoke, she pulled the pillows from behind her back so she could lay flat. "Hold up, handsome," she whispered, and when the human lifted his head from her sex, she slid a pillow under her hips, exposing herself for everyone's enjoyment.

"Slow and wet, just like I like it," she commanded him and he bent his head again.

She exhaled softly, rotating her hips in smooth circles under his tongue.

"What do you need?"

It was hard enough to speak when your tongue was split but when a gorgeous creature such as her was enjoying her lust so immensely that the smell of her heat wafted up, it was definitely a stuttering moment.

"The mas-master wants you."

"For?" One long finger snaked down to her swollen clitoris and she elongated it between two fingers. Watched his eyes as he fought not to stare. The human between her thighs focused his attention on forcing his tongue as high as possible into her slippery vaginal entrance.

He'd lost his thought. "Oh, Jenesi…I mean Keara. Something to do with tricking her."

Natalya smiled widely. But the poor errand boy was far too entranced to notice it.

"You have two tongues."

His eyes cut to hers at the sudden change of subject. "Y-Yesss."

She tapped the human on the head. "Up for a second," she commanded. "Now you," she said with a smile. "You have two tongues, I have two holes. Fill them."

He didn't know what to do. Everyone knew that Natalya was a very real candidate for the demon queen, should things fall through with Keara. It wouldn't do to get onto her bad side this early in the game.

He bent and inserted part of his tongue deep into her vagina and the other piece deep into her anus. Her skin was silky-soft and slippery.

"Oh, yes," she wailed as her pussy flooded with more liquid. She spread her labia open with her fingers so that her clitoris poked stiffly into the air. "Now suck it," she commanded the human.

Why didn't she ever think of this? A tongue in her pussy and a tongue in her ass. By a little virgin demon errand boy, no less. He'd be a prize stud in no time. He just needed a little schooling behind Enishka's back.

Her human in training settled onto her swollen clit as she commanded and began to suck fiercely. Her body clenched tightly. And when the little demon began to slide his tongues in and out of her, she screamed with the ultimate pleasure. She grasped her nipples and twisted as the biggest orgasm of her life, one with the permission to hunt her hated enemy Keara, slammed through her body.

"Oh, fuck," she yelled.

When Natalya finally calmed from her earth-shattering climax, she dressed in a filmy white, see-through gown that left nothing to the imagination. And then attended Enishka's court.

The pompous demon lord sat on his throne as he normally did. Today he took the lower half form of a chimp, and she was glad he sat on the bulbous red globes of his ass. They would look totally incongruous should he stand. She hoped he understood she wouldn't be living in his disgusting swamp after their marriage.

"Natalya, how kind of you to visit."

"I believe you summoned?"

"Surely you would not attend me only in the event of a summons?"

If nothing else, Natalya knew how to be political. She hadn't got as far as she had by not accepting that much about social climbing. "Of course not. But I am eager to please and I understand you need me?"

"Yes, my sweet. I have a delicate project for you."

Natalya approached sultrily, lifting her skirts to the top of her thighs so she could sit at his feet. Watched his face as he appreciated her body. She curled herself delicately around his legs and kissed his hairy shins just under his knees while he spoke.

"I want you to find Keara. Take her new boyfriend from her, leave her devastated and alone. She needs to learn her place, yes?"

She could barely keep the smile from her lips.

"Understood." Then on an afterthought, "Master."

Keara would have had the best sleep of her life, wrapped in her lover's arms. She had no idea her dream was about to be invaded.

"Hello, my child."

Keara turned her head, the thick headiness of the dream making it difficult to move properly. "Is this truly a dream? Or a visit?" she demanded of Enishka.

"Which do you think it is?"

"I don't know or I wouldn't ask. I can't imagine it's a real visit, for why wouldn't you just summon me into your dimension?"

The painful thrust between worlds was the power she'd given her demon master when she began to suck pieces of putrid human souls. But the surge was so worth it. Even now, she craved the rush that ran through her veins.

Enishka smiled at her. But he never answered her question. "Why have you not broken the bastard who hurt you?" he asked.

She'd thought about it, of course. The taste of revenge was always so sweet. But was it her human side that craved the darkness, or her demon? "Dean was a good human man. He simply made a choice, one that I feel was the wrong one but his nevertheless."

"Good man? Bahh, good and human don't belong in the same sentence. There's a reason why Earth is referred to as hell. It's for the creatures that inhabit it."

"Certain humans believe in hell also. And that horned demons roam the darkness of the dimension. That mystical swamplands cover most of it."

He stared blankly at her before erupting into laughter. "Such an imagination you have! As if our situations could be reversed and humans thought we were the ones that lived in hell."

Insisting was futile. Enishka only saw things one way. His way.

"Nice change of topic, but let's get back to the human. He was using you, my dear. Are you really so sure he was being noble in returning to his wife? Perhaps he didn't confess his relationship with you to her. Maybe she believes her husband is innocent and you chased after him, trying to break up a solid marriage."

"Of-of course not. He told me he'd explained everything to her and they agreed to attend counseling to save the marriage."

"Would that be the first lie you caught the human in? Maybe, just maybe, my dear, he blamed you to make her jealous. To get her to think a beautiful woman was interested in her husband. That he was a real catch, instead of a selfish, spoiled liar."

"I don't follow?" Perhaps she did catch Dean in a couple of white lies, but only to keep her from being hurt. They weren't deliberate or spiteful. Were they?

"Do you think he really told her he planned on marrying you? She probably had no idea he was even seeing you. What if he was sleeping with both of you while telling you they didn't have a real marriage?"

She'd never thought of that. Of course, it was possible, and it made so much sense. Her heart started to beat a little heavier. Surely the evil one couldn't be on the same page as Caleb. Did everyone see that track as truth and she was the only one who refused to acknowledge it? No, Dean was human and therefore good. "That can't be. He wouldn't have done that. His marriage with Annie was dead, they were only living together for the sake of the adoption."

"Are you so sure, Keara?" The demon lord's voice was a bare whisper, making her strain to listen.

She wasn't sure. A sickening lurch twisted in her belly. No, this was Enishka. It was a trick, things were always tricky with him. But still, Caleb had hinted at the same thing. Was she that much of a fool that everyone saw Dean for what he was but her? That she was blinded by love like the idiot she apparently was?

Enishka stepped in closer behind her, so close she felt his hot breath in her ear. It was surprisingly sweet-smelling. As if he decided to mimic Caleb.

Desire curled in her belly at the reminder of Caleb. But no, this wasn't him. She was a fool, this was simply a dream.

"Come, my love. Walk with me."

"I don't go anywhere with you, Enishka." She felt proud of herself, letting him know she saw through his treachery.

But he only smiled. "We can stay, I suppose," he said, glancing around the room.

Keara looked also. To her surprise, her dream turned into her bedroom, except now it was more sexy than normal. Instead of black and white, it was black and blood red. The human half of her wiped away in an instant and filled with sex instead. Sex and demonality, a powerful combination that she fought daily.

Slick, satiny sheets that invited sensual images of male and female limbs entwined. Hardness and softness.

He laughed when he saw that she changed her mind and would indeed walk with him. Rather than stay in that erotic bedroom alone with him.

The moon outside was full and shining brightly. Stars glowed in the clear sky as they walked through garden paths. "Would marriage to me be so difficult?" he asked softly. "You'd be a queen, as you were meant to be. After all that suffering as a child? You are the only one who deserves it. But I have to choose soon and only you and Natalya are in the running." Reaching down for a tender rose, he plucked the flower and handed it to her as though it were a prize possession. She reached for it with slender fingers, smelling the sweetness as he spoke again. Urgently, as if he couldn't hold back sharing with her. "Speaking of which, she wants the human you are toying with now. Caleb."

Keara vowed to show nothing. To give away nothing. Simply looked at him with deliberately blank eyes.

"You remember what her power is? Anyone who mates with her becomes impotent with anyone else. Naturally, she has a rather large following of men."

"Why would she want Caleb?"

"Merely because you have him now, sweet. She's always wanted what you have."

It was just a dream. There was no way Natalya could travel to Earth, even if she desired it, in order to torment her. While Enishka might be able to conjure the power to send someone, he would have to exert an awful lot that would leave him weakened. He'd never do it. Not with an impending showdown.

"Think about it, Keara-mine. Think, and tomorrow, remember."

Those were the words she heard as she awoke the next morning. As if they chanted on their own in her head, over and over.

Think, and tomorrow, remember.

The powerful demon lord returned to his own body in the swamp where Natalya had no idea he'd even left.

"I can be your wife," she hissed. "You don't need her."

Enishka looked at her thoughtfully. The idiot had no idea what he needed. She was so jealous of Keara, it clouded her vision.

"You are aware that it's a temporary job?" he reminded. "My breed will eat their mother when they hatch."

The horror in her eyes showed she wasn't aware.

"I never have enjoyed children."

"I imagine I can learn to live without passing along genes." He rolled his head on his shoulders, the neck bones popping loudly in the silence. "Let's put you to the test, shall we, my dear?"

Natalya looked at him eagerly.

"Let's see if you can get Keara to strike out at the human Dean. If we can get her to rise to violence, we've got her. Take a human form and go seek him out."

Natalya took a dark haired form, mimicking that of Keara. "How's this?"

He nodded. "It'll do, if necessary. Or you can use it to hunt her new pet, Caleb. A handsome human man you might have fun with. As long as we can get her to strike, we have her. Oh, and Natalya?"

She looked back at him.

"Do not fail me."

"Never, master. But how shall I get to the hell dimension?" Her voice was sweet, knowing that he had the means to send her. It was a tremendous draw on his power but if he wanted this badly enough, he'd do it.

"Tell me what you would pay for the trip, my dear."

"Pay?" The look in her eyes was confused. Surely he didn't expect her to give him something for his own favor requested of her?

"Yes, pay," he said firmly. "You don't expect I would be weakened by sending you, *and returning you*, from the hell dimension?"

It was the tricky *returning you* that got her. The subtle threat of being left forever in hell that sent cold shivers down her spine like frozen little fingers grabbing for her. There wasn't much Natalya feared, but this was a childhood scare. Things like that stayed with you forever.

"What is it you'd want?" she asked slowly, cursing herself mentally for underestimating him.

"A blood promise. You will never betray me and will serve me always."

Blood promise. A ritual of blood willingly shed from demons and a promise made at the same time, unable to ever break. It also meant that once she became his wife, she could never rule the dimension. For how would she kill him off if she promised on her own spilt blood to serve him?

Yet, should she refuse, he could slaughter her here and now for attempted betrayal. Dammit, why was it the politics became more difficult the higher you climbed on the social steps of society?

"Of course, master," she smiled sweetly, because she had no other choice in the matter.

Chapter Seven
The Sweetness of Revenge

ॐ

The next morning, Keara did remember as per Enishka's last instructions. It was the first thing on her mind when she awoke. He was going to send Natalya after Caleb. Was that his game when he said he only helped out his own? She'd go crying to him and he'd turn her away unless she bartered her soul? Or gave him her powers? Or even agreed to bear his children?

Natalya couldn't have Caleb. Keara knew how she worked, the blonde demon would seduce him. He wouldn't be able to resist, no man could. Once that was done, Natalya had the power over men to cause impotence except with her. A tough lesson, to pick up a stranger in a bar and never have your Johnson work again. To have her disappear and you never again have sex, ever.

The only fate worse than that was following her into her dimension to serve her. Willingly. For that was the only way humans could get in. Short of the ones who had bartered their souls.

She could keep Caleb safe from getting tricked by Natalya. She could make him fall in love with her. The Punisher of Luciefyiore.

It was the lesser of the two evils. The Punisher and The Huntress. Herself and Natalya.

But then she'd run the risk of accidentally stealing his soul. And it would condemn her to a lifetime with Enishka, for she'd be proven demon if that happened.

She'd never deliberately forced a good human to fall in love with her. Not since the accidental high school incident.

Was it fair? Hell, why should she care? Life wasn't fair. She certainly hadn't been treated fairly in either dimension, so why should she worry about another?

Was she deliberately going to do this? Force his love, take away his choice? His humanity? Her father did with her mother. Obviously it was how she was wired, for it was in her genes.

Was she doing it to save him from Natalya? Or was there a less heroic reason? Like the excuse to keep him forever tied to her? Was her demon speaking? That selfish, rotten core of her that surfaced over and over?

When she was an innocent teenager, she discovered she could cause men to fall in love with her to the point of madness. Back then, it was merely by focusing her wants and desires on them. Now however, her bitterness was like a screen filtering the love. Now she'd have to do it differently.

She'd have to focus during sex. And fight hard not to suck the soul. She couldn't condemn his life along with hers.

Tonight.

A slight vibration in the dining room caught her attention and Keara concentrated on not looking directly into the room. Peering through the curtain of dimensions was easy now that Enishka kept sucking her through the portals. She may have given him the power to summon her against her will, but without realizing it, he gave her a weapon in return.

Her abstract sight saw the faintest shadow on the white wall. A feminine shadow…with horns.

Natalya.

"How did you get here?" Keara hissed.

"It doesn't matter," Natalya said, morphing fully into her body and trying not to look surprised that Keara had spotted her. Surely that was impossible? She circled the table opposite her, like a hunter stalking its prey. "I was given permission to hunt you."

"Hunt me? Not possible," Keara spat. "I have more power than you ever will."

Keara was right. How else could she have sensed her arrival? But trying for the element of surprise, Natalya struck hard with a blow to the center of Keara's chest.

Keara flew across the room and through the open doorway to land against the living room wall. Natalya ran after her with the dagger in hand to finish the job, but to her surprise, Keara wasn't lying on the floor. She wasn't even in the living room. Natalya paused in confusion before looking around her wildly. She grunted when she was kicked in the middle of her back. She flew head first into the wall where Keara was supposed to be.

Her horns tore holes in the wall and she was stuck midway there. Keara grabbed the back of her neck and pulled her out.

And held her up with one hand until her feet dangled above the ground.

No one had ever knocked the breath out of her before. Certainly not a half-breed piece of...

Fingers tightened around her throat.

"Yes, I know what you're thinking," Keara said.

If she could have, Natalya would have shivered at the coldness in the voice. Keara's eyes glowed even worse than Enishka's did. Her heart beat faster in her chest and the adrenaline surged in her limbs. Maybe the rumors were right. She'd made it up back then, but maybe the intense glow of Keara's eyes did cause the fire that destroyed their school. And had her banished from Luciefyiore.

"So, replace me, hmm? You'll be the demon lord's next bride? For the opportunity to poison him and rule?" Keara asked.

"Never. I wouldn't have him with a ten-foot pole."

"Liar."

"Wait," Natalya croaked.

"Why?"

"I…I have information to barter."

The hand from her throat dropped so suddenly, her oxygen-depleted legs gave out beneath her. She collapsed onto the floor, gagging at the tightness in her dry throat.

"Out with it."

"The human. Dean. Wasn't your…mistake."

"What do you mean?"

"He traded…his soul…to Enishka."

"Before or after meeting me?"

"Before." She took a deep breath. "He knew what you were. All along. He was being fed information about you."

"His purpose?"

"Enishka sent him to tempt you into a testing phase."

"His reward?"

"Money at first. He was a millionaire when he met you, wasn't he? After he traded his human life in, he was to receive power. The end result? Status in our dimension."

"So money plus power equals status at the end of his two lives."

"Yes."

"And are you telling me because he's now your competition on the social ladder? What's it going to take to get rid of you?"

"That slimy human can't compete with me. But if you take revenge on him, they have you."

"You do know that Enishka wants me as his bride? That's why he sent you, the best huntress in Luciefyiore, to seek me?" Keara asked suddenly.

The hiss of indrawn breath told her that Natalya didn't know.

"I take it he made certain promises to you?"

Slowly, Natalya nodded. "He did. He never mentioned you as a possible candidate for bride."

"Well you can have him. I have every intention of staying in the Earth dimension."

"I don't want him."

"Then I repeat, what will it take to get rid of you?"

The energy expended during the fight with Natalya exhausted her, both mentally and physically. Mentally because she knew it was a preparation for the showdown with Enishka that was sure to come.

Physically because…damn. Demons have inhuman strength and she still wasn't sure how she defeated Natalya. It must have been that desperation streak in her that had surfaced one other time in her life.

The time she burned down the all-girl school she attended back then. Luciekynokus.

Much as she hated it, she had to lie down for a nap. And hope that she could actually rest this time instead of dreaming, which sucked time and energy from her.

Or maybe she could get really lucky and Enishka would summon her.

Keara sighed. At this moment, she was too exhausted to care. She collapsed onto her bed and immediately drifted away.

She was in Dean's white SUV, driving down a path she remembered well.

And somewhere, Caleb was with her, commanding this dream.

Not this one, Caleb. Please.

You can do it, love. You've already lived through it. You just need to learn from it. I'm here for you. Be strong.

He knew the "be strong" would get her, Keara thought. Dean pulled up in the curved driveway and came around to open her car door.

"Well, baby doll? What do you think?"

"It's gorgeous."

"And all ours. If you like the inside as much as the outside."

The house was magnificent. A corner home in a prestigious neighborhood filled with attorneys, stockbrokers, and investors.

The front door was opened as they approached the steps. "Welcome folks. You must be Dean and Keara? I'm Matt."

Matt held out his hand for Dean's handshake first.

"Yes, Matt. I'm Dean, this is my fiancée, Keara. She's the one who'll decide if this is a make or break deal," he joked.

Matt shook Keara's hand next, the charm already lighting his salesman's eyes. "I guess I'd better be extra nice to you then, hmm?"

She forced a smile. Stupid human. Treating her as though she were a half-wit like the rest of them.

Keara refused to allow this scene to continue. She woke herself up, slowly coming to reality to find herself staring at her bedroom ceiling. The familiar sight strangely comforting.

It didn't matter that she'd refused to dream, because Keara knew what originally happened anyway. They'd decided to rent the home instead of purchasing immediately. They'd just signed the paperwork and had gotten their keys when the realtor left and Dean paled as he stared out the window.

He'd forced her to hide, because Annie had driven by and noticed his SUV.

Annie. The wife who supposedly he had no real marriage with. The wife who knew he was engaged to another. The wife who agreed to their amicable divorce with the understanding that he'd get visitations with Carissa.

He'd had a private conversation with her outside on the front porch while Keara crouched in an upstairs closet.

She refused to relive those feelings she felt back then. The humiliation, the doubt. The sick pit of something deep in her belly.

The ever-so-brief knowledge that she was being used. That maybe, just maybe, Annie wasn't aware of her.

She jumped when pounding sounded at her door. She stumbled to it, throwing it open to the real-life Caleb.

"You have to relive these, baby."

She regretted that she'd long ago given this human the power to invade her dreams. Unfortunately, as a child away from the teachings of her demon father, she had no idea what powers existed inside her when she drew Caleb to her.

"I'm tired. I don't have the energy to dream. I just want to sleep. Is that too much to ask?"

"You won't be able to rest until you can get your mind to relax, too. You have to go through this."

"What is the point? What's done is done. I loved and lost. He returned to his wife, he's happy. I learned to live without him. Big deal."

"But Keara, you've never gotten angry over Dean. You allowed him to make you feel like you were crazy for feeling normal emotions. You never understood they make you human, especially rage."

"I don't get angry," she said coldly.

Not since the fire at Luciekynokus. No one knew quite how the fire started, but Keara did. It was the reason why she didn't allow her eyes to glow for long periods but Caleb didn't need to know that.

"Everyone gets angry. It makes us human. We're not angels, we're not demons. We're human. When you suppress your feelings, you may dull the pain, but you also numb the pleasure. You are human, baby. Not demon. Live, Keara. Live and love."

Live and love? Such an odd phrase, almost as odd as Enishka's *think, and tomorrow, remember.*

"I do love," she said slowly, because she couldn't really remember. It was all so confusing, Enishka telling her one thing and Caleb giving her another.

Still, his voice was soothing and calm when he said, "Tell me about the breakup with Dean. You'd shut me out by then. I have no idea what happened."

Keara sighed. He wasn't going to give up and sleep was obviously lost. Again. Maybe it would help to talk to his calming force. Although she wouldn't go into the humiliating scene as she crouched in the closet, like a scared and humiliated rodent. "It was a normal, bright day in April. We met at ten in the morning, Dean had rented us a house. The owner handed us each a garage remote and a set of door keys. Everything was fine. He called me later like he always did and said that Annie had called him over to see Carissa. He laughed because every time he was around Annie, she would kick him out of the house. His last comment to me was, 'Let's see if I can get kicked out a third time'. He was supposed to call me on his way back home from there and at nine-thirty, it dawned on me that he never did. Just then an email popped up. It read, *Don't freak. Will call you in the a.m.*"

"Selfish bastard. How could he send you something like that and not expect you to stew about it all night?"

Keara shrugged, the hurtful emotions turned off while she told the story. For once, Caleb took pity on her and allowed her to hide her raw insides.

"The next morning there was no phone call. I was up at five after not sleeping all night. Finally at ten there was another email. *Attending church with everyone. Will call later.* All

I could think of was that to attend church obviously meant he spent the night there."

Keara took a deep, painful breath and decided to turn down the hurtful emotions. Her voice became monotonous, the deadened gaze focused on a spot on the wall behind him. She forcibly relaxed her hands. The hands that clenched together, white knuckled.

"He finally called around noon. Said we had to talk. In a sarcastic tone of voice, I said *no kidding*. When he arrived, he had all of the stuff that I'd ever given him dumped into a plastic trash bag. He handed it to me and said he'd decided to reconcile with Annie. That he couldn't leave a family behind, not even for love. He walked out and left me in shock."

"Is that the last time you had contact with him?"

"No. About a month later we had a phone conversation. It was…pretty nasty. He told me to get over my bitterness."

"As if he wasn't the one that made you bitter? Being bitter is totally normal."

"No. Being bitter is what thrust me into the testing phase. I have to leave it behind."

"No, baby. Emotions make you human. Being bitter is what made you human. You'll have an emotionally stable life while Dean will always remain unhappy and unsatisfied no matter which direction he takes."

"Then why am I being tested?"

Caleb's expression was unreadable. "I can't answer that. But I'm sure there's an answer somewhere."

Keara rubbed tiredly at her eyes. When she opened them, Caleb was staring at her. God, he was beautiful. Smooth, chocolaty eyes contrasted with dark blond hair. So ruggedly masculine, it curled her insides.

He could be hers for eternity. Worship the ground she walked on forever. Only have eyes for her.

She'd never, ever have to worry about him returning to his wife. Or meeting another woman in spite of claiming how beautiful she was. For he'd only have eyes for her.

When she had a bad day and her hair was a mess. When her horns protruded and her eyes glowed blue. He'd only have eyes for her.

If she made him.

She was going crazy. Lack of sleep was definitely getting to her. She was planning to seduce Caleb and make him fall in love with her.

It was insane. What the hell was happening to her? Was she turning evil? Was she going full demon?

"Come here, baby," he whispered. He wrapped her in the comforting strength of his arms and tucked her head under his chin. She could feel the sweet kisses he pressed to the top of her head.

She could smell the faint cologne that marked his warm skin. Feel his loud, steady heartbeat beneath her ear. Barely feel as he quietly and easily lifted her to head into her bedroom. Pulled the covers open and gently eased her in.

Finally, there was semblance of rest when he curled next to her. Where she could breathe easily, safe in his arms. Nothing could get to her when she was wrapped up tightly.

He was gone when she awoke, but it was okay. She was a new person with a little rest in her. A rejuvenated woman who knew what she had to do.

Shower and a killer hairstyle. Perfectly seductive makeup. A quick study in the full length mirror.

She looked good tonight. The tiniest dab of perfume at her pulse points and one more sweep of the long, glossy locks that she would run over Caleb's sensitive body later.

Red dress, high heels. Dressed to kill.

She took a deep breath to calm her nerves. It was Caleb. It'd be fine. She didn't need to feel guilt at his forced love. She was doing it to save him, after all.

Not because she wanted him. Forever.

She thought about her conversation with the demon Natalya. She didn't trust a word of what Natalya said about Dean. Oh, she didn't doubt that Enishka sent Natalya after her, but Dean trading his soul for wealth and power? If that was the case, he certainly wouldn't have returned to Annie when he had those.

No, Natalya had made it up and she'd have to tread carefully there to find out what the traitorous demon was up to. She'd have to watch to keep her from backstabbing her no matter what arrangement they'd agreed to.

She knew it was necessary to manipulate Caleb's love, but why did she feel so damn guilty?

Because she wanted it?

She morphed into Caleb's loft apartment and left him a note. *Come find me tonight. I feel like dancing.*

It didn't take him long to find her downstairs in his own bar. The seductive red dress was a dead giveaway, as was the crowd of men dancing around her, vying for her attention.

The sway of slow, smooth hip circles caught his eye and he had no other care as he pushed easily through the crowd to her. She immediately pressed herself to him, wrapping slender arms around his neck.

"Hi," she whispered.

"Are you being naughty?" he asked, the barest hint of jealousy in his voice.

"I'd like to be naughty," she said with a laugh. "I was waiting for you."

"Waiting for me, huh?" As if he couldn't believe she was serious.

She twined her tongue with his, right there on the dance floor.

"What's gotten into you?" he whispered.

"You, Caleb. I want you. Now," she whispered back. "Let's go upstairs or let's put on a show for the bar." She made her point by sensuously pressing her hips into his and circling slowly. "Imagine you, deep inside my warmth as I clench and unclench around you."

There was a bulge in his pants that he couldn't fight. That desperately wanted to be set free.

He grabbed the tiny, feminine hand in his larger one. "Let's go."

They could barely race upstairs fast enough. He kept stopping her on the stairs to slide his hand underneath her skirt.

To groan when he found no panties. Just warm, wet femaleness, waiting and swollen and eager.

She slowly unbuttoned the top half of his shirt and parted it wide. Right there on the deserted stairwell, halfway up.

She let her gaze linger over the magnificent chest bared before her. He was beautiful, hard muscle and tight skin. Nipples, the color of dusky cocoa.

She drew a finger over the taut abdominal lines and felt his stomach tighten. She then pressed kisses to those very lines.

That was it. She grabbed both halves of his shirt and pulled. Remaining buttons popped everywhere. They rattled down the stairs, like tiny echoes, all the way down. She yanked the offending garment off broad shoulders. Leaning forward, she captured a nipple between her lips and nibbled lightly.

Her fingers trailed the spiral of hair down to his waistband. Further down, to feel the enormous bulge through his jeans. He groaned when she pressed lightly against the rough fabric to feel how ready he was.

He was just as ready as she.

He pulled her up the rest of the stairs, leaving his buttons scattered on the steps.

By the time he locked his front door behind him, she was gone. However, a trail of clothing led to his bedroom. Like a man half crazed, he burst into his own room to see her lying naked on his bed.

On his bed.

Warm, sweet woman. With thighs spread and fingers touching her own sensitive flesh. Giving him a show.

He stood at the edge of the bed, just watching. But when she glanced at his cock, he was the one to roughly yank the snap on his jeans so she could push them down his hips. Then she was on her knees, kissing his hipbones and letting the softness of her hair bathe his erection.

With her hands on his thighs, she began to kiss his testicles. Small, gentle kisses and then sweet jabbing licks with her tongue. Soon she licked every spot of his ball sac but ignored his hot penis.

"God, that feels good," he whispered.

He grasped the back of her hair and turned her head directly to his throbbing cock.

Her laughter was musical. She gave one small lick to capture the sweet pre-cum that glistened on the tip of its smooth head. "Is this what you want?"

He groaned.

"I think so."

She took his whole throbbing head into her mouth and sucked the delicate sweetness of it. It was swollen and pulsed as she held it in the warm recesses of her mouth.

"Keara, baby," he muttered. She slid her lips down the side of his cock, wetting it thoroughly, up and down.

"My turn again," he commanded, and pulled her up alongside him. He bent his head to hers to kiss her deeply, then twisted away. "Up on all fours."

Keara turned over and rose, shaking her ass in the air. She spread her legs slightly just to give him a teaser.

He slid fingers over her swollen slit, then parted the slick flesh to look at the pinkness inside.

"Sweet," he told her. "Like this?"

His finger curled into her.

"Ooh," she moaned softly. "I do like it."

His finger slowed to the slightest movement deep within her. She thrust her hips harder at him, trying to force his fingers to move deeper, go faster, do something.

He chuckled under his breath.

"More," she insisted.

"You want my cock instead?" While he spoke, he grabbed a condom and slid it on.

His words and movements sent a rush of heat to gather in her pussy, to fill her up with liquid slickness. And then the thick head of his cock rubbed up against her. Parted her sensitive nether lips intimately. And slid in the barest half inch.

She thrust her hips backward and forced him another inch. He buried his cock head into her warm wetness, but then pulled back again.

"Are you going to give it to me or what?"

He chuckled. "I am. Patience, love. If you hold still, I'll give you what you want."

"I promise," she moaned. Ready to do anything he asked.

He gripped her hips in his hands to hold her steady. And slid in slowly, all the way to the hilt.

She felt like a velvet glove, gripping his cock. Hot and wet and sucking at his tender flesh. Pulling him in and holding him tight while he fought to slowly inch out.

It was a struggle between her body and his. She was grasping and gripping, he was trying to withdraw. They worked against each other and it was so deliciously wonderful.

Her breathing was slow and ragged. Just like his.

And when her cunt began to quiver, she started to struggle against the hands that held her hips still.

"Harder," she moaned. "I'm starting to come."

He reached around and pulled on her clit. He slammed into her, hard, over and over, a quick beating rhythm. She exploded, clenching his cock with her inner muscles.

"Keara," he groaned.

Geez, it wasn't supposed to happen like this. She was supposed to be driving him wild, not the other way around. Selfish woman, concentrate. He's supposed to love you. You have to make him love you.

She was supposed to think about how much she wanted him to desire her. Not how much she desired him.

She turned over and slid down to where he was still on his knees. She bent her head and gave a delicate flick of her tongue on the purple head of his cock. And tasted their combined fluids.

His and hers.

Concentrated on the feelings he made her feel. The emotions she alone could give him. Felt her eyes glow.

The joy, the happiness.

His and hers.

Let him know as she sank his stiffened flesh deep into her mouth that this was what she wanted most in the world. The combination of them.

The lust. The passion. The want. The need.

His and hers.

He began to rock his hips. Slowly, like he just couldn't help himself. He slid wetly from her mouth with a groan as she tempted and teased. Groaned louder when she sucked him back in and made him hers with the passion that she would only admit to at this moment.

"I'm too close, Keara."

She sucked harder, gripped his cock deeper into the wetness of her mouth.

"Baby, I mean it." Desperation tinged his voice.

Still, she refused to let him pull away as she gripped his muscular butt with her hands and held him against her.

She felt it when his climax exploded. Felt it roll upward from his balls and out into her mouth. So unlike the power sucking she often did.

His cock spurted his release into her throat and she swallowed the essence of Caleb. The pure, human sweetness of him.

"Baby," he gasped as he pulled out and collapsed on the bed.

So this was a blow job. A real one. Her first one.

He was still hard and she crawled up alongside his muscular body. The most perfect body in the whole world, all dimensions included. She straddled him and slid his wet and still hard penis slowly into her sheath.

He looked up questioningly.

"Shh," she whispered and began to leisurely rotate her hips on him. Then she leaned over and sucked at the tender skin of his neck, marking him as hers. Fought the inner rage as she tried to control both halves of her personality.

She had to concentrate. Force his love.

Harder and harder she rocked as his cock refused to soften. Their heartbeats raced and their breaths came in quick, heated pants.

She felt the demon coming to life inside her, trying to take over.

He pumped his hips into her, pressing so deep she gasped at each thrust.

This time when the explosion hit, it was simultaneous with his.

She was powerless against it. She had no strength left.

"Oh my God," Caleb groaned, his eyes looking into hers before they rolled back in his head as he lost consciousness.

Missing the heavy wet tears that cut trails down her cheeks. Dripping slowly with heavy wet plops onto his still chest.

When all was said and done, she had been unable to control the demon.

For she'd stolen his soul.

Chapter Eight
The Challenge of Liberation

Ꙅ

No one was more aware than Caleb that Keara would need some personal space. In the meantime, he had his own work to do. He entered the most popular of his rival bars and sat up at the counter.

"Bored with your own place?" asked Alan, the owner, as he slid him a drink.

"Just scoping out the competition," Caleb responded with a grin. "What are you doing working the bar?"

Alan shrugged. "Good help's hard to find. I'm covering for my bartender's maternity leave."

It was convenient that Alan had been in the thick of things for a while. He'd be just the one to answer a pertinent question. "So you got any interesting new faces? Particularly female?"

"A blonde that's been hanging out a bit. Attractive. Something strange about her, though I can't put a finger on it. She should be coming in soon."

"Thanks."

He'd wait. Because it should be worth it. It wasn't long before that same blonde found him, moved in next to him and sat down. Moved in with a purpose. Exactly like Keara had been months ago.

The blonde never bothered to wait for him to notice her. Yet she halted at his next words. "Missing your horns."

Natalya angled her head. "Keara warn you already?"

"She didn't need to. I can spot you a mile away."

"Then you sought me, human. Big mistake. I'm your worst nightmare."

* * * * *

She had just sat down with her salad when the chair opposite her table was pulled out and someone sat down.

"Keara."

"Dean! What the hell are you doing here?"

He looked exactly the same as he always did. Soft blue eyes, angelic blond hair. The tiniest dimple near his sensuous lips.

And yet there was something missing.

"Baby doll, I miss you. Bad. I-I had to see you. Talk to you. Tell you I've never stopped loving you."

"You left me, Dean. Remember? Six months ago. You chose another woman over me."

"No, my love. I chose not to damage my kids, but you know what it's like with Annie and me. I finally realized, it's pointless to try to stay together for the sake of the children, even the one we just adopted. She'll never change. Especially when I'm so in love with you. That kind of love only comes along once in a lifetime. Who am I to throw such a precious gift away?"

"It's too late. Go back to Annie and your family."

"No, don't do this. Don't make the same mistake I did and toss our perfect love aside."

"Perfect love, Dean? *You* tossed that aside, remember?"

"I'm rectifying it, Keara. You and I, we were meant to be together. Always. Soul mates." He tried to reach for her hand but she yanked it from his grasp.

"Please. Let me just talk then."

"Talk about what? You and I are done. There is no love, there's no anything. I wish you well, good luck to you and your family. Those kids, remember?"

"Keara, just a few minutes of your time. Please."

She took a deep sigh. "Ten minutes, Dean. That's all you deserve and then you are out of my life, got it?"

He nodded eagerly. "I have so much to tell you, baby. Ten minutes is going to shoot by."

Keara looked pointedly at her watch and forked a bite of salad into her mouth.

"Thing is, I will never stop loving you and I realize that now. Well, I've always realized that but I felt like I had to stick it out for the sake of my family."

"Then why are you here?"

"Because I realize I made a major mistake. I can't live without the love of my life. There will never be as pure a love between a couple as what you and I had."

"It really wasn't pure, was it?"

Dean looked confused. "Of course it was. We loved each other unconditionally."

"I loved what I thought you were. What you tricked me into thinking you were. But somehow, you knew exactly what I craved in a partner and gave it to me. How did you do that?"

"I...don't understand. I can't read minds, baby. I simply was what you loved."

"No, you weren't. You pretended to be the caring, romantic family man in order to lure me in." *Like her father. To give up everything he ever knew for her mother.*

"That's ridiculous, baby."

"No, it's not. How amazing that you took your food prepared like mine. That you enjoyed the same music as me. That you loved exactly the things I loved."

"We were meant to be together."

"Or a little too much of a coincidence. You knew what I wanted and played it up."

"No, how could you even think that?"

"A little birdie told me you've sold your soul, sweetie. That your entire mission was to ensnare me."

There was complete silence on his end, and Keara took another bite of her salad impatiently.

"I don't know what you're talking about. I do know I have a lot of making up to do. But that's what I want. I want to make it up to you for the rest of our lives. I want to take care of you. Prove that I'm the man made for you. We could travel, just like we planned. Remember? Make love in every country before we die of old age?"

He stared at her earnestly. She continued to eat her salad. Had he not heard?

Dean sat back and folded his hands across his midsection expectantly. Smiled at her with his baby blue eyes, the way he always did.

His eyes would crinkle at the corners. A happy dimple would appear next to his sensual lips. And Keara realized that she would have fallen for it. In the past.

She would have forgiven him and chalked it up to a misunderstanding on her part. Maybe she expected too much of him. Perhaps Natalya lied about him.

And he fully expected the same reaction now.

"Is that it?" she asked coldly.

His perfect smile faltered. "What do you mean?"

"Is that all you have to say? Because I've pointed out everything I've learned."

"Do you want me to beg? 'Cause I'm willing. I will beg for you, Keara. Want me to say I'm sorry? I was wrong? I'm all of those and more. I made a mistake, I'm human."

"Yep. You made the biggest mistake of your life. I was too good for you but willing to settle for a loser anyway. And almost did."

He was such a disgusting mess she didn't have time for. Last night the demon in her arose and sucked the soul of Caleb, and here was Dean whining about his life mistakes?

"Hey, my love," she leaned in close enough to kiss him. The way she used to. But she didn't. "I'll call you. Sometime."

With that, Keara rose and left, leaving him to pay for her salad with all his millions. She hoped his money bought him some happiness somewhere down the road.

She headed directly to the bar, where she knew she'd see Caleb. Wondering how she felt about Caleb now that she'd seen Dean in person. Of course, she also wondered what it would be like to see Caleb now with guilt clouding her vision.

Once she got to the bar, she pondered where to sit.

"Keara?"

"Rod. Hi, how are you?" She knew of course, regretfully he was her minion and she would always know his mind now.

"I'm great. Mike and I are...you know."

She smiled at him. "Yeah. That's good."

He smiled back. "We're happy. So what are you up to?"

"Waiting for Caleb."

"Are you seeing him?"

"Yes, I am."

"Good. You deserve someone to make you happy. I was so unhappy being a divorce attorney and I didn't even realize it. Life is about balance, isn't it? It's so much easier to deal with the nastiness at work now that I can leave it behind me when Mike and I are together. He's meeting me tonight, we'll shoot some pool."

"Business is good, then?"

"Booming, as always. The divorce rate is up, you know."

"Does it ever go down?"

Rod laughed. "Not really. The success comes in what kind of clientele you can snag. Everyone wants high end clientele and I just reached a pretty high. A couple of weeks ago I received a phone call from someone who'd heard about my reputation. She knows her husband is a rat bastard and suspects he had an affair on her, but can't prove it. As soon as she can, she's taking him for everything he's got. All we need is a clue as to who the other woman was and we can search her phone records, emails, etc. The good news is, they're a multi-millionaire couple. She's already kicked him out of the house and filed for divorce, so it's just about the fight over the money, now." Rod rubbed his palms together gleefully.

"Got a name? You know how many men I run across."

"Well, it's unethical for me to share this much of my client's story. But if you just smile at me, I'll know where to look to service her."

"Okay."

"Her name is Angela Williamson." He paused, waiting for Keara's reaction. The reaction was slow in coming, she just stood frozen, looking at him for long moments.

"Hmm. If my name was Angela, I'd shorten it to Annie."

Surprise stole across Rod's face for a moment, followed by happiness. "Not many people would associate Annie with Angela. Would you happen to know her husband Dean?"

Keara smiled. This time she'd listened to her instincts, knowing something was up when Dean had come crawling back. Now she knew why. He didn't decide their love was too great to throw away.

His wife had left him.

Bastard.

Red hot rage boiled over her body and threatened to let loose the glow of her eyes. One lone voice broke through it, soothing her, like a familiar loving caress.

"Keara," Caleb said calmly.

"Okay, then, take care," Rod said before turning on his heel with a look of disgust at Caleb's arrival. Thankfully missing the reaction.

Keara turned to see Caleb, grateful for the distraction. He looked good in his black dress shirt that unbuttoned at the throat, exposing sexy male flesh.

Sexy male flesh that was unmarked by the love bite she'd left him with earlier.

Puzzled, she stared at his neck where it should have been.

"What's wrong?" Caleb asked.

"Where'd the hickey go?" she asked softly. As if she wasn't sure if he was tricking her somehow.

"What hickey?"

"The one from me."

He laughed. "You've never left me one. And I've never left you one, silly. Besides, it's been a while since you visited me," he murmured. "If you'd like to get together and leave one, I could be talked into it. If it's somewhere discreet."

Not been together in a while? Did he not remember?

"What'd you do last night, Caleb?"

"I just worked. Like I always do."

"Did I come into the bar?"

"Not last night. What's going on? Are you okay?" he asked, suddenly concerned.

Keara forced a smile. "I'm fine."

"Sure?" he said, looking into her eyes.

"Yes," she responded, with one last look at his neck. She had marked him last night, hadn't she? She had made him fall in love with her? Right? Did he love her? As much as she loved him?

Oh, hell, where the hell did that come from?

Keara walked from the bar, quickly. Glancing over her shoulder, her mind still on Caleb. She got out the front door when the wind hit.

Followed by the painful thrust between dimensions.

She landed on her knees before Enishka's raised threshold, where he stood sparring with the Rot Demon.

"I am getting really sick of being sucked through the portal by you," she said.

"Bitch!" screeched the Rot Demon as he kicked at her. "Show some respect for our lord and master."

Keara glared hotly at him as she gripped her thigh. The spot where he'd kicked still burned and would bruise tomorrow. She focused her gaze on him. He took a step back as he watched her eyes glow.

"My child. How kind of you to visit," Enishka called.

Keara was distracted enough to turn her bright blue stare toward him. "I didn't request a visit," she pointed out.

"And yet you can't refuse," he smiled.

Keara sighed. "Why am I here?" She took a look around. Enishka was naked from the waist up, for once his legs in his original form. Mighty and muscular, huge towering powerful thighs, necessary to carry the rest of his bulging body. Speaking of which, she looked at the rest of him. His chest and biceps were powerfully built and gleaming of sweat from the practiced swordplay.

As she watched, he cut the sword in a pattern through the air.

Simply a show-off.

"Why am I here?" she repeated.

"It occurs to me you were never tested along with the other children at Luciekynokus. I have no ideas what powers are held in that half-bred body of yours."

"I was never tested because I was considered different from the others. Human. Aren't I a little too old for testing? That's done before puberty."

"Normally. As demon lord, I have the right to know of which powers each demon has inherited."

"But I am a half-breed and no longer of your dimension. If I'm injured or killed during testing, it violates the Human Protection Act."

"Oh," he grinned. "I'll be ever so careful not to kill you."

Keara knew exactly what a caged bird felt like. Better yet, a gladiator. Forced to fight and in a life-or-death situation, who knew what powers might be revealed?

Enishka angled his sharp blade slowly toward her cheek, daring her to flinch.

She didn't.

When he struck, he sliced across her cheekbone. Bright red showed before it dripped down the side of her face.

"Eeww," muttered the Rot Demon. "She bleeds red. Like the humans."

"Exactly my point," Keara said.

Enishka narrowed his eyes. "You will fight, Keara."

"Or you will be punished for harming me, master," she retorted.

Fury blazed in his watery, reddened eyes. With a frustrated screech, he jumped before her, and thrust a nine inch blade deep into her belly.

Keara stood absolutely still, the handle of the dagger protruding obscenely from her abdomen. Plugging the well of blood that should be pouring from the wound like a waterfall.

There was a gasp of horror somewhere. Dismay over the idea of upcoming punishment from the actual harming of a human. A direct violation of the law imposed upon them by the ancient Greek council. And they'd been known to punish the demons as a whole for the actions of the demon lord.

A look of confusion, followed by fear, ran fluidly across Enishka's face.

"Bitch," he muttered. "You did that on purpose."

Tinkling bells rang, louder and louder, but Keara wasn't aware if it was her imagination or actual ringing. Lightheadedness had hit, like flashing stars behind her eyes as her blood pressure dropped.

And then they appeared.

Protection Fairies. Tiny, winged beings with a golden glow circling around their heads. They buzzed, wings fluttering so quickly they were but a blur. Round and round they flew around Enishka, who paled. Some laid tiny fingers on Keara. In an instant, the knife was no longer there.

Nor the pain.

That was when Keara realized why Enishka paled. The pain would be magnified on the blade now. Tenfold.

And it was being handed off to her.

The smallest fairy buzzed at her. Keara tore her eyes from the dagger she'd reached for, and focused on the fluttering fairy.

She was the queen. Her flaxen hair was the length of her entire body, floating in the wind. Her voice was light and flowing, like a summer breeze.

"*Lex talionis.*"

"Mirror punishment?"

The queen nodded. "An eye for an eye."

"Thank you," said Keara softly.

"For your compensation, human. Free passage back to your world, for the painful way you were dragged here." The creature continued. She then flew up and kissed Keara on the forehead. The spot tingled for a moment, then penetrated like a kiss of peppermint oil.

The swamp was quiet and still when Keara turned to face Enishka. Without warning, she plunged the dagger into his abdomen in the same spot where he'd stabbed her.

An eye for an eye.

He let out a long, torturous howl.

The fairies immediately flew around Enishka, making sure he suffered the torture he'd doled out first, but refusing to allow him the reprieve of death.

Crazy with pain, Enishka swatted at the winged beings, earning a tsking sound from them. Keara's clotted cut disappeared from her cheek. In trade, Enishka's cheek split open.

He howled and stomped, certainly not taking his medicine like a man.

Keara smiled grimly before nodding to the fairy.

The kiss on her forehead tingled again before her body winked. The dimension around her faded, replaced by the figures of her own dimension as she materialized there.

Enishka's throne was replaced with a bed. He lay in it, dark circles under his eyes.

Gently, Tobias changed the bandages on his abdomen.

"Will it scar, Tobias?" Enishka asked tragically.

Tobias studied the angry gash Keara had made with the blade.

"Yes, master," he said quietly.

"Not that, you idiot," Enishka screamed. "My face."

Tobias glanced up quickly. What would one more scar matter on such ugliness?

"That bitch," Enishka muttered without waiting for his response. "I'll enjoy watching her suffer when I get her here."

Tobias wondered if she'd be the one to suffer. Truth was, Enishka wasn't in his right mind ever since his twenty-five year banishment. He was still powerful, but mentally unstable.

Keara was more than a match. Mentally, she was whole. Physically, no one quite knew her strengths or weaknesses.

She reminded him a lot of Natalya.

Chapter Nine
The Bitter Taste of Betrayal

ဢ

Keara was exhausted the next morning. Short tempered as though she hadn't slept. Obviously she had, for she had the dreams to prove it. In fact, it felt like she hadn't slept in quite a few days instead of just last night.

She was run down and crabby. And more than a little guilty. Confused. Bewildered.

Was it any wonder that she picked a fight with the man she loved? She needed her space and how else did a demon obtain it?

It didn't help that he wanted her to relive another damn issue with Dean. Why did she have to go through that? It was pointless, dammit. What's done was done.

It wasn't like she wanted to fall in love. He was just supposed to love her.

Besides, she had to store up some more reserves.

So when Caleb called, she point-blank told him she was going to a bar "with a little more action" than his.

The pause on the telephone made her feel a little shrewish. Especially when he asked, "What's going on?"

"Nothing. You know I'm out…seeking. There's nothing different."

"The difference is you have me."

"I told you, I never wanted a relationship. Why is that too much for the male ego to comprehend? The sex has been great, but that's all it was. Sex."

"You can belittle it as easily as that? It's only sex to you?"

"What else is it supposed to be? You aren't my boyfriend, we aren't exclusive."

"You're bitter."

"I'm not. I'm realistic and I decided a long time ago after I loved someone unconditionally, that the pleasure of that love isn't worth the consequences of the pain afterward. I'd rather not have love any longer."

Ashamedly, Keara knew he only felt differently about the emotion because she made him. She'd forced his love. He didn't get a choice like she did. Like everyone should.

"Dammit, Keara, when will you wake up and see what's in front of you? When it's too late?" he said before hanging up on her.

Frustrated with life, Keara sat in her living room and pondered whether or not to call him back. But the choice was taken from her when the phone rang again.

She answered on the first ring. "Hello?"

"Boyfriend troubles?"

The pit of her stomach dropped, but she couldn't tell if it was from disappointment from it not being Caleb or instantaneous dread that it was Enishka. Of course, if he was calling, it meant he didn't dare pull her through, so she was safe for the moment. Perhaps he was still weakened from his wound. "How are you able to keep dropping into this dimension?"

"You gave me a link to you when you embraced your demonality. Sever it by coming back to Luciefyiore."

Keara sighed. "Where are you calling from?"

"Are you sure I'm calling? Perhaps you fell asleep on the sofa and think you answered a ringing phone. Maybe I'm just another dream of yours."

"I don't care if you're a dream or a real phone conversation. You're taking up my time and I'd like to know why. What the hell do you want from me?"

The tone of his voice snapped. "I want you, period. You are owed to me, Jenesi. Your mother was trained to be mine and tricked by my second in command. You are that offspring and *owed to me*."

"Do I not have a choice?"

"Did I?"

"Maybe I love another. A human."

"Ahh, yes. This Caleb. Are you so sure he wants what's best for you? Why is he making you feel all this rage? Dredging up all that water under the bridge with the old boyfriend?"

"He's not bringing it up for his own purposes. He just wants me to see it with open eyes."

"Open eyes? So he can look good. If that's how you feel, Keara. But is that how you feel? Do you believe him?"

God, she wasn't sure. She was tired, so very tired. All the time, even when she slept she felt like she hadn't. The only time she was relieved was when Caleb rocked her to sleep.

It was like the nights were wasted. Sometimes she couldn't even remember if she actually fell asleep.

And she was hungry. All the time. Addicted to power surges, like a junkie to heroin. And as confused as hell.

"Go away. I don't want the job." She hung up the phone and waited to see if it would ring again. It didn't.

A power surge.

Maybe that was what she needed. She needed to seek out some fresh meat.

Inside and out.

A rival bar was what she needed, just like she'd told Caleb. One where she wouldn't run into him. She found one across town and sat at a bar stool to study her surroundings. Blue eyes watched every movement in the bar. Who was sober, who was drunk. Single, married? Attractive and not.

It didn't matter.

A group of men in the corner laughing and drinking. As yet, not even looking for single women. They would be by the end of the night.

The usual hairy-chested, gold chain-plated men who thought they were irresistible.

And a blonde woman in a slinky dress. Stalking the same men she was.

Natalya.

"Would you like to dance?" The voice broke through her thoughts and she acknowledged with a distracted smile before really looking at the specimen before her. She accepted his hand as he led her to the dance floor and then allowed her concentration to focus on him fully as her attention zeroed in on him.

Attractive. Lean and slender. Quiet, that was a plus over the usual cocky men she met.

"What's your name?" he asked.

"Keara. Yours?"

"I'm Jason."

She took a closer look at him. Fake tanned skin that obviously came from a tanning bed. Strategically placed highlights in his brown hair.

Vanity. It could bring him down.

Keara gave him the full force of her sexiest smile. Watched as he caught his breath. She moved closer to him, her body twisting to the music.

One leg maneuvered between his and the other was outside his leg, so she straddled his thigh. Wriggled deliciously, then stepped away.

A teaser.

He followed in, deliberately making eye contact with her. Keara tried not to grimace at the leather-looking skin around his eyes from the damage of the sunbed.

She couldn't do it. Realization sank in as quickly as a bucket of water dousing burning flames. She didn't have the patience to tempt and tease, to find out how much corruption ran through his body.

Her dancing slowed and she took one step to distance herself from him.

Someone moved in behind her, moving in time to the music. She heard a soft, feminine voice in her ear.

"You are The Punisher. You need power in the event of a showdown, which we both know will happen soon. You allowed the Earth dimension to soften you. Suck it up, Jenesi." Natalya's hands gripped at her hips and moved her to the same beat she moved to.

The disgusting human smiled widely at the sight of two women, dancing to please him. "What's your name?" he asked over Keara's shoulder.

"I'm her friend. Natalya."

"Nice to meet you," he said, while checking out her goods. "I'm Jason."

"You single, Jason?"

"Technically. I'm still living with a girlfriend, but if I could find someone to replace her, I'd boot her out in a heartbeat."

"Could you take two?" Natalya smiled charmingly, her blonde looks nearly angelic.

The human blinked as his good fortune sunk in. "Hell, yeah."

Natalya looked at Keara and wriggled behind Jason. She thrust her hips into him from behind, and reached for Keara's hands, pulling her into them. Slowly, she maneuvered Keara's hands around their waists, and Jason began to thrust his hips back and forth, into the two of them.

Keara was close enough to whisper to. "You can do it, or I can," Natalya said, not even caring that he could hear. "Now, I never have, so I'd hate to try to find out I love it."

Keara understood exactly. Stealing power was tricky, just once and you might find yourself permanently caught in the trap, stealing until you turned into a Rot Demon.

Natalya would be just the type, which is probably why she'd never done it.

Keara's eyes went blank and she lifted her parted lips to Jason. Natalya pulled them close. Their lips touched, softly at first.

The lights in the bar flickered and darkened as the music cut. There was silence in the bar before personnel scrambled to find out what was wrong.

A few minutes later, the music and lights returned.

Keara was gorgeous, flushed pink, her full lips glossy and moist. In comparison, the human was pale, the fake-bake tan looking incongruous as it sat upon his leathery skin. The strategically placed highlights in his hair were also odd, almost disproportionate, until one realized that there was now gray threaded through his hair, giving him a frosted appearance from the eighties.

"It was nice to meet you, Jason," Keara said as Natalya moved closer to her side.

"Yeah, uh, I'm not feeling all that well."

Natalya's smile was harsh. "Go home to your girlfriend. Maybe she'll take care of you."

"Yeah," he muttered, as he turned and stumbled before moving away.

"Then again, maybe not," Natalya said. "I sure the hell wouldn't." She turned to Keara. "Let's go sit."

They found an empty table in the back—empty of people anyway. The top of the table was littered with drinking glasses. Natalya approached it and with one sweep of her arm cleared it, spilling everything onto the carpet below before sitting in the booth as if nothing was wrong.

Keara sighed. "You haven't changed."

Natalya grinned, a devilish grin that reminded Keara of when they were children at their school, Luciekynokus. "On the contrary, I learned to take care of myself."

"Is that why you're aligning yourself with me?"

"You got it, sister. You think I don't know Enishka would squash me like an insignificant bug should he get the chance?"

"I thought you craved the power. You've always craved it in Luciefyiore."

"I assumed climbing the social ladder meant safety. If you have importance, no one would dare harm you. What I didn't understand was you still have threats as you climb, even more so as demons try to take you out for your status."

"So what's the answer?"

"I want the top. The throne."

"How?"

"I originally planned to marry Enishka and get rid of him. But now I realize that's not even an option. He has too much power. Any wife he obtains, he'll simply get rid of after gaining her power and rendering her useless. So I'm aligning myself with you, especially if I'll be stuck in this dimension."

"He sent you here and left you?"

Natalya nodded grimly.

"I still don't trust you."

Natalya smiled. "Smart girl. Never trust anyone. I don't."

"Then why are you aligning yourself with me?"

"You pissed him off, Keara. And he's scarred. It's a permanent reminder of you. You're going to have to strike hard and fast. Before he gets you first."

"I can't strike first. That would make me no better than him."

"If he strikes first, he'll hit you hard enough that you'll go down. You won't be able to defend yourself. You'll be done for forever." Natalya rose from the table before leaning her face into Keara's and saying bitterly, "And I'll be stuck here forever."

* * * * *

It was still early when Keara left the bar. She drove by her parents' house to find her father sitting alone on the front porch.

Turning off her headlights, she walked up to the porch swing and sat with him. She tucked her legs beneath her and curled up.

"What's wrong, babisna?"

She smiled against his shoulder and twined her fingers with his. His hand was so much larger than hers. "Why would you think something's wrong?"

"I can feel the tension in you. Tell me you're not sucking too much power?"

"No. You feel a little because I just did some tonight, but I can't remember the last time I had any before that, it's been so long." A slight lie, but one she didn't feel guilty for. Her parents certainly didn't need to worry about her.

"As long as you don't do it too often. It's too addictive for any demon, and you're only half."

"Daddy," Keara said suddenly. "Tell me about when you met Mom. How did you know you loved her?"

"How could anyone not love your mother? How could a soul stay so pure when sold by their very own parents? How could an infant be raised by an evil demon lord and still stay untainted?"

Keara understood exactly. There was no one on Earth or Luciefyiore like her mother. Almost as if her mother didn't belong in either dimension but had surfaced from another.

"Did you know Adolpheus, the Rot Demon, once tried to suck her soul?"

Keara gasped.

"It's okay," her father assured her. "That's the beauty of it. He wasn't able to. There wasn't an impurity in her."

"He's Enishka's right hand now."

"Interesting," her father murmured, lost in his own thoughts.

"How did Enishka not kill him instantly for trying to steal her soul?"

"He knew Adolpheus was in the middle of his addiction and unable to help himself. In fact, I think Enishka was the one who encouraged his power sucking to make him into a Rot Demon. Plus, it helped that the attempt failed and she was unharmed. Although," he said slowly, "I guess he also could have had another reason in mind. Perhaps he wanted to see how uncontaminated her soul was to see if it could be sucked? Like a live experiment. That tricky bastard," her father said, more to himself than her.

"How did you get her away?"

Her father turned down to look at her. The gaze in his eyes was solemn. "I planned against Enishka for many, many years. He has the power of the entire demon realm within him. It takes more than just strength to win, it takes cunning also. I hear he's insane now?"

Keara shrugged. "I didn't know him before so I have nothing to compare him to."

"You're safe in this dimension, babisna. Enishka can't cross portals."

She didn't need to worry her father with the news that she'd given the demon lord the power to summon her over. And that he'd sent the Huntress after her. Her father would fight for her and she could protect both of her parents by keeping them out of this fight.

There were so many unanswered questions running through Keara's head. She wanted to ask her father how to fight the evil that brewed inside her, but did he even realize they were wicked? That the humans weren't the evil beings in hell they'd always suspected?

Chapter Ten
The Sweetness of Revenge

ॐ

Natalya brushed her blonde hair, the waves curling the ends nearly to her waist. The ring of the telephone broke the stillness of the posh hotel room she stayed in. It shouldn't, for who would be calling? The hotel was owned by one of Enishka's minions and he should be the only person who knew about her in this dimension.

Yet the person on the other end of that phone knew where she stayed. Warily, her horns descended as she picked up the receiver, knowing the caller could only be bad news.

"Yes?"

"Hi, um, I was told to call you. The Huntress? My name's Dean."

"Who had you call me?" She knew, of course. Who else would have him ask for the Huntress but Enishka? Just as Keara would be referred to as the Punisher. The two highest-ranking demons, based on power, under Enishka himself. The third in the running was the disgusting Rot Demon.

Dean's voice was a reverent whisper. "The demon lord."

"And why does he want you to contact me?"

"He thinks we can work together to bring Keara to him. Look, I've already contacted her. She's not as trusting as she was before. Wouldn't agree to meet me and barely talked to me. I don't see how I could help."

"Then why are you calling me?"

"He wanted me to call you. I'm indebted to him."

Natalya sighed. "I'm the Huntress. I'm not used to working with incompetent humans. Fine. I'll draw her out, get her to that nightclub called The Silver Rose. You think you can handle it from there?"

"Yeah."

His voice sounded confident enough to raise Natalya's curiosity. "What will you do, human?"

"What the demon lord instructs me to do. This time, work on her human protectiveness. Play on her sympathies."

Exactly what she would have done. For even as a child, Jenesi could be tricked, over and over. Show her the smallest amount of kindness and she'd be wary. But run to her crying with a scraped knee and that silly maternal human gene would kick in. The file on Keara was an inch and a half thick on her weaknesses.

But only half an inch thick with her strengths. To rank as high as she did, she had to be hiding some of those powers. Just like her father did before her.

Sneaky Horntreau clan.

"Okay, then. Tonight? Ten?"

There was a pause while he checked whatever calendar he had before him. Natalya rolled her eyes, inspecting her fingernails while the dimwit tried to act important. "Yeah, ten will be fine."

"She'll be ready."

"Will I meet you?"

"Perhaps." *Over her dead body. Backstabbing human, to sell his soul and crucify one of his own.*

* * * * *

She was supposed to meet Natalya here. So far, the blonde demon hadn't shown up. No, she wouldn't be at Caleb's bar like Natalya had originally suggested as a meeting place. Keara nearly had a heart attack when the name was casually slung out.

Keara had suggested this place herself. Far enough away to not be recognized. Close enough to steal some power should she get the urge.

"Hi, baby doll." Dean stood before her, pulling out a chair and sitting down.

"What do you need, Dean?" Where the hell was Natalya? Shock hit Keara's midsection as she realized this was a setup. Natalya had no intention of showing up. Dean had instead.

Did he know he was being used? Was everything about him a lie and he was a poor innocent human being manipulated by demons to have her fail her testing phase? Or was he really working with them?

"I'm in trouble, Keara. Someone is stalking me."

It wasn't what she expected. Her eyes looked sharply at him, especially when the next word was mentioned.

"Almost...hunting me."

Dean fought the urge to smile. Enishka had slyly mentioned playing the Huntress against Keara. A girl fight, that was a huge turn on.

But as soon as the urge to smile came, it was resisted. He turned soulful blue eyes to her, knew that his pouty lower lip was getting to her when her eyes dropped to it.

As if she remembered the sweet kisses they'd shared.

That was the one thing he regretted about ending their relationship. He would have liked it to continue a bit longer because she was damn hot in bed. But Enishka commanded the breakup, the time was ripe according to him.

He would never point out that it obviously wasn't a good time since she hadn't gone all demon like everyone expected.

She was still as sexy as hell, that was for damn sure. He wondered how many good fucks he could get in until she caught on to who he worked for.

"I need help, baby. I know I don't deserve it, but you're the only one I can turn to."

"What do you expect me to do?"

"Just make the night terrors go away for a little while. Stay with me. Please. I miss you so badly and I love you so much."

"Annie's not going to object to that?"

He leaned in as if to tell her a painful secret. "Annie will never change. Our marriage will go nowhere. I know that now, and I've left her. I'm staying in an extended stay motel downtown."

Keara stared at him, as if trying to see into his mind. "I'm not moving in," she warned. "One night is all. Then it's over."

"I know, sweetie." His lips were very close to hers and he moved them in, the tiniest bit. Just the way she liked it. Sensual and erotic, and when she didn't stop him, he slid over hers.

The kiss was the way it always was, perfectly played out, soft and sexy.

But nature called at the most inopportune times. He murmured against her lips, "I just need to head to the bathroom and we can leave, if you're ready?"

She nodded.

"Be right back," he murmured, kissing the tip of her nose. Like he used to.

He slid from the seat, trying to ignore the semi-erection that rose in anticipation of a good fuck. And then got harder as he thought of the condom machine in the bathroom. He could stock up for the wondrous night ahead.

Keara sat and waited for him to return from the bathroom as she stared into her drink. Wondering if she had the strength to do this.

"What are you doing here?" asked a familiar voice.

"Caleb," she said. Shock rounded her eyes. Panic hit when she realized Dean would arrive any minute. She couldn't have Caleb see how low she'd stooped. "I'm having a drink, what are you doing here?"

"Looking for you." His voice was nonchalant.

"Do you always look at rival nightclubs?"

"Do you always go to rival nightclubs?"

There was a pregnant pause as she tried to be flippant. "I don't owe you anything. No explanations, nothing."

"No. But you know how I feel about you, there's no denying it."

Keara raised her eyebrows. "Really? And how is that?"

"You care about me. If you would let yourself, you'd love me. As much as I love you."

It wasn't real. He thought he loved her because she'd forced him. And she couldn't tell him she exerted demon power over him.

"Caleb, look. We barely know each other. You can't possibly love me."

"Why not?"

"You don't know me."

"I know more than you think."

"You don't know the real me."

"Only because you try to hold me at arm's length. You try to distance yourself, but I'm not going to let it happen." With a tug, he pulled her to her feet and molded her body to his. The long, lean length of him, thigh to thigh, hip to hip, breast to chest.

And spiked her interest. Like Dean never had.

"Then you know me well enough to know I'm here with someone else."

"Who?" he growled.

"Someone with money. Lots of it."

"Materialistic, are you?" he joked.

"What are you doing?" she gasped as his hot tongue rasped against her throat.

"Teasing you. Leave with me."

"What will I tell him?"

"Nothing. Let him come back to find you gone."

Oh, hell. What was one last time, especially if she'd never see him again? She nodded, the barest semblance of a smile on her lips. She slipped her hand in his and let him lead her from the bar into a waiting taxi. She scooted right up next to him on the seat, no holds barred.

"Your place or mine?" he asked, nibbling on her earlobe.

"Mine is closer." Her voice was breathless.

Caleb gave the address to the driver and pulled her onto his lap, facing him so the driver couldn't see. With one deft hand, he unsnapped her jeans and eased the zipper down. He traced calloused fingers along the edge of her tiny panties, slowly feeling the contrast of the silk and lace scraps. He left a trail of heat in his wake before slipping inside the seam, where his touch literally burned. Once inside, he just pressed his hot palm against the heated core of her.

He could turn her on like no other.

She moaned. "Why?"

"You said you're hornier than most women. Yet you won't have anything to do with me. So let's see how long it takes you to throw me down."

"Are you insane?"

But she felt like the insane one. His finger stroked her damp, plump lips that had swelled before she even left the bar, before it pressed into her hot, slick shaft. It felt so incredibly long and thick, she wanted to press against it. Uncontrollably. Force it deep. To fuck herself on his hand and ease this enormous need.

Still, she tried once more to refuse. As if his finger wasn't in her pussy. After all, it wasn't supposed to be like this. She should be the one in control, not him. "I told you, it'll just be one night of fun sex. I don't want a relationship to trap me and you're getting possessive."

"It's just because I love you, isn't it?"

But that magical finger, the one that was hot and wet from her juices, circled her clit with heat. Her hips surged forward of their own accord, wanting so desperately to force him to press against it, but instead he circled again. And again.

She was on fire. Her heat phase demanded satisfaction. Power. She wanted to suck it from someone. And this time…release along with it. Turning it into something else entirely, something she had no real definition for.

Against her backside, she felt his cock making demands. Stiff, full grown and ready for her. Pressing against her buttocks, full of sweet promises, of hard fullness. She wondered how it would feel plunging again and again deep within her. Over and over, until she could take no more.

"Dammit, Caleb, you have to stop. Before he sees."

"Stop me. You know how," he said against her lips.

"How?" she moaned, before his tongue snaked out and licked her full lower lip. Nibbled gently until she opened and met his tongue with her own.

"A promise. Trust me enough to let me love you."

He'd want her love in return. They always did.

She didn't need to stop him. The cab rolled to the curb and he withdrew his hand as she zipped up and maneuvered from the car.

She wasted no time. She left him paying the driver while she unlocked her front door. When he finally stepped inside, she closed the door behind him and unsnapped his jeans. "It's about time, slowpoke."

"I don't see you naked yet, baby," he said.

"But you will."

Her hand brushed against the swell in his jeans while she unzipped him. She dropped to her knees, tugging his waistband down to expose the cotton underwear that barely covered the bulge beneath.

She pulled them down and he sprang forth. She rubbed her cheek onto his sensitive flesh, loving how warm he was against her face.

She licked along the length of him and he groaned. His penis jumped slightly, with a mind of its own. As if it were excited to be kissed by her sweet lips.

Excited it was. It nearly leapt into her mouth when she opened her mouth over the head. He gasped when her mouth enclosed the crown of his penis. She sucked softly, almost rolling the head of his cock in her mouth.

"Keara," he groaned as he caressed her cheek with his palm.

In response, she kissed along the shaft of his hardness, all the way to the base. And kept kissing, then ran her tongue along the area where his cock met his balls. She kissed all along his tender ball sac, and then took one testicle into her mouth, sucking softly as she rolled his balls gently in her mouth.

"Oh, sweetheart," he said, looking down. The visual of her worshipping his body was almost too much to bear. There she was, on her knees before him, sucking his balls with those luscious full lips.

The lips that hinted at her mixed heritage of not quite human.

If he could only get this woman to worship him completely. The way she was meant to.

"Get up," he said softly.

She rose to her feet and stood up on tiptoe to press her sexy lips to his. He inserted his tongue between her lips and she met him with her own.

They blended their tastes, soft and sensual, mouths sliding against one another. He unsnapped her jeans so her waistband would gap. He slid his hand down the back of her pants to cup the smooth, round globes of her ass. His skin slid across her silky flesh and he squeezed softly. Soon he withdrew his hands and pushed her jeans slightly lower, below her hipbones. Which was easy enough to do in this day of low cut jeans.

His thumbs massaged her hipbones and her lips parted slightly at the erotic feelings being transferred from his fingertips.

He pulled her thin cotton t-shirt up over her head and she lifted her arms to help him. Then she stood before him in jeans and a front clasp bra in blood red.

He twisted the tiny clasp between her breasts and the bra popped open, spilling pale skin into his hands. Her nipples were hard points of pleasure that he massaged gently with his thumbs. Her moan was too much to take and he bent his head to lick at the pouty little rosy tipped breast.

Her nipples were perfect. Hard and pointy and so eager to be teased with his tongue.

He lapped at the stiff peaks before sucking one in.

Her response was worth it. She arched her back, thrusting more of her hard tipped breasts at him. She cupped a breast with her own hand, massaging it as she held it to his lips.

He pushed her jeans down completely over her hips, taking her panties along with them, leaving her bare to cup the warmth between her legs in the palm of his hand. His middle finger inserted deep into her sheath, finding her hot and soaked, ready for more than just a finger.

"That feels so good," she moaned, clenching her muscles around his finger. "Deeper, Caleb."

"How's this?" he asked, kissing her sexy lips as he curled his finger to reach her spongy G-spot. He stroked the soft skin there and she exhaled, smiling lazily with her lush lips.

Her eyelids were heavy as her sultry blue eyes gazed at him. "Are we going to make it to the bed?" she asked.

"Yeah," he said. "Because I want you to lie on it and spread your legs wide. I want to see your entire pussy before I taste it. Do you have any clue what it looks like, silky and swollen? The most intimate part of you?"

She gasped as he caught her clit under his thumb and pressed in.

"Oooh," she breathed. "I want you so much."

"We were made for each other. We fit each other perfectly, we complement each other."

She closed her legs, pulling his hand from her body with regret. She brought his finger up to her mouth and enclosed in her warmth. She sucked his finger clean, watching him with those exotic blue eyes. He jerked the rest of his clothing off, reached for a condom, and watched as she undressed also.

"Come to my bed," she whispered.

"How about this way?" he asked, and lifted her body to his waist. She wrapped her long legs around him, and he sank his stiff cock into her.

"Ohh," she groaned, and he walked with her, his body imbedded in hers, all the way to the edge of the bed.

She climbed off him long enough to lie back on the bed, spreading her legs in the fashion he'd just told her about.

She pressed her knees against her chest, then opened her legs. He stared at her spread pussy and she snaked a hand down to spread her inner lips apart. To let him see all the tender pink folds inside, the petals of a soft rose.

He lowered his face down to her nether lips, licking one swollen side into his mouth and then paying careful attention to its twin.

"Yes," she hissed. "That's it. Exactly."

His tongue found her clitoris, jabbing at the sensitive nub while she squirmed deliciously. She began to thrust her hips at him, and he clamped his mouth over her mound and sucked. She found her release, her flesh contracting in quivering bursts as she grabbed the back of his head and pulled his face harder against her vulva.

She breathed deeply as her muscles relaxed, and he laid his cheek against her thigh as he watched her continue to quiver. After she rested for a few minutes, he climbed on top of her and said, "I think I'll fuck you from behind."

He helped her turn over onto her stomach and pulled her up onto weakened knees. He entered her so slowly. It felt so right, as if they were made for each other. Their bodies fit perfectly, his imbedded deeply within hers.

Hot, warm sensitivity as their flesh slid against each other. In and out, as if the swells of her pussy wanted to tightly grip at him against his withdrawals.

He plunged back in, inch by inch, letting her feel the strength filling her. He groaned into her ear, "I want to fuck you faster. You're so tempting, I just want to fuck and fuck, all day long."

"Ride me harder," she encouraged. "I'm so close again."

He began to buck his hips faster. He ran his hands over her naked back and said, "Play with your clit, baby. Pull it."

She reached down between her legs and he could feel her fingers brush against his balls. He shivered and began slapping harder against her.

He was so close, he just had to feel her tightly strung body burst all around him so he could find his own release.

And then she collapsed her head onto the bed, which made her delectable ass rise higher into the air. "Ooh, Caleb," she screamed as her body spasmed in wondrous rhythmic clenches around his cock.

Her climax was too much for him. Heat rose from the joining of their flesh and he felt the cum shoot from his cock in long, hot spurts.

He collapsed onto the bed, spooning her from behind, bodies still joined, dampened skin drying. He stroked her soft skin as they fell asleep.

It was perfect to wake up still in his arms. The sun was shining into the window and it was so unlike the hot, orange sun of Luciefyiore.

She could feel Caleb awaken and he murmured into her ear. "I love you so much."

She froze. Stark daylight and he loved her. Unconditionally. Because she made him.

And one day soon, as he lay on his deathbed, he would find that she'd stolen his soul. At that point, he would still love her, no matter how evil she was. Because she made him. Dammit.

All was lost now.

Without a word, she headed into the shower. When she was done, she re-entered the bedroom, where she hurriedly dressed. Caleb followed along at a more leisurely pace. She tossed his clothes at him from various points of the house.

"What's got you panicked?" he asked.

"Nothing. It's morning. Bright and early. I have things to do, places to go. People to see."

"So you're tossing me out?"

"Course not." She leaned in with a quick peck to his lips. "Stay if you want. But I have to get out."

Truth was, she had an uncontrollable need to hurt someone. An addictive urge to suck souls.

The urge was getting too strong to fight. For in the beginning she could, but now she wanted it all. Not a simple power surge, but a whole soul. At this moment, she didn't even care about becoming a Rot Demon, as long as she could suck souls for the rest of her life.

Who cared if it was in Luciefyiore? Why was she even fighting to stay in the Earth dimension? She knew there was a reason, but it didn't seem important anymore.

She was too far gone.

Caleb pulled her to him. "You can go if you need to, sweetheart. But I want you to know, I love you."

She should feel something. There it was, a tiny little tingle of excitement in the pit of her belly. She looked at him, wonderingly. How could three little words stir her this way?

"I love you, baby," he repeated softly. "Everything about you."

"I'm a demon."

"You're a human."

He refused to see what she really was, dammit. He was trying to make her and himself believe she was better than what she was. She wasn't, his love wasn't even real.

"No, Caleb. I'm a demon."

Chapter Eleven
The Consequences of Revenge

ଇ

"I'll always love you."

She closed her eyes against his words. He was running true to form. What had she done? Dammit, why had she done it?

"I don't love you, Caleb," she said softly. "I don't love anyone. I can't. I'm not capable of it."

"Of course you are."

"No," she said gently. "I'm not. And I'm no longer going to see you. I'm sorry if it upsets you, but I tried to warn you. I'm not human enough to care."

She turned and walked away, but he called out to her. "I will always seek you, Keara. Just like in the past. You can't just walk away."

She had to keep him from her. She had to keep him safe. She shut down her links and she shimmered from her physical form, right before his eyes. Because she was stronger now, being with him for that little bit had strengthened her. Was she uncontrollably stealing power from him now that he was her minion? Was she on her way to becoming a Rot Demon even now? Panic ensued at the thought.

She morphed into Caleb's apartment without his knowledge. It was the one place he wouldn't think to look for her. In his bedroom, she stripped off all her clothing and studied her body in the full length mirror. Searching, studying her naked form. Looking for the tiniest spot that had softened, like the beginning of an overripe tomato.

A squishy spot which will have turned color, either green or black. Where the skin would slowly peel away and the flesh beneath would mush like bad fruit.

Where liquid pus will form and spew to the surface.

Keara stared at her naked body before giving a harsh laugh. There was nothing unusual on her, it was all her imagination. Sure she felt stronger from the lovemaking with Caleb. Not because he was her minion but because...

She'd fallen in love with him.

Real, live human love. Although he'd never know. He couldn't know, not after she'd forced his love. After she'd stolen his soul.

She turned to the bed where they'd spent countless hours. This would be the last time she saw the inside of Caleb's apartment. She couldn't bear to make herself leave. Not yet.

There was a t-shirt of his on the bed. She brought it to her face and inhaled the faint scent of Caleb. Suddenly, she whipped the shirt over her head and felt the soft cotton against her skin where it enveloped her. Just as it had him not long ago.

Maybe she'd keep it. She pulled her panties back on and then looked longingly at the bed again.

He wouldn't notice if she took a little nap here. Where it was safe and the room smelled like him. Where she felt like she had a connection to him.

Exhausted, she curled into his bed for the last time. Alone this time. She swung the covers up over her shoulder and closed her eyes. Why was she so tired after she'd just felt so strong? Was something draining her?

Enishka snapped up from his throne, his eyes glowing a bright red. "We got her!" he exclaimed.

His underlings cheered.

On the stage near his throne, Enishka began to dance. Today he was in the form of a pig and, as usual, it was just from the waist down. It was an incongruous display, a half-pig doing an irrational dance.

And then it all stopped. Immediately. Enishka raised his hands high and the reddened clouds parted, flying across the skies according to his demands.

He began the ancient ritual of proclamation. *"Jenesi...Keara Knight, half-breed child of Elizabeth and Demitris, you are being decreed. Inside your soft human form burns the blood of your Horntreau clan, the last of its kind. Your inner blood burns stronger than your outer form. So from your eggs you shall spawn a new breed, with characteristics of Horntreau, and characteristics of...mine."*

Keara's eyes snapped open, wide awake. She jumped out of bed. Enishka was summoning. He was going to suck her through the portal which he used to bring her over. She fought it, knowing this was it. This was the showdown.

And she wasn't ready.

Dimensional walls shimmered as they appeared in her line of vision, mingling with the reality of Earth. Right there, where she should have been safe. Caleb's bedroom. She fought against the pull, knowing if Enishka yanked her into Luciefyiore she wouldn't have the strength to return.

He called again. *"Come, Earth child, come home where you belong. Where I alone have the power to decree where you belong. Where you have the duty to continue your dying race."*

Keara's eyes glowed bright blue and her horns rose in defense. A portal shimmered in the air next to her, opening slowly. Soon the difference in oxygen between the dimensions would create a vacuum strong enough to suck her through. She couldn't allow that. The electric glow of her eyes fixed on the portal and focused. She concentrated, the sweat pouring off her forehead. The walls began to seal shut. A portion of the wind blowing in from Luciefyiore stopped.

Keara took a breather, her strength higher than Enishka's for the moment.

Demons everywhere felt the struggle, the turmoil between the two powerful beings. Walls of the material dimension, previously invisible, continued to shimmer and waver hesitantly. As if they were unsure who to obey. Fear hit the bellies of the sensitive demons in Luciefyiore, whereas excitement hit the spiteful ones.

This was it. The showdown. Time to take sides.

On Earth, tension was high. Insane asylums had trouble calming their patients, even medications had little effect. Burglaries were up. Couples fought and kept the police force busy with domestic abuse calls. And the weather was violent. Tidal waves roared and winds screeched.

In the demon realm, sweat poured down Enishka's face as flames grew higher, giving off extreme heat and drying up the swamplands. Just as they had years ago, back in the school of Luciekynokus. "Dammit," he shouted to no one in particular. "She shut down one of the portals."

The faces of several underlings looked up at him in horror.

Enishka realized what he said. How could a half-breed child have enough power to shut a portal? And a child she was, alive for less than a quarter of a century, while he'd been alive for several millennia.

Enishka didn't like the expressions on the faces of his demon servants. The same fear that was usually reserved for him instead showed in reverence to Keara.

The little bitch.

His dark head twisted to one side. "Form a circle," he demanded. "And join hands."

His underlings made the mistake of hesitating. Burning rage flowed through Enishka. Electricity cackled and sparked at the dry ground, catching one demon's leg and flaming up his foot.

Enishka ignored his screams, but didn't intervene when another demon tossed him into one of the scum-soaked ponds to douse him.

The rest of the creatures scurried to grab hands as they formed a large circle around Enishka and his throne. Even with the circle of thirteen demons, he knew it would be difficult to pull her in.

* * * * *

Caleb searched everywhere for her when she morphed from him. She wasn't at her parents', she wasn't at her house. He tried desperately to link with her mentally.

Keara never heeded his calls. So instead he sought out the only other demon he was aware of. Natalya.

"Where is Keara?" he growled.

Natalya barely glanced up at him, not even caring that somehow he had found her. "She's being summoned into our world. Can't you feel the turmoil? She was decreed demon over human, although I don't know how, and must live out the rest of her life there in order to mate. It's her role as the last of a dying breed."

"Take me to her."

"I can't, human. I can't even get myself back."

"Liar. How did you get here then?"

"I was sent to have her turn demon. One way or another. I'm stuck here with a bunch of useless humans and unfortunately, enough power to attract them. So don't threaten me, fool. I'll break you like a stick."

"You have two choices. Either figure out a way to return to your dimension or I'll send your horns back. Without you."

"Listen to me, human male. I can't even get to where Keara is trapped. Once you're there, you're stuck until your duties are done."

"Where?"

"Arashnoks. Where demons are spawned. She'll be released when she produces fertilized demon seeds. If she's made Enishka's queen, she'll have several hundred to bear. If not, you'll be lucky, it's an earlier return."

"So in either case she can be released back to Earth?"

"Not exactly. It gets worse. For if she's made Enishka's queen, her litter will devour her once they're hatched. No one wants to be the mother of that brood."

Before his eyes, he watched pain twist through Natalya's features, forcing a low moan. Her features began to twist and swell and she was sucked through another dimension that shimmered even while he watched.

"Stay away from her. She doesn't need to be distracted," was the last thing she warned before the portal closed with a slurp as if it swallowed her.

Keara was also being sucked through the vortex which opened in the middle of Caleb's bedroom. She was halfway in, up to her waist, while her hands gripped the cold metal legs of his bed. Her horns reached out to sense any nearby power she could seize, but there was none. Not even Rod and Mike in the bar below.

Except for Caleb, who was trying desperately to link with her after the horror of watching Natalya's pain when she was pulled away. Trying so urgently to keep Keara safe and out of that portal and away from the demon dimension.

Keara could feel his determination in trying to help her. But didn't he realize he was provided a direct link to himself through her? She refused to let Enishka obtain any source of connection to Caleb. She'd die first. She'd do this alone without risking him.

So she dug in. And plunged into the portal.

The flames in Luciefyiore continued to burn according to Keara's will, but Enishka saved a lot of his strength. For he used the souls of the thirteen underlings to get her in.

When she was yanked violently through and the portal door was shutting on its own, Enishka glanced around. The thirteen underlings which made up his council were now thirteen piles of ash forming a circle around him.

"Sweep that up," he commanded another demon who tried to hide behind a tree. A temporary underling who would become a part of his new council. Out with the old, in with the new.

Keara had been hurled through light, time and space, panting and gasping, into Luciefyiore. More specifically, to the portal of Arashnoks to breed.

No one paid any attention to her as she came to her senses on Enishka's stone altar, where the supposed forced marriage would take place. One demon was calmly sweeping up burnt ash and this time the swamp was strangely subdued.

As she caught her breath, Natalya landed near her, obviously hurled through space also and looking so much worse for wear. It was obvious she wasn't as used to the mode of travel.

Enishka stood from his throne and everyone curiously tried to listen in.

"Natalya," he snapped. "Arise."

She was so weak, her muscles twisted and spasming, that she had to be helped. A couple of the more brave swamp creatures lifted her by her arms, supporting her weight with their own. Showing a unity they normally didn't have.

"You failed?" his voice was deceptively sweet. "I don't see either one of Keara's human toys here."

He swiveled his protruding bug eyes to the empty cages which had been set to either side of the altar. Keara felt sick when she realized it wasn't going to be a wedding stage, but a torture chamber. He had been prepared to torment Caleb.

The blonde demon barely glanced at Keara before dropping her eyes in reverence to the demon lord. "Yes, master. I was unable to steal either one."

The swamp went loud with whispered chatters. As far as anyone knew, Natalya had never before botched a mission.

"How in the world could you have failed?" Enishka asked suspiciously.

"Keara was able to spot me when I arrived in her hell dimension. She weakened me and thrust me back here before I could make contact with either one of them."

"And did you return?"

"Yes, which sucked nearly all of my power."

"Then?"

Keara's voice rang out. "It was too late. Caleb's soul was already gone."

Enishka's head turned slowly toward her, the creaking of his neck bones popping as though his head would fall off. "What do you mean?"

"His soul belongs to me now."

All hell broke loose.

"Damn you," Enishka screamed at her. An image of his angry face glowed as it flew across the swamp before it zeroed in on her, hurling at her so quickly it made her sway with dizziness. "You knew I wanted the human. You knew I sent Natalya for him."

He raised his arms and the wind picked up loose rocks and sticks. One swing of his arm hurled the objects at her.

Keara curled on the ground. When it was over, a pile of debris buried her. The swamp was quiet. Bravely, the little two-tongued demon named Tobias moved to find her. When no one stopped him, he began to cautiously dig her out. An airway was dug first around her head and she coughed and sputtered as he lifted more rocks and wood out of the way.

She was filthy, covered with cuts and bruises. Scratches everywhere, stained red with her odd human blood.

But there would be no Protection Fairies this time. For she'd been decreed demon. "Are you all right?" Tobias whispered

Keara glanced up. Her eyes were completely blue. A strange glowing color that was completely opposite to the red glow of Enishka's. And yet offered an unexplainable comfort, like coolness for the fire.

In the background, Enishka stamped his feet angrily, as a small child would. "Lock up Natalya for failing. And dress her in wedding finery as my backup."

"It's too late," Keara said calmly. "Fretting is pointless. His soul is gone. There's nothing you can do. It's mine."

"Then yours will belong to me, half-breed. Along with your powers."

With that, the world as Keara knew it went black.

Chapter Twelve
The Failure

ဆာ

She was groggy when she woke up. She tried to raise a hand to rub at her eyes, but it wouldn't lift. She opened her lids to see both tied at the wrists to the headboard.

Enishka sat patiently on the edge of the bed.

"While you slept so peacefully, I arranged the ceremony. It doesn't matter to me who becomes my queen, you or Natalya. But be prepared to know that before you serve your time in Arashnoks, I will have you watch your human lover's torturous death. You see while you slept, I tapped into your psychic link to see how to draw him here. I may not get his soul, but you will miss out on your happy little human lives with his death."

Her barely coherent brain was too exhausted to try to figure whether or not he lied. "You lie."

"Willing to take that chance? Get him here or I will. Of course, if you willingly marry me, I can agree to leave him alone."

"I refuse to summon Caleb here."

"Then you have exactly one day to decide to marry me, or I'll get your human here myself."

"I will not."

"I'll just tap into your link with him while you sleep again, then." A red beam of light shot from his eyes and hit her painfully in the chest.

Keara awoke more slowly this time. She was half sitting and half lying on a bed, fully dressed in a black lace gown. A wedding gown.

Hers.

"Welcome to Judgment Day, my bride."

Once again, the swamp creatures giggled hysterically and remembrance snapped into Keara like a rubber band.

Desperately, she struggled against the ropes that bound her to the bedpost. Who'd ever heard of a bed in the middle of a swamp? It would be just like Enishka to take her on it in front of everyone. She'd obviously struggled while unconscious, the blood that marked her wrists proved it. Of course the cuts and bruises that covered her skin looked incongruous with the wedding gown.

"As you can see," he hissed, "you've been proven more demon than human. You're mine, Jenesi," he said, reverting to her original name.

The swamp was loud with the racket the demons made as they cheered for their master.

"You can't do that," she shouted over the din.

The demon lord ignored her, choosing instead to accept congratulations from the new underlings which surrounded him.

She knew what would get his attention. "Enishka!"

It earned her a slap from the slimy, rotted demon who guarded her. The force of it whipped her hair about her face and reddened her cheek. But it served its purpose, for there was silence in the swamp.

"You wish to speak, wife? What gives you the right?"

"You are wrong. I am human."

"Prove your humanity, Keara. What good have you done in the midst of all this rage-filled man-punishing?"

"Goudy and Malet."

"You choose to use the humiliation of two macho men in order to prove humanity?" the demon lord snickered before bursting into full blown laughter.

She waited until the laughter died down before saying, "They have never felt humiliation."

"Funny. We all winced in shame while we watched." Several of the swamp creatures tsked.

"I gave true love to Goudy and Malet. A happy-ever-after. Human love." Her voice rang.

Silence met her statement. "What is true love?"

"Complete unwavering happiness. Total fulfillment for both parties. Male or female, it doesn't matter."

There was a lengthy pause of silence in which he stared at her incredulously. "Tobias!" Enishka barked. "Show me the damn humans."

Tobias inclined his head, his twin tongues snaking out nervously from his lips like an overgrown serpent. Raising his arms toward one of the moons, he closed his eyes and whispered.

Energy hissed, like an electrical current being released.

Slowly, the overgrown moon was pulled toward to the swamp. As it maneuvered, the shapes and shadows began to shift. A pattern was formed and Keara realized it was like watching a movie on a big screen TV.

The movie was of Goudy and Malet.

They sat on the front balcony of Malet's apartment, watching the human moon and stars. Goudy's head rested on Malet's shoulder.

"I'm glad Keara got us together," he whispered.

"We owe her," Malet responded, pressing a kiss to the top of Mike's thinning hair which he wore sticking straight up in what used to be a crew cut when it was thicker.

"Enough!" boomed the voice of Enishka.

His demon servant pushed outward with his scrawny arms and the moon shifted back into place, the feature film in the center returning to the shapes of craters and shadows, becoming still once more.

The swamp was thick with sudden silence.

"You tricked us?" Enishka spoke slowly. Succinctly. "Clever girl. Clever, clever...clever girl."

He strummed his thick fingernails on the arm of his chair, making a horrible clicking noise like some kind of exotic insect. His face was tight with frustration as he thought of a way to keep her anyway. Or at least her power.

Then his face cleared as his awareness caught at the realization of what she had done.

"Yes... Clever girl. You turned revenge into true love. You *caused* true love. Then you must have inherited your father's gift?" His interest was piqued, at full attention. The last of the Horntreau line inherited the most prized power, and prophecy had foretold it would be at full strength. This was proof. Keara was the prophecy. Just like he'd suspected.

Keara took a deep breath. This was it. Her confession. While it proved her humanity, it was very possible that upon hearing her answer the evil bastard would insist that she stay to be his bride anyway. He'd want to own her power and if she was his wife, he'd take it. Yet it was the only way to save Caleb. She'd have to extract the promise from Enishka after the admission if he wanted her power. She'd even be willing to bear his cannibalistic brats, as long as Caleb was safe. She opened her mouth to admit to the truth and sacrifice herself.

Because he couldn't have Caleb. She'd die before allowing him to have his soul.

"No." A voice rang out.

Every head in the swamp turned toward the sound and watched as a male materialized among them. A powerful being obviously, if he had the ability to listen and speak in their dimension without yet physically being there.

Caleb. Where had he come from?

"Who are you?" the demon lord hissed.

"Caleb Van Trump."

Satisfaction waved over the features of the demon lord. "You are what, since you materialized in my world?"

"Demi-god. Descended from Eros."

Aggravation laced the demon's voice. "Eros? The patron of male love?"

Caleb smiled though there was no joy in the smile. "You got it."

"An old enemy. And why have you invaded my home, Son of Eros?"

"You summoned, did you not? And I'm following Keara. She's mine."

"On the contrary, Van Trump, she is my bride."

"She's human."

"She's demon."

"Will that be your decision?" Caleb's voice rang out, the phrase oddly formal.

The demon lord paused. If he wrongfully chose her to be demon and a pack of gods, that damnable Eros included, decided she was not to support his precious offspring, it was an offense punishable by demotion. He would lose his crown, his dimension, his everything. For good this time, after his twenty-five year suspension. Was one little half demon worth it?

He turned to assess Keara. Absolutely. If she was the one, she had untapped power waiting for him. Caleb Van Trump looked at her also. The demon lord watched as Caleb stared at the half-breed. Dammit, he hadn't counted on that. Caleb was obviously in love with Keara and would fight for her humanity.

But the ability to drive others insane. Especially those of his own kind. To own that one little power nearly made him drool with lust. And the right to fuck the offspring of his enemy Demitris and his lost love, Elizabeth.

The fact that he never loved Elizabeth didn't matter. She had been his, dammit.

"She's owed to me," he hissed. "She is to mate in the underworld. She can't reproduce otherwise, I have decreed it. She is the last of her race."

"You don't want to fight me over this."

"I'll cause your death, little demi-god."

"Not before the son of Eros gives you your own true love, Enishka. Eternal love. With anyone I desire. Think about the consequences. I'm sure Natalya has."

For the first time in his rotten life, Enishka felt true fear. It froze his thinking. It was a horrible feeling, a helpless feeling so unlike the power rush he obtained when he caused others terror.

He took a deep breath. He'd have to bind Van Trump's power before the bastard pierced him with his arrows. Tied him forever to the ruthless demon bitch, Natalya, who would slit his throat before he even slept. Where could his power originate?

Cupid. God of Love. Descendent of Aphrodite. Perhaps the mouth? Kisses? A gag should do it. It should render him useless. It was a good a shot as any.

"You cannot use your power in my underworld, boy. Just as I am not allowed to use my original powers in the human dimension."

The cackling and twittering erupted. How had the stupid son of Eros forgotten that? Enishka allowed himself a smirk of satisfaction before striking out and binding a tie around Caleb's mouth while he was distracted.

It was amazing how the gag worked. Caleb was immediately weakened as sure as Samson was by Delilah. He sank to his knees, although his eyes blazed with fury.

"Well, look at that," Enishka cackled. "It appears I found your Achilles' tendon. Tobias," he barked and waited until the demon aid scuttled forward. "Toss him into the cage. Is Natalya preparing as my bride also?" Enishka asked his demon underling.

"Yes, m-master."

"Then bring Jenesi."

She was grabbed by her arms and half carried into the ring of fire. Left standing in the center, she couldn't speak as she'd been gagged when Caleb morphed in. Instead, she returned the curiosity of all the eyes all focused upon her.

"We have two choices, my sweet bride. You can willingly marry me or you can watch your helpless lover's death. What will you do to save his life?"

An underling stepped forward to rip the tie from her face so she could speak.

"How dare you touch a human?"

"Who's gonna know? You feel the need to tattle to someone? Little winged creatures, perhaps?"

"Laws are in place for a reason, Enishka."

The rotting demon stepped forward in reference to his name, but the instantaneous blue glow of Keara's eyes forced him to take a step back without the usual slap. Everyone was quiet as they witnessed the exchange and an undercurrent of excitement ran through the swamp creatures.

Enishka watched all as he strummed his fingers on the wooden cane he carried. Today his form was the legs of a goat with the snout of a pig. He wiped his hand across his snout, draping a wet streak of mucus across it.

"I guess I won't break any laws by touching a human. Instead I can banish him to the Insanity Dimension."

The Insanity Dimension. Where no one knew what would happen once you entered, for no one who entered ever returned without the madness of dementia.

"You wouldn't," she whispered, ignoring the banging on the cage by Caleb.

"I would. How long he stays depends on how long it takes you to say I do. And to prove I mean business…"

Enishka turned his glowing gaze to the cage where Caleb was held and the man inside shimmered into another dimension.

"No!" Keara screamed, running to the cage as he vanished.

"Relax," Enishka said calmly. "I just sent him to the border of Insanity. He's hanging on by the strength of his hands. When he gets tired, he'll drop in. Unless you say *I do* before then. What's it going to be, Jenesi?"

"Send for the damn minister."

Demons scuttled back and forth in preparation for the upcoming ceremony. The swamp thickened with the usual fog, adding an eerie quality that equaled her mood. What better place for a marriage from hell, than hell?

Keara waited to see who the minister would be. None ever stepped up. Then, the Rot Demon retrieved a small book and took the round stage before them.

Enishka stood before him and turned to raise an eyebrow at Keara. Two demons scuttled forth to guide her to stand beside her bridegroom. They left her to take her vows with hands still tied at the wrists.

"Dearest Loved Ones…" began the Rot Demon.

Keara tried to ignore the plop, plop, plop as he read the vows to them, much as she tried to ignore the drips from his nose that landed into the book he read from.

"A demon king shall take his queen, and combine her powers with his for the benefit of our kingdom…" he continued. His voice droned on and Keara barely heard the words, she was so enraptured with watching the slime slough off him. Pieces of tongue slipped off and stained the pages before him as he spoke, like drops of spittle flying through the air.

And when he turned a page, a finger plopped onto the ground below. Another dropped, striking directly on top of the first finger and breaking it in half. As she watched, the broken pieces of fingers slithered as though they wanted to run away, only to curl up and shrivel suddenly, like slugs opposed to sunlight.

She felt sick.

And then there was a pause in the service as everyone turned and looked expectantly at her.

"I do," she said automatically.

Enishka clapped his hands in glee.

In the far off distance, a slight howl was heard in the whistling wind. It grew louder and louder, a tortured, gut-wrenching sound.

"What'ssss that?" asked Tobias.

"Sounds like pain," Enishka said slyly. "An inhuman scream that pierces dimensional walls. Could it be the lover?"

Using a long finger, Enishka reached out and sliced a wavering wall near them. He gave a look to his underlings who stepped into the other reality without question and brought a weakened Caleb back with them.

They'd been gone just a second or two, but when they stepped back over, Caleb was severely bruised and bloodied.

"Leave him be," yelled Keara, lifting her full, lacy skirts to run to him.

"Or you'll what?"

Enishka grabbed her slender arm, yanking her roughly, and Caleb charged him.

It took four demons to subdue the man she loved. Four to one...until she couldn't stand it anymore.

"Stop. This solves nothing, you must leave him alone."

"Why?"

"He's mine."

"But you're mine, wife."

"You got what you wanted, now honor your agreement."

"But there's more I want. Children."

"Are you insane? I won't bear brats of yours! You promised you wouldn't kill him if I married you."

"I will have your powers, Keara. You will be my cooperative bride and breed with me or the human loses his soul."

"You can't have his soul," she whispered. "It belongs to me."

Enishka clapped his hands. "Thank you once again for that admittance. I have you! After all these years, you're mine. You stole a soul, for that I can declare you demon to the heavens above!" He screamed the word "decree" to the skies and the clouds darkened in threat before they parted to a bright, glowing light.

The swamp chattering halted for once as another dimension merged into Luciefyiore. A dimension that was glittering and golden, with men and women dressed as ancient Greek gods. For all she knew, they may have been.

And the glittering little protection fairies, fluttering about like busy hummingbirds.

"Do you hear me, Council? The prophecy is demon," Enishka's gleeful voice rang to the table in which the strangers were seated.

The swamp was still as everyone waited for a reaction of the strange newcomers.

The men and women dressed in white and gold appeared oddly out of place in the incongruous swamp. Their demeanor was completely opposite the chattering and giggling drama of the demons. They sat utterly calm, almost robotic in contrast.

The head of the table spoke, his hands clasped on the table before him. "Why has she been decreed demon?"

"She has stolen a soul."

"Release her."

The ropes that cut into her wrists were untied and Keara stood in her black wedding gown before the two dimensions. The swamp was still, save for the plop, plop of the blood that dripped from her sliced wrists.

Demon blood.

One lone man stood from the head of the golden table. "Is it true?"

She dropped her head. "Yes. I did."

"No," rang out Caleb's voice as he dropkicked two demons. Somehow, the binding gag had fallen from his mouth during the previous struggle and he was no longer helpless. Six others moved in to take their place and the head of the council boomed, "Enough! Do not touch him. He's one of ours."

"Caleb Van Trump. Did she or did she not steal your soul?" continued the golden man.

Caleb was as calm and collected as the council members when he replied. "She is not able. I gave it to her freely."

The demons in Luciefyiore looked at each other around the room, panic stricken.

"Enishka. Did you force the prophecy to marry you?"

The demon lord wanted to lie. Keara could see it in his face. "She is my wife," he finally admitted. "But rightfully so. She is demon and therefore her powers belong to me."

He never fully answered the question. It seemed the council didn't really care, however.

"We will convene and discuss our decision. In the meantime, Keara and Caleb are confined here. They will not be touched or harmed and are free to go about as they wish."

"This is my swamp," Enishka reminded.

"And for the moment, she is queen of it, is she not?"

Keara ran to Caleb as the portal dimension wavered and disappeared.

Blood trickled from his split bottom lip. She wiped at it tenderly with her thumb, because there wasn't enough fabric on her dress to sop it up. Black lace wasn't known for its absorbent properties anyway.

Caleb reached for her hand and turned it over to examine the blood clotting on her inner wrist. "You're hurt," he muttered in spite of his lip.

"I barely feel it. You're more hurt," she smiled tenderly at him. "What were you thinking, taking on all those demons?"

"They looked a little puny compared to what I'm used to."

Keara looked puzzled. "What are you used to, Caleb? My father didn't surprise you and knowing that I used to reach for you mentally didn't shock you either."

"I think we need to talk, somewhere a little more quiet."

"Can you get up?" she asked as she reached for him.

He accepted her help in rising. The swamp was hushed, but both seemed to know it was an illusion and there were demons everywhere listening in.

Keara pursed her lips in a semblance of silence and Caleb touched his to hers, wincing slightly.

"Let me show you where I grew up." There was an angry hiss nearby and Keara smiled knowingly. "It's sacred ground. Pure demons can no longer enter, preventing them from eavesdropping."

"I thought you had been decreed demon? Losing your humanity?" he asked. "You can still enter?"

"Yes, I'm decreed. Not pure-born. Follow me."

They walked in silence, ever aware of being spied on. Finally, Keara's hand tensed in his, and he tightened his protectively.

They rounded the corner of an old, burned out school. The school in her dreams. He turned questioningly to her to find her staring straight ahead, as if locked in a trance.

"Luciekynokus. It was the most prestigious school here when I was growing up."

"Ahh. I remember. This is where you were stuck back when you first contacted me."

"Exactly."

"Why is it sacred?" he asked as they stepped over the burnt threshold to get inside.

"It was rumored to have been 'cleaned out' back then. Blessed by the council, I later figured. No demon has ever been able to step foot on the grounds."

"Back during the murders that had you banished to Earth?"

"Yes. The accidental fire."

"Baby, that wasn't blessed by the council. That's your doing. You burned out the school."

Keara was truly puzzled. "Yes, I admit I burned the school, though I don't know how you knew. But I had nothing to do with cleansing it sacred."

"But you did. Keara, don't you realize yet? You are a powerful being. I've been protecting you for years."

She gave a bitter "hmmph." "Powerful? If I was, I wouldn't have been decreed. And what do you mean, protecting me?"

"Keeping you from harm. Helping you keep your sanity so you didn't unfairly turn demon with all the ploys being thrown at you."

"Then you failed miserably."

"You're not full demon, no matter what that fool decreed."

"Caleb," she whispered. "Do you know what I did that allowed him to decree me? I did something very wrong and lost my humanity on my own. I forced you to fall in love with me. What you're feeling isn't real."

"No offense, sweetie. But you didn't."

She looked blankly at him. "I didn't cause you to fall in love with me?"

"No."

"Caleb, my father is a Horntreau Demon. The last of the breed. He has the ability to cause humans to fall in love with him. I have that same ability, only stronger for some reason. Don't you see? You only love me because I made you." Her voice fell to a soft whisper with her guilt.

The silly human man had the audacity to laugh at her confession. "You can't make me fall in love with you, sweet stuff."

"Yes, I can. I did."

"Keara, I love you of my own free will."

"No, Caleb. You don't understand. I inherited my father's ability. I caused *you* to fall in love with me. What you feel *is not* real."

"What'd you do? Purposely exert your power?"

Her voice was a whisper as she admitted the horrible truth. "Yes."

Still he laughed. "Sweetheart, you can't make me."

"I can and I did."

"I'm not human."

"What?"

"No, baby. You can't. I love you, just like I told you. But I'm not fully human. Your power is to make *humans* fall in love. "

"You already knew about my power?"

"I told you. My job was to protect you from the demons."

"You're not pure human? I'm not able to… Are you sure?"

"Yes."

"Do you know how guilty I was?"

"Yes. I felt guilt myself. I knew I was supposed to save you," he whispered. "You just had to let me. I'm a demi-god, remember?"

How could she forget that little fact? He was right! She couldn't exert the power on anyone but humans, although it was possible the original power through her father was strong enough. For a moment, happiness as bright as sunshine pierced her dark desire. Until the thought of the power inherited through her parent reminded her of another issue.

"Caleb, I'm still half demon. An evil, ugly creature."

"You could never be ugly."

"Not my outside package. Inside. Inside I'm tainted. Rotten and foul like the rest of them. I can't help it, I was born that way."

Caleb's eyes had softened.

She didn't need his pity, never that. "Dammit, don't you dare look at me like that."

"Keara, is your own father a horrible creature?"

She paused in her reply, torn between love and loyalty and the truth she'd always believed. When she finally answered, it was carefully worded. "My father doesn't mean to be. He's as good as he can be. But there are some things internally we can't control."

"Like?"

"He forced my mother's love. While he's always treated her wonderfully, the crux of the matter is, he manipulated her life for his own benefit."

"Isn't she happy?"

"Yes, but that's not the point."

"Then what is?"

"She doesn't get a true choice."

"Then am I evil also?" The voice that echoed throughout the hollowed room sounded remarkably similar to Caleb's but didn't come from his mouth. A look of peace came over Caleb's face before the other materialized.

Keara recognized the figure. Eros. God of love. Also known as Cupid, the offspring of Aphrodite. Caleb's ancestor. And one of the High Council. He reached for Caleb and hugged him as if the two were long lost twins separated at birth.

He turned to Keara. "I repeat, child, am I evil as well?"

"Of course not," Keara protested.

"But your father simply did what I do, did he not?" The voice was gentle.

"That is your gift," she found herself saying.

"It is also your father's or he would not be able to."

"You don't do it for yourself. He did."

"Well, little one, then I have a confession. I caused the love between your parents."

"Excuse me?"

"It was my arrow. I pierced your parents."

"You did it? My father didn't?"

"No. It was me."

"My father thinks he forced my mother's love."

"He didn't. I knew she was a good soul and had to get away from Enishka. I knew your father would be wonderful for her."

Keara was flabbergasted. She stared at Eros.

"Are you saying—"

"Your father isn't an evil creature because he forced love upon someone. For how can true love be evil, child? True love is a magical gift. One which certain people have the honor of bestowing upon others. Because your father deserved it, I bestowed it upon him to love your mother forever. She loves him completely and honestly, which is his gift to her."

"But I'm half demon," she said as she glanced quickly at Caleb and then looked away.

"I see the problem," Eros said slowly. "There's a story you need to hear. For years an ancient prophecy was foretold to each generation. The origin—a half-breed child born of a pure human soul will grow into the most powerful being, in time inheriting all the powers of the dying demon breed of her father. In hearing of this prophecy, Enishka went searching for this pure soul to mate with. He found your mother. Now keep in mind we had no idea whether or not your mother was the one. But I was sent to ensure that the mating didn't occur, for if you had been born of Enishka's seed all hell would break loose. The balance between good and evil would have been unfairly tipped. He would have raised you as evil instead of allowing you to find your own choice. Purely for his own benefit, of course."

"He wants all the powers of the dying breed."

"Exactly. If he had been your father he would have had access to manipulating his child's gifts. And if you had been forced to marry a demon, your power would have reverted to your husband. He saw the opportunity to hook his claws into the greatest source in the world—the power to turn love evil."

"How do we know I'm the prophecy?" Keara murmured.

"Was it coincidence that you were named Jenesi? A derivative of Genesee? I think not. No, my dear, we've been looking for you for quite a while. But back to your father. He fell in love with your mother because I pierced his thick demon hide with an arrow," Eros smiled as though Demitris were a close friend, "and you father sacrificed his entire way of life for your mother. That's not evil, little one. She was willing to follow through on the marriage with Enishka because she was sold to him by her own parents as an infant. The only way she would renege on the promise was for true love. So your father gave her true love even though it banished him forever from the demon dimension and forced him to learn to live as a human for the rest of his life. A huge adjustment, since he was revered as second in command in the demon world."

She looked over at Caleb who pulled her toward him. The warmth of his arms enclosed her and she sank her head into his shoulder. Keara was still stunned by the wealth of information she'd obtained from Eros. It explained so much that her emotions were overwhelmed.

"Are you okay, love?"

She nodded and kissed his collarbone that lay so temptingly against her lips. "I'm sorry I lied and pretended I didn't love you, Caleb. I didn't want you hurt."

"I know."

"I can see I don't need any of my arrows with you two," Eros said, laughter tingeing his voice.

Keara's head shot up. "Did you… Had you…"

"No," Caleb growled. "I'd be immune. I love you on my own."

"Never. And furthermore," Eros spoke gently now. "Because you had so much of a struggle through your childhood in being raised on Luciefyiore, the grand council has decided that you and your family, your mother and father included, can live wherever you desire, without banishments, for the rest of your time. You've surpassed your demonhood, surpassed your humanity and in time will prove to be as pure as your mother. Now, let's get back to the swamp so the council can convene, shall we?"

Chapter Thirteen
The Conclusion

ဢ

A buzz of excitement covered the foggy swamp. The only creatures that were silent were the twelve in the council who sat round the stone table. Each member looked stoically ahead, as if frozen statues in stasis. One by one, they began to come alive although they still did not speak.

Keara stood on a round, raised stage still dressed in her wedding finery. The finery fit for a queen. Whether she stayed the demon queen was to be determined by the council.

A few feet from her, Enishka stood on his own platform, his bottom half the form of the legs of an upright alligator.

She could hear the steady beat of tapping. Her eyes sought out the source of the annoying clicking to see the end of the demon lord's alligator tail, rattling against the ground like an overgrown serpent. Impatiently beating out a rhythm.

"So?" Enishka snapped. "Is she my queen or isn't she?"

"The council has ruled…"

Enishka's tail stopped beating as he leaned in for the result.

"To allow the marriage to stand instead of annulling it. She is your wife. She willingly gave her vows. Although we all know it was to save Caleb's life."

Pleasure stole across the face of the demon lord. Turning to face her, he blew a kiss at her, causing her stomach to lurch.

"But…" the man at the head of the table continued, "on the flip, she is proven human instead of demon as you had decreed."

"What? My decree cannot be overthrown. I am in charge, it is my duty. My right to pick. And she owes me a new breed of children."

"The council certainly can overthrow your decision based on our own duty to protect the innocent. In this case, Keara. In fact, the Protection Fairies have notified that you've already earned punishment for her harm."

"Lies! How can that be? Favoritism!" The demon screamed. "Innocence! Bahh. You know she's been sucking power from corrupt human souls such as that cop and divorce attorney."

"Yes, but in only sucking the evil spots from them, she saved the humans from their own hellish fate. She taught them love, that it starts with each other. Soon enough, it will spread."

"And you will ignore that she stole a human soul? Like the demon that I decreed? That she is on her way to becoming a Rot Demon?" He waved his arm toward the demon who always waited hand and foot on him, who stood slimily dripping.

"She stole Caleb's soul to save it from your order of harm. You, on the other hand, have intentionally threatened a human who happens to be a descendant of the council. For that reason alone, you are sentenced to a permanent banishment following your previous twenty-five year commitment."

"What? You can't banish me! Who'll rule Luciefyiore?"

"Why, your...queen would be next in line."

"No, you can't do that!" Enishka roared. "Her powers are mine! They are owned by me. I am more powerful than any demon around. I will—"

His voice was cut off as a nod was given to Tobias by the head of the Council. Tobias raised his arms and the red moon of Luciefyiore descended. Enishka was sucked into it, still kicking and screaming like an errant child in the throes of a tantrum.

The head of the council turned to Keara and spoke calmly. "He will, of course, get your powers, Jenesi. It is his right. Unfortunately, they are rather useless on an empty moon."

* * * * *

Keara made her way to where the old school still stood. The building was only half standing, the roof burned away to show the faint glow of the red stars above.

So different from the burning brightness of the Earth dimension's stars which lit the night.

It seemed like a lifetime ago since she'd attended this school. It *was* a lifetime ago. She was Jenesi back then and was truly Keara now. The human woman she'd grown into.

"Are you here?" she called out.

Leaves crackled in the dryness as Natalya turned the corner, her black dress trailing the dirty ground behind her. "I am."

Keara turned to face her. Surprisingly, they were dressed very similarly. Keara's black lace wedding gown was just as full and trailed behind her. The corset top pushed her breasts up and over, but she had dainty little sleeves that slid over her pale shoulders, while Natalya's gown had none.

"All my life, I wanted to be you," Natalya said, her voice emotional and belying the hardened look she always wore in her eyes.

"And all mine, I didn't," Keara retorted wearily.

"As a child, I knew you were the prophecy. To think, you never cared about being the ruler of our world. My childhood mind couldn't comprehend that."

"You forget, I'm half human. I had a prophecy to fulfill in that dimension also."

Natalya nodded. "For as much as I reminded you, I did forget. Often."

176

Her admittance meant a lot. It meant that Keara was much more accepted than she knew. Not that it mattered any longer.

"He's overthrown?" Natalya asked.

"He was when the council reconvened. He forced me to marry him against my will."

"You'll be the ruler still?"

Keara shrugged her slender white shoulders. "I'm next in line since my father's banishment is still in effect."

"You'll uphold your part of the bargain?"

Keara raised her brows. "Luciefyiore needs a demon lord, doesn't it? I can't be here full time. I'll appoint you in my stead as we agreed."

Natalya inclined her blonde head. She may not ever care for Keara, but she had to respect a slimy human who held her part of a bargain.

"Thank you."

Keara inclined hers also, although neither woman noticed it was the exact opposite angle of Natalya's.

Night and day.

Black and white.

Totally different colors. And somehow, it no longer mattered.

* * * * *

Keara peered out the window at the scene below her. It was a perfect cloudless day. The grass was bright green and laughter sparkled from the guests below. This time, she was being married in white lace instead of black.

There was one demon present at the wedding of the century. Her father didn't count, of course. He was considered a demi-god in his own right and was fitting in with the

Council. Rumor had it that he would be the first representative from Luciefyiore to be asked to sit in.

But the demon… Natalya appeared angelic enough, with her horns descended, to look like anyone else. And without the usual black she wore, she could easily have been mistaken for one of the Greek gods who dressed in white and gold. But those who had been exposed to her knew otherwise. She was full demon, through and through.

The door whispered open behind her and Keara didn't bother to turn around. "It's bad luck to see your bride before the wedding."

Arms snaked around her middle and Caleb whispered into her ear. "We make our own luck, baby. You and I."

She smiled and turned to face him. "Have I mentioned lately how much I love you?"

"As much as I love you?"

"More, sweetheart. As much as life itself."

He leaned his forehead to hers. "And if you ever try to save me by sacrificing yourself again…"

She laughed. It was a warning he'd repeated more than once since they'd gotten out of Luciefyiore.

He leaned in for a kiss, a promise of what was to come later that night. His lips slid over hers and their breathing deepened with the usual need.

Natalya poked her head in the door to witness Keara in Caleb's arms, mouths mashed together, hot and heavy.

"My father will be here any minute," Keara whispered with a giggle.

Keara was to be given away by her father. Natalya had never actually met the Horntreau demon, he had been banished when she was an infant. Still, there was a certain amount of awe there for the man who had beaten Enishka.

"Break it up, lovebirds. Geez, you two disgust me." Natalya's voice did have a certain amount of queasiness to it, she made sure of it.

Caleb kissed the tip of Keara's nose before turning to face her. "Go find yourself a man," he muttered.

"I have several hundred back home, thanks," she reminded, blinking her eyes innocently. "I just came to warn you before your father got here. The gravitational pull of our moon is weak tonight and with the entire council busy with the wedding, rumor has it that Enishka's followers will try to set him free with a portal."

"Not possible," Keara said. "I learned something interesting when Enishka and I battled. The power struggle between us caused amazing things back on Earth. The moon was full when people in asylums went a little crazy. They felt the energy, it opened up a tiny link in their brains."

"Yes?" Natalya said.

"So in order to make things more balanced, there are certain demons in Luciefyiore who will go insane along with the humans on full moon nights. Adolpheus, the Rot Demon, for instance."

Natalya smiled. "Along with every one who worshipped Enishka?"

"You got it."

"How is that possible? You still have some power? Enishka didn't get it all?"

Keara smiled. Her demon eyes glowed blue and her horns slowly rose. Caleb was tanned and blond next to her.

An angelic image to balance Keara's demonic looks.

Epilogue

ॐ

Natalya was on her back, legs wrapped tightly around the hips of the human male who was thrusting deep into her.

"I'm coming," he muttered, voice husky.

She smiled. "Mmm. Fuck me harder, lover."

It tossed him over the edge, his hips bucking wildly into her as his climax hit, spewing hot semen from the tip of his cock.

He collapsed onto the luscious woman, her sexy breasts pushing into his chest.

Natalya somehow reminded him of Keara. She was blonde while Keara was midnight, but each had large blue eyes and even larger perfect breasts. Round sweet globes tipped with rosy pink nipples. Hard nipples, always poking stiffly. For him.

Sweet pussies, swollen and hot and wet, shaved smooth underneath.

He'd met Natalya in a bar tonight and she sought him out above all others. It did his ego good to be so wanted. Especially after his wife left him and Keara refused to take him back.

When Dean looked up again, Natalya had horns.

"What the fuck?"

He tried to pull his dick from her, but it was gripped tightly within her passage. And then it began to burn, as if her juices were acidic.

Again and again he tried to pull out, to no avail. All his panicked mind could think of was washing off his cock.

"You're welcome, Keara," Natalya said to no one in particular but looking into Dean's eyes. "You'll be impotent with anyone but me," she told him. "And soon, you'll be headed for our dimension, won't you, sweetie? By the way, *I'm the Huntress*."

DEMONIC PLEASURES

જી

Dedication

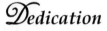

To Laura, who's not into vampires.

Trademarks Acknowledgement

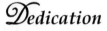

The author acknowledges the trademarked status and trademark owners of the following wordmarks mentioned in this work of fiction:

Barbie: Mattel, Inc.

Glossary

Luciefyiore (Loosh fyoree) — The demon dimension

Luciekynokus (Loosh Kyin ah kiss) — A prestigious all-girl demon school

Yanka (yanka) — Title of respect for a teacher used before their actual name

Horntreau (horn troe) — A demon race. Jenesi (Keara) is the last of the line and she's diluted with human blood.

Natalya Hershkle (Hersh lee) — Full-blooded demon known as The Huntress, appointed to rule Luciefyiore for Keara who wanted to live in the Earth dimension.

Prologue

ℬ

Natalya was on her back, legs wrapped tightly around the hips of the human male who was thrusting deep into her.

"I'm coming," he muttered, voice husky.

She smiled. "Mmm. Fuck me harder, lover."

It tossed him over the edge, his hips bucking wildly into her as his climax hit, spewing hot semen from the tip of his cock.

He collapsed onto the luscious woman, her sexy breasts pushing into his chest.

Natalya somehow reminded him of Keara. She was blonde while Keara was midnight but each had large blue eyes and even larger perfect breasts. Round sweet globes tipped with rosy pink nipples. Hard nipples, always poking stiffly. For him.

Sweet pussies, swollen and hot and wet, shaved smooth underneath.

He'd met Natalya in a bar tonight and she sought him out above all others. It did his ego good to be so wanted. Especially after his wife left him and Keara refused to take him back.

When Dean looked up again, Natalya had horns.

"What the fuck?"

He tried to pull his dick from her but it was gripped tightly within her passage. And then it began to burn, as if her juices were acidic.

Again and again he tried to pull out, to no avail. All his panicked mind could think of was washing off his cock.

"You're welcome, Keara," Natalya said to no one in particular but looking into Dean's eyes. "You'll be impotent with anyone but me," she told him. "And soon, you'll be headed for our dimension, won't you, sweetie? By the way, *I'm The Huntress.*"

Chapter One
The Punishment

∽

Natalya Hershkle had a hard time not staring at her image ever since she'd been dehorned.

Not that she always wore her horns but knowing they were gone made her feel as naked as a newborn. Exposed. Maybe even vulnerable. Which was not acceptable for the recent ruler of Luciefyiore.

She sat in the quiet coffee shop waiting to meet Keara, the original bitch from hell. Technically, her boss. As the demon queen, Keara had appointed her as ruler. But Natalya shouldn't have chosen the small seat by the window because her eyes kept straying to her own reflection.

"Well, well, who's the human sitting alone in a coffee shop? Oh, sorry, didn't recognize you."

Natalya whipped her head from the glass to see Keara, huge with a human mixed-breed brat in her belly. "Cow."

"Cow with horns, baby," was the queen's response.

Natalya mumbled under her breath, low enough that Keara couldn't actually hear.

"You know, Talya, they had to dehorn you. It's the only way your power could be reversed."

"So I got a little carried away…"

Keara snapped. "A little carried away? You have a powerful gift. To cause impotence with any male who mates with you. You took over all of Luciefyiore."

"It was the tiniest fantasy…"

Keara looked incredulous. "Fantasy? That every man in our dimension could worship only you?"

"Well, geez." Natalya squirmed uncomfortably. "It's not like I ask you about your hidden desires."

"How the hell is Luciefyiore supposed to continue if everyone is impotent? What happens to the demon dimension when no one is able to breed? It becomes a world of lesbians?"

Natalya shrugged sullenly. It wasn't something she'd actually thought about. "I don't know. It's not like I meant to do it."

"I guess we could have just invited a bunch of humans in to make us a half-breed community."

That got Natalya's attention. She turned horrified eyes to Keara. "You're kidding, right? That's disgusting."

Keara cleared her throat. "Need I remind you your queen's a half-breed?"

"That's different. You were at least raised with us."

The queen's voice was still somewhat cold. "My child is mixed-breed."

"And I'm sure it'll be cute, even all toothless with a round head," Natalya patronized.

Keara's eyes glowed slightly, a bluish tint that was always unnerving. "I want you to serve your time and clear up your mess quickly. I have to rule Luciefyiore during your banishment to Earth and I don't want to be stuck there long enough that my child is born there. Got it?"

Carrying the little parasite obviously made her crabby.

"So I don't have a set amount of time here?"

"You're banished to this dimension until you cause unselfish love without the use of demonic powers. Learn quickly. You can stay in our house since Caleb and I will be cleaning up your mess in Luciefyiore."

"Thank you," Natalya murmured meekly, for she had no other choice in the matter.

"Here's the key. Caleb's waiting, we're heading straight there."

Natalya walked the short distance toward Keara's house. She passed the train station and looked with interest at the scrambling humans hauling suitcases to and fro.

Lord, they were ugly. It was rare to find a handsome human, only then were they trainable. To service her demonic pleasures, of course.

The consequences of punishment—to be stripped of one's horns—was humiliating enough. Like going naked in public. Not to mention dangerous, since one's power originated from their horns. But to be banished to hell, er, Earth until she could earn passage back by causing unselfish love? Bah, nearly impossible. The scrambling humans were so unattractive, wimpy with no inner powers. No sexy horns, making their heads look like round volleyballs sitting on their shoulders.

And the babies! They were horrifying—toothless, with their huge heads and…ick, bald. No demon babies were ever born bald. They usually had a head full of hair the length of their bodies. A personal comfort blanket. Not those humans.

It would take her powers to get the ugly creatures to fall in love but she had none without her horns, dammit.

It's not like she meant to cause every man out there to become hers. She wasn't stupid, after all. She just bored easily and lost track of how many she had in her harem. On top of it all, Keara had quite a lot of nerve to threaten her. Being so humanly pregnant—which was disgusting on its own for in their dimension demons hatched from eggs—but the high and mighty Miss didn't want her precious mixed-breed born in Luciefyiore.

The good news was Natalya would be held in awe when she returned to Luciefyiore. Demons had always thought of the Earth dimension as hell. She would be considered much more powerful for sustaining such a torturous banishment here.

She scanned the street before her. What little humans looked desperate for love? An older woman sat on a bench, handbag beside her. She was as ugly as a stump and looked as though she hadn't been laid in decades. Hell, she probably couldn't even hold her bladder. Natalya sat down next to her.

The old shrew grabbed her bag protectively and scooted farther down the bench.

Natalya sighed and moved closer to her. "Old woman, you look like you need a man."

"Hmmph. You look like you need one yourself, hussy."

Natalya inspected her nails magnanimously. "These males are beneath me. However, at your age I'm sure you're not as picky."

"Well, I don't need me no man, see? What do I need some old geezer for? They can't cook, they can't clean and I don't want some old fart trying to stuff his dirty old dough into me. I got me my pride, you know."

"Did you just say his dirty old dough? Is that what I think it means?"

"You got it, sister. Now scoot, you're getting on my nerves."

"You don't have many friends, do you?"

"I don't need me no friends. Bunch of users. Get lost."

"Shrew."

"Slut."

With that, the old hunchback rose from the bench, leaving a trail of garlic mist in her wake.

"How the hell am I supposed to help the stupid creatures if they don't know they need help?" Natalya murmured under her breath. "And if they don't brush their teeth?"

"Excuse me?"

"Oh, nothing." She turned her head to the masculine voice and felt her mouth drop open.

Maybe the old shrew was right. She could use a man. And there was a truly amazing one right before her. He very nearly reminded her of a demon. His eyes were brown with a golden tint that hinted at a glow should he get sexually aroused, his jaw was hair-roughened and she lowered her eyes to check out the swell in the tight jeans he wore.

Very acceptable.

She returned her gaze to his face, where he stood watching her with an almost amused smile. "Are you finished checking out my goods?"

For once in her life, Natalya Hershkle, Ruler of Luciefyiore and the queen's right hand, was almost embarrassed. Heat came to her face and her palms actually dampened. It was the strangeness of this dimension. Had to be. Why else would she feel like throwing up in front of a totally fine man?

Hu-man, she corrected herself. A disgusting breed only fit to service her as a sex slave. Well, along with any other man of any breed, her own dimension or this one.

"You have a very nice package," she told him with her nose in the air. "I'm curious as to what it contains. If I cared to stay here long enough, I'd find out. However, I'm staying with a...friend and don't know my number, so I can't give it to you."

"I didn't exactly ask for your number, princess."

"Of course not. But you would have," she assured. "However, I don't have time for a dalliance. I'm on a mission."

He raised his brows a fraction of an inch. Then cleared his throat. "Okay then. I'll leave you to your mission. Good luck to you."

"Thank you." She waved her hand airily. "Off you go." She then searched out more humans.

Problem was, should she look for the desperate ones? Ones that looked horny? The ugly ones? Would they be lonely? There were so many questions and no one to give her the answers. Besides, the strange yellow of the Earth's sun was fading so she'd best find Keara's house.

For back at home, things shifted at night. It wouldn't do to be caught in a strange place when it happened here.

Good thing she left. Since she was walking, it took longer than she could have imagined. She remembered the huge house, of course. Oddly enough, it looked much like her own back in Luciefyiore.

She inserted the key into the lock and yawned. The door pushed open softly. It seemed eerily quiet at first and she realized she'd never been in a completely empty house.

Ever.

Not when she had so many studs to service her. There was always one or two hanging around and lately, well lately there had been many more than that awaiting their turn for her bed. More like fifteen or twenty.

Her house had gotten a bit crowded, that's for sure. By this same time back home, she probably would have had at least five or six orgasms and would be sitting down for dinner. Handfed.

Tonight she was tired from the dimensional hurling and guess what? She didn't have to eat dinner if she didn't want to. There'd be no one there to coax her to keep her strength up. To offer to prepare the finest delicacies.

She entered the master suite. It made the most sense to bunk there, since she'd been banished with nothing but the clothes on her back. She'd need to borrow Keara's. She stripped her own clothing from her body and slipped a soft, sheer nightgown over her head. Hell, it wouldn't fit Keara for a while anyway.

The cow.

She'd have to explore the house for a guest bathroom to find an extra toothbrush. She walked down the hallway from the double doors of the bedroom.

Jere couldn't believe his eyes. A blonde goddess, slinking half naked in a whisper of see-through fabric. He could see the pink of her stiff nipples poking through. And farther below, her puffy labia were clearly outlined.

He instantly hardened. His cock rose slowly to full attention at the sight of those luscious lips. She was riffling through a bathroom drawer and he followed quietly. She had the curviest ass he'd ever seen, like an upside down heart extending from her tiny waist. Smooth golden skin. Everywhere.

She must sunbathe completely nude. His heart raced as he wondered if she was tanned even lower.

Her pussy.

Wondered if she'd ever spread her legs on a beach, shaven smooth and let the sun kiss her nether lips. Felt them swell with the warmth of the sun's rays.

Dammit, he was horny. As usual. It was a curse he lived with daily.

"You! What are you doing here?" Instead of sounding panicked, she was annoyed. After all, she was The Huntress. Men were her snacks.

He leaned against the door frame, arms crossed. Watching her as though he had a right to.

"I'm checking out *your* goods now. Fair's fair."

"How'd you get in? Did you follow me?" It was at this moment that she missed those horns. They'd rise about now, strengthening her with an infusion of power the human could only wonder about.

He simply raised an eyebrow. "Follow you? Hardly. This is my…cousin's house. I arrived earlier and got the key from Keara's dad, Demitris."

Wow, this was hunky Caleb's cousin? The guy from the train station with the acceptable package? Speaking of his package, how did the man walk? Just like earlier, he had a huge bulge in his jeans. But this time, he stared just as eagerly at her body. As he should, she was a beautiful woman. Fit for worship.

"How many inches do you have?"

He blinked. "Excuse me?"

"Your size. How big? It's always so disappointing to get someone naked and see no reason to continue."

"You're kidding," he said incredulously.

She looked puzzled. "Of course not. That's never happened? You both get naked and see what a man calls average and it's smaller than the length of your hand. I know, I know, size isn't *supposed* to matter but it does, don't you think? Sometimes a woman just needs to be filled."

"You're not from around here, are you?"

"No. Why?"

"You are absolutely the oddest woman I've ever met."

"Why?"

"You're standing here half naked, talking to me about my cock and don't feel the slightest embarrassment."

"I'm beautiful. Why should I be embarrassed?"

"You have no modesty."

"Is that bad? Wait a minute. Are you trying to distract me from the question I asked you? How big you are?"

"No! I mean, I'm not comfortable measuring it for a complete stranger."

"We wouldn't be strangers after the act," she assured him.

"I am not," he growled, "measuring my cock."

This woman completely baffled him. It was obvious she was a loon, yet she knew Caleb and Keara well enough to stay in their house. And crazy as she was, she turned him on like nobody's business.

It was beyond the constant state of arousal he always lived in. She was magnetic and demanding. Not at all what he was used to or even wanted.

Only what he craved.

"Fine, little human." She walked right past him as if he wasn't there.

"What do you mean by little?" he called out as she walked down the hall, completely missing out on the word *human*.

"You know exactly what I mean. Below average. Not worthy of me, Ruler of Luciefyiore."

Jere felt sucker punched. Socked in the gut. His breath left his body before he snapped to his senses and followed her into the master bedroom.

"You're from the demon realm?"

"I rule in Keara's stead. While she follows her Earth destiny. Please, be gone. I'll need my beauty rest."

The woman certainly did think she was a queen.

"Princess, you're half naked and I can't decide if we should talk or do other things. Either way you fascinate me."

"Like I said, you're not worthy of my attentions."

He looked mildly irritated. "I'm not smaller than average."

"I still do not want you."

Obviously she believed he was a lesser man and didn't care to find out otherwise. He stepped toward her and watched her take a step away.

He stepped forward again, a stealthy hunter stalking his prey. She watched him with those icy blue eyes, the coloring of an angel yet the cunning of a demon. He was an inch from her, his breath mingling with hers.

One finger trailed over the thin material of her nightgown and traced the lightest circle around her nipple. It stiffened and reached for him as she hissed air deep into her lungs.

"Someday before I return, I'll allow you to please me," she whispered, her lips parted and moist.

There was silence for the briefest moment before he spoke. "One day, I'll allow *you*."

And he was gone.

Chapter Two
The Suffering

ဢ

Her eyes snapped open immediately. How the hell did anyone sleep with the Earth sun rising so damn early? And it was bright, not at all like the pale shade of the sun back home.

She was as uncomfortable as a train wreck. Her eyes watered from the light, her body was sore from the long walk yesterday and she felt painfully odd.

What was wrong? It was the strangest feeling, yearning and incomplete. Aching. Surprise hit her as she realized what was wrong.

She was unsatisfied.

She couldn't remember ever being unsatisfied. Not in her entire life. She groaned and tried to drown out the light with a pillow over her face. Nothing helped. Her swollen labia rubbed between her legs, so she reached out and grabbed a pair of lace panties and pulled them up, making a mental note to herself. Never go to bed without undies. Too sensual apparently, for a girl wakes up in the mood.

Sleep was elusive.

Her body had a mind of its own, her passage was silky and wet and she kept imagining a hunky man sliding his thick cock into her. Girth. There was nothing like girth.

Not just any man either. The one in the same house.

He'd make a fantastic lover, she was sure of it. He was strong and virile and at this moment, she could imagine kneeling before him, worshipping the length of his cock. Running her tongue along the underside. Sucking delicately on the head.

She flung off the wisp of panties and kicked them under the sheets.

He'd have a tiny bit of moisture at the hole of his cock. She'd lick it up, it'd be sweet like tasty honey.

She spread her legs, bending at the knees so everything was wide open. Her clit was swollen and hard under her finger.

He'd groan and begin to move his hips. She'd suck everything, his balls, his cock, until he'd beg her to let him come down her throat.

The more she swirled her fingers, the more juice she gathered, until they were soaked. She brought one up to her mouth and licked. The sheer eroticism of the act seized her body. She bucked her hips and came, rolling waves of lust just as strong as if someone trainable sucked at her cunt.

She panted for breath and enjoyed the tiny aftershocks that rolled through her body. Slowly she began to relax and clasped the pillow back over her eyes to drown out the dreadful morning light.

She lay quiet, trying to fall asleep again. For ten whole minutes.

And then the strange smell hit her. Gagging, she scrambled from the bed to head from her room to follow the ghastly odor.

The sexy human male she'd just fantasized about was clad in loose pajama bottoms and nothing else. He stood at the stove with a sizzling skillet, which emitted a foul stench that migrated throughout the entire house.

"Breakfast?" he asked.

"What the hell do you people eat?"

He grinned. "I know, I remember when Keara first came here. She'd wake up cranky too. Vegetarians, huh? This is bacon and eggs, princess. Get used to it. A man likes his meat."

"Bacon? And eggs? Like cannibals?"

"Cannibals?" He truly looked puzzled. "I don't follow."

She shook her head to clear it.

"Oh, you mean because of demon eggs?" He grinned again. "We eat chicken eggs here."

"That's right," she mumbled under her breath. "I forget. You give birth to repulsive little parasites instead of hatching your young. And bacon? Is that the disgusting smell?"

He sniffed the air. "Disgusting? That smell makes your stomach growl."

She covered her mouth with her hand. The thought of it made her want to dry heave. "What is it? More flesh?"

"Yup. Pig."

Her eyes widened in disbelief. "Pig? The little pink creatures? You eat them?"

"So will you."

"No way. I'll starve first. They're ugly. And pink."

"Suit yourself, prima donna."

The bastard turned his back to her and continued sizzling the smelly pink and white strips on the stove.

"What is your name and how long will you be in this residence?" she asked in her haughtiest voice.

"Jere Rousseau. I'm staying until Keara returns. She doesn't want her father unprotected while she's gone, so Caleb called me over to stay."

Keara's father? The ex-right hand of Enishka, the banished demon lord? The man had enough power to rule their dimension if he wanted. "Why in the world would Keara be worried about Demitris? He has the strength of an army."

Jere shrugged. "Pregnancy hormones. That protective maternal gene kicks in."

"Well, you can't stay in the same house as me. Especially with those horrible odors you emit. You must leave."

"Nope."

"No? What do you mean?"

"Demitris gave me the key to stay here. Here I'll remain."

"Clearly, he didn't know I was arriving when he gave you that key."

"Maybe not. But why should I be inconvenienced? After all, I'm family." The bastard gave another grin and slowly lowered his eyes to her exposed body.

As if.

Yet her traitorous flesh heated from the inside out. Nerve endings tingled, forgetting they'd had a very recent release.

However, Natalya Hershkle would not be ruled. Certainly not by a mortal.

"I'm not into humans," she retorted and spun on her heel. Straight to her room, where she hurriedly showered and headed out to find the house of Demitris and Elizabeth.

Searching while not having horns was a problem. How did one do anything in this dimension without them? She had to lower herself to find the posh hotel where she'd stayed at once before when sent to this dimension. Enishka had a minion who owned the hotel. Through his help she'd be able to find Demitris' home.

She didn't walk this time. A taxi dropped her off at the hotel. She was sure Keara wouldn't mind her using one of the little plastic cards in her office and signing her name carefully. *Keara Van Trump.*

Natalya walked to the front desk. "Hi," she said brightly to the acne-covered kid who stood there. "Dave in?"

"He's busy."

Fine, she could wait a few minutes. She was patient.

A child scuttled past her. "Twick or tweat," she hollered. "I'm practicing for Hollerween."

Natalya pulled away enough so the chocolatey little fingers couldn't touch her. And then she noticed them.

"Hey, little girl, you have *horns*."

"My mommy bought me them."

"Where?"

"They're clip-ons, see?"

Barrettes. The stumpy little human wore barrettes clasped into her rat's nest.

"I really need those," Natalya murmured.

"Whatcha got?"

Natalya raised an imperious eyebrow. "You wish to trade something?"

"Yup."

"What is it you want?"

"I like your watch."

"Done." It was Keara's anyway. She unclasped the watch and handed it over.

The negotiations were quick. A pudgy hand unsnapped *one* barrette and handed it over. Natalya stared after the child in amazement. "The other?" she reminded.

"Oh, you want the two of them? What else you got then?"

"Why you little…"

"Mom!" the child screamed.

The tiniest little wave of a finger and the dirty child looked wide-eyed in amazement back at her. The spots where Natalya's horns once were actually tingled. She wondered if she had enough residual power for the smallest scare. "I could make your hair curl, little girl."

Instead of looking frightened, the child replied slyly. "I like curls.

"You do?"

Nodding, a little hand reached out to twist her own lock of hair, winding it around a fat finger. Talya concentrated on the scalp tingle and beneath the kid's touch, her hair spiraled into ringlets.

"Woa! Lady. Amazing. My name's Karah. It's been a pleasure doing bizzy-ness with you." The other barrette was quickly handed over.

"Whatever." Impatient now, Natalya headed back to the acne-covered desk clerk. "Okay," she snapped. "I'm sure Dave's not busy anymore."

"Yeah," he started, "but you can't just walk in there—"

"Too late," she tossed over her shoulder with a sweep of her blonde hair. She opened the door and walked through, closing it firmly behind her.

"Hi, Dave."

His face paled in the presence of The Huntress. Of course, he didn't know her horns were gone, he would just assume they were hidden. He also had no idea she hadn't been sent by Enishka this time. Enishka was too vain to let his human minions know he'd been banished from Luciefyiore.

"Wh-what can I do for you?"

"I need to find someone. A man, of course." She grinned, the sexy smile that had no humor. And watched as he swallowed.

The phone on his desk began to shrill as if it were angry. It rang continuously while the idiot stared. "Go ahead," she encouraged. "Take your phone call."

He warily lifted the receiver as Talya fought the urge to laugh. Who did he think would be on the other side? Enishka himself?

She wandered around his office while he tried to act normally with his conversation. Behind him was a small hallway nook, complete with a mirror.

Natalya clipped her barrettes into her hair.

It was just like the old days. Although she knew the horns weren't real, looking at them made her feel as if she still had all her powers. Sure it was an optical illusion but damn. She looked good. She stood a little bit straighter.

When she turned the corner to face Dave again, his eyes widened with fear. She fought the urge to laugh.

He hung up the phone.

"I need your help," she said.

"Anything, Huntress."

It was amazing what accessories accomplished in this world.

* * * * *

The taxi cab dropped her off at the house of Demitris. Natalya walked up the front steps. She knocked politely at the door, then bowed to one knee, waiting for the acknowledgement when it opened.

"Natalya?"

She raised her head. "Master."

"Not any longer. I'm human in this dimension. Well, as human as I can be." Demitris grinned at his own joke. In this dimension, he masked his true face to others but she saw his demon form.

"You'll always be my master."

"No, my dear. Anyway, come on in. Are those horns?"

She'd forgotten about the stumpy human's play toys. "Oh, um, yes."

"I thought my daughter said you'd been dehorned?"

"Well, yes," she squirmed. And then reached up to unsnap one.

Demitris stared, round eyed. "I don't want to know."

"It's best if you don't."

Once, she wouldn't have cared. Now she almost felt ashamed of herself. Fake horns, bartered for with a human child. The shame bordered on disgust that she got the shaft with the child. Practically a little con artist.

The little trampling.

Yes, almost felt ashamed of herself. This dimension had her all screwed up. She was aghast that she, *The Huntress*, would feel shame over anything.

How she longed to go home where the title still fit. Maybe at home, she'd be allowed to have horns. Surely there was some sort of magic spell to do it.

"What can I do for you, Natalya?" Demitris asked as he showed her inside.

"I seem to have inherited a problem. Keara left me her key during my banishment."

"Yes?" He gestured to a small seating area and she sat politely, taking care to cross her legs.

"To stay in her house. But it's inhabited by a human. A human is staying in Keara and Caleb's house. With me."

Realization dawned in his eyes. "Jere. I'm sorry, Natalya. But it is a rather large house, is it not?"

"Yes, it's a large house. It's still inconvenient."

"I'm sure it is, my dear. But Jere needs to stay there. There's a reason but I can't share it with you. Let's say he's in hiding and will be found in my home."

"Hiding? From what?"

"I really can't say. If you find it that abhorrent to stay in the same house as him, you are welcome to move into our guest room. But trust me, he's a good man. Honest and honorable."

Talya thought about it but Demitris' wife was a full-blooded human also. She'd just be trading one of them in for another.

"No," she sighed. "That's fine. I won't put you out. I'll deal with him myself."

* * * * *

Who was she really? The woman stirred him beyond belief. It wouldn't take long to wander through her stuff, to search for clues to the real her.

Jere slipped into her bedroom, as quiet as a mouse, aware that she wasn't home but still stealthy from years of habit. Faint scents of Keara and Caleb lingered but more powerful was the aroma of her.

Hot-blooded demon ruler, Natalya.

Innocence and lust. Sweet and sinful. Tenderness and passion.

His extra senses picked up the exact spot where she lay in the king-sized bed last night. The sweet aroma of her sexy skin lingered. Along with something else.

Her lacy panties. Scented with the rich smell of desire.

They'd been wet, creamed from her body. She'd flung them off sometime during the night. Wait, they were too wet. Was it this morning? His imagination ran wild. Did she separate her slim thighs and touch her slit with her long fingers? Did she moan as she spread her labia, found her clit and massaged herself to orgasm? Was it his face she pictured?

His cock was as hard as a rock. He released the snap of his jeans and felt his erection kiss the air. It was swollen purple with need and he gripped it tightly with one hand as he clenched her panties with the other.

Lace drenched with her essence.

His hand pumped the strength of his sensitive cock and pre-cum dripped from the tiny hole at the tip. He imagined her sweet mouth there, lapping the droplets of juice while her fingers spread apart her pussy for his view.

Did she lie on this bed last night with her nether lips flushed and excited, rolling her hips as she imagined him thrusting deep into her?

His hand stroked faster and with his other one, he cupped her panties around his tight balls. Knowing her intimate flesh had been against the very fabric excited him beyond belief.

Excited him even more to bring her wisp of panties up to inhale deeply.

His cock ached as he pumped harder. He was so close and her panties were rich with feminine desire. He needed his release, a massive rolling orgasm to satisfy his needs, if only for the moment.

His heart raced and he threw his head back and growled. His orgasm started deep in his balls and jerked free in great streams of cum.

* * * * *

Natalya slammed the front door, still irritated beyond belief. She went straight down the hallway to her room.

Something was different. Dammit, she felt like an amputee might, as though she could reach out with a missing limb. In this case, a vital limb. Her horns. They would have ascended about now and she would have found what was different.

But they were gone. Useless. She had nothing but the barrettes, a child's toy. This time tucked into her purse.

Nothing was amiss. Everything was exactly the way she'd left it earlier that morning.

Except for the scrap of black lace panties on top of her bed. Those had been under the covers.

Even without her horns, she knew. She knew who'd been in her room and what he'd been doing.

Her bedroom door slammed behind her as she headed down the hall screaming his name. He opened his door as she reached it.

"Yes?" he said casually. Eyes hard.

"You were in my room," she accused.

"Yes," he agreed.

It threw her for a loop. "What? You aren't going to deny it?"

"Why should I?"

"Because you have no business invading my territory."

"But you invaded mine. I was in the house first, remember?"

If she'd had horns, they would have extended about now. As it was, the best she could do was grit her teeth.

"Stay out of my room." At her commanding tone, he raised an eyebrow. "Please," she said sarcastically, knowing he'd insist on the word. Then she thought about it. "Why were you in there, anyway?"

He took a step closer to her, so close she could feel the heat radiate from his body. Smell the faint aftershave on his skin.

She wondered how that warm skin would feel bare against hers.

He leaned his face close to hers, almost touching her cheek but not quite. "I wanted to learn about you."

How she longed to stretch her neck and encourage him to kiss the outstretched tendon. Her voice was breathless when she replied. "What did you find out?"

"That you brought yourself to climax while you thought about me."

There was dead silence after his statement. For the briefest moment.

"You are somewhat pleasurable to masturbate to," she returned. No sense in denying it.

"Glad I could help out, honey." There it was. The tiniest tip of his tongue, tracing along her sensitive earlobe.

"Still, the pleasure was all mine," she reminded. And then thought about it. "Or was it yours also?" Her voice practically purred with pleasure. "Did you grow hard thinking about it? Did you touch yourself in return?"

"How could I not? With your scent there in the bed and with the image of your body nearly naked each time I've seen you."

"Did you rub yourself to completion, Jere?"

"With hard, sure strokes, sweetheart. Your scent in my nose."

She knew exactly what he was talking about. "You sniffed my panties?"

"The next time, I'll have my face pressed against your pussy, not a wisp of worthless fabric."

"Tell me more."

"I'll lick along the seam of your lips, over and over until you separate them for me."

The thought made her shiver. "Don't you have a girlfriend?"

"No."

"Amazingly built human like yourself? I find that hard to believe."

"Believe it. I'm single. What about you?"

"Me? I'm, well… I guess you could say… Well, I have a few men back at home. On Luciefyiore."

"But not one is your boyfriend?"

Natalya squirmed. "Not exactly. They were my…servants."

"Servants? I asked if you were single and you tell me you have servants?"

"They were there to service my needs," she said meaningfully.

"Oh."

For the second time in her life, Natalya Hershkle felt ashamed of herself. "I prefer to be single," she told him. "I do. For if I weren't, my option would be Enishka, the demon lord."

"The same one that had Demitris and Elizabeth banished? Keara's first husband?"

Natalya nodded. "The one and only. So back to you, why are you single?"

She almost regretted the question when he stepped away from her. Taking his warmth with him.

"I guess you could say I've been a little bitter since my fiancée left me."

"Why'd she leave you?"

"I was sentenced to do time."

"Do time? What is that?"

"I was a convicted felon, princess."

"Really?" So much made sense, the hardened look in his eye. The mistrust. Like a puppy that had been kicked from early on.

"Do you want her still?" she whispered.

"No."

But if the fiancée hadn't left him, he wouldn't be bitter. And alone.

And some odd little hidden part of her wanted him to be happy. She reached out to his face and ran her thumb alongside his hair-roughened jaw. Traced the line to his lips. Smoothed his lower lip that jutted out slightly.

Felt it move as he whispered against her. "I thought you didn't want a human. That I don't turn you on."

She sighed. "You turned me on from day one, Jere. Let's just go with the flow, have some fun. Okay?"

He brought his mouth closer to hers and she tasted him. Finally.

Their tongues meshed, slid alongside one another, alternating between seeking pleasure and tasting and giving satisfaction in return.

"What do you like?" she asked. He'd never know that she, Natalya Hershkle, had never asked a man that before. She was to be pleased, she'd never given it. Not in the past.

But she wanted to with him.

For once, she wanted to make someone else happy.

"I'd like you to do whatever you want, baby."

Chapter Three
Sensual Pleasures

ᔓ

Well, if that wasn't opening up a whole lot of options. She lifted his shirt and ran her fingers over the warmth of his skin. Upward, until she reached his nipples. Small and flat.

She tried to undo his waistband. Her fingers were unpracticed.

"Having trouble?" he asked, a hint of amusement in his voice.

"You know, I don't think I've ever undressed anyone," she said, wonderment in her voice. Now that she thought about it, her minions serviced her already naked. According to her demands.

He unfastened his own button deftly. The smallest little movement. Pushed his jeans down his hips and over muscular thighs.

She took his hands and led him to his bed. He allowed her to push him onto his back and she feasted on the scene spread before her.

He was a luscious specimen. Smooth skin pulled taut over muscles. Perfect color, tanned to a toasted almond. She leaned over and licked a line from his navel up to his breastbone.

Saw the hardness in his boxers swell.

She used her tongue to taste a nipple and he shivered beneath her lick. She inserted a finger into the waistband of his boxers, lifted and let his rock-hard erection burst out.

It stood swollen and proud, veins protruding through the silky skin. Soon, very soon, that thick piece of male flesh would be plunging into her, hard and fast.

With one fingertip, she traced a vein. Followed it as far as she could and then traced the seam at his head. A small amount of moisture leaked from the tip, she swirled it over the engorged head.

His balls were quite satisfactory. Large and heavy, they should slap against her sensitive flesh nicely when he rode her.

She leaned between his spread legs and sucked one of his testicles into her mouth. She rolled the delicate sac with her tongue, vaguely hearing him hiss with pleasure.

Wrapping both hands around his massive rod, she licked the head of his cock. Twisting her hands up and down his length, she slowly sucked his head into her mouth, creating a vacuum.

"Holy shit," he gasped.

She took his entire length in and then slowly let it back out. He began to buck his hips. She alternated between deep-throating him and sucking the head of his cock. He felt like concrete encased in warm silk and she knew he wouldn't last long. He was engorged, so hard he'd shatter.

Hey, while he was this hard, she might as well see what it felt like deep inside her.

She quickly pulled off her panties and hiked her skirt up around her waist. Before he even looked up to see what she was doing, she impaled herself on him.

It was good.

Thick and completely filling. She began to ride him, up and down, wantonly. When he raised his head to look at her, she spread her lips for his view.

Saw the lust drift over his face when he watched his cock disappear into her hot pink sheath.

"I'm gonna come," he warned.

She climbed off him and he made a small sound of protest. It stopped when she began to lick his cock clean of her juices.

"I can't take this," he said, flipping her onto her back and trapping her.

He sought out her lips, thrusting his tongue into her mouth as if he craved her taste.

"Mmm," he growled.

"Like that?" she whispered, fully aware what taste lingered. The combination of them both.

But Jere was done with speech. His mouth locked to hers again, searching for something unfathomable in her soul.

He inserted a finger into her soaked pussy, feeling the heat that emanated from deep inside.

She moaned. If he knew how wonderful his plunging finger felt, he'd be impossible to deal with.

Soon she was filled with three fingers. In and out, stroking her sheath, widening her entrance, stretching her wonderfully. One thumb reached upward to press against her clitoris.

She was going wild. She was panting uncontrollably, making goddawful little grunting noises.

Yet she couldn't help herself.

She wanted that huge, thick cock to replace those talented fingers. She was squirming, bucking her hips.

"Jere, give me more," she demanded.

"Princess."

Demands didn't seem to work with this odd human male. How else was she to make it known what she wanted, craved?

Oh. The one little word she used earlier, albeit sarcastically.

"Please," she begged. "Slide your cock in me."

He gently bit the side of her neck and pulled his fingers out of her sheath to grip his swollen member at the base. He teased her with it, not doing anything more than rubbing the head of his cock against her lips. "Like it?" he asked, smearing her wetness up and down her swollen labia, which parted eagerly as if they wanted to swallow him.

She quickly swung her hips back against him, forcing the huge head of his cock in a mere couple of inches. Both groaned at the instant pleasure.

"Naughty girl," he whispered against her throat. And then rammed in, right to the hilt. Slowly he pulled out, only to thrust in again. Again and again he rocked, filling her then releasing.

She clenched her vaginal muscles around him, gripping him tightly as he tried to pull out.

"You're so tight," he said, his voice strangled.

"Kegels," she informed him. "Faithfully."

He stared at her blankly for a second but then thankfully continued his passionate rhythm. Faster and faster he plunged, until she just couldn't take it.

Her world exploded with him locked deeply within her. He ejaculated into her, still moving and groaning into her throat.

He was heavy and sweaty lying over her, catching his breath. But it felt good. She rubbed his lower back, massaging gently. He was warmth and strength.

She yawned against his neck.

Sometime later she woke up wrapped in his arms. He said something to which she mumbled a reply.

He left her curled up in bed, exhausted. She was vaguely aware of him pressing a kiss to her temple and of water running in the background.

Hours later, she awoke to darkness in the house. After a long hot shower in which water beat down upon sore muscles, she smiled into the mirror as she blow dried her hair. She felt good. Better than she usually did after sex. Why was that? It had been a while. And Jere was amazing. It must have been a fluke that they meshed so well.

He was, after all, human.

Normally that would have been fine. It wasn't like humans didn't service her. But that was the key.

Humans serviced *her*.

She'd never cared whether they reached their enjoyment or not. With Jere, she wanted to give him the utmost pleasure. What made him different?

It was this strange dimension that made her feel guilty for bartering with a sneaky little child. Made her feel guilty for having a harem. Made her feel guilty for thinking humans were beneath her. It had to be.

The mirror that she peered into wasn't quite right. It was growing dim inside. Natalya blinked to clear her eyes.

Her image was beginning to shift and distort. A hole was swirling in the center, like a beam of light.

The council.

The circle grew until it became the mirror and Natalya raised her hand out to touch it. The force pulled her into the swirling vortex, into another dimension.

A golden, glittering dimension. As usual, when the councilmembers met for business, they sat around a long table, all dressed in white robes with golden accents. The last time she'd been before them, it was to explain why there had been no eggs hatched in Luciefyiore recently.

She still clung to the excuse that she wasn't aware of how big her harem had grown.

The bastards in charge had dehorned her to reverse the power of impotence over the males she'd acquired since her rule in Luciefyiore. She still kept her original minions but like old toys they no longer held her interest. Especially since she was banished from home.

"Natalya Hershkle."

Natalya walked forth, stopping before the table where they all looked at her with their expressionless faces.

"How do you fare with your banishment?"

"Well, I haven't been able to cause true love yet." If her voice was a tad sarcastic, she sure didn't mind. "Of course, my power's been taken and it's been but one day on Earth."

"We have a small problem that was unforeseen. Enishka has heard of the predicament and has demanded a hearing. He claims his wife Keara should be the one to rule Luciefyiore instead of appointing you. Unfortunately, with the harm you caused the demon realm, his case is strong."

"His *ex-wife* doesn't want to rule. That's why she appointed me in her stead."

"Technically, only a blood relative can rule long-term. With your mistake, he's now pushing that issue, claiming you were appointed and your reign can't last forever."

"So what am I to do?"

"You have less time than originally thought. If you do not cause love for your lesson, your powers will not be returned. But you will be."

"Returned to the demon realm? I thought I was banished to Earth?"

"You will be returned to Luciefyiore as a helpless demon. No horns, no power."

"You can't do that!" Her voice was desperate but still the emotionless bastards showed nothing. Surely they remembered a time centuries ago when a demon had been stripped from his powers. He may as well have been road kill.

There was a reason why the boundaries between Luciefyiore and Earth were sealed. Those without defenses would be slaughtered by the more powerful beings. Humans or dehorned demons.

"The only thing you will have are your minions that had already been called. Although freed, they can protect you."

"My minions? That is all that protects me from certain death?" Her voice was harsh but what alternative did she have? They may as well send a bolt of lightning to strike her out easily instead of the slow painful torture she'd be exposed to later.

"You still have time for the original agreement. Cause true love to regain your horns and with them, your powers upon your earlier return."

"How?" she snapped. "There's even more pressure now with a shorter time frame!" She stepped toward the table and an electrical impulse shocked her from the foot up.

The burn tingled her toes, traveled up her leg, growing hotter as it rose.

Still, she refused to remove her foot from the invisible trigger.

It hit her midsection, then her chest. She was on fire, burning inside, her head felt like it would combust. She took one step backward to jerk from the trigger.

And fell screaming into the whirling black vortex that opened to swallow her whole.

When she awoke, she was in bed.

Near the bed, Jere sat in a chair, watching her. "You're awake."

"Yeah," she said, slightly groggy.

"I was worried. You've been out for a while but Demitris was over and checked you, he said it was just a state of stasis."

"How long was I out?"

"Three days."

"What?"

"I couldn't find you for the longest time. I thought you stepped out somewhere. I was getting worried and checked your room one more time and heard you moan on the bathroom floor. You weren't there before, I'd swear to it. I picked you up and carried you to bed."

"I had just showered and a portal opened through the mirror," she said as the memories came rushing back to her. "I now know the consequences of my failure."

She wasn't even sure if she could discuss it. The idea of the return home while powerless was too much to comprehend. She was a sitting duck, a piece of meat thrown to a pack of hungry humans.

The council may as well paint her pink and attach a corkscrew tail for the savages here to eat for breakfast with their *eggs*.

She was so happy with Jere recently. Well, it had been three days but to her it felt like a few hours earlier.

He stroked her bangs back from her forehead. "Go on. What happened?"

"I-I'll have to return home without my power. Enishka is challenging my ruling because of my mistake. And things look good for him."

"How can he have any challenges while he's banished?"

She shrugged. "He's still the rightful lord, born to the throne. Keara rules by default, as his wife and Demitris' daughter. She appointed me as ruler but I called too much attention to the legalities of doing it and gave him a way to challenge by my own actions."

"You didn't mean to cause a problem."

"No, I didn't mean to. But I did. And it can't be undone."

It felt good to admit that. She realized it was the first time she admitted to making a horrible mistake. She'd abused her power.

Jere's hand was rubbing the top of her temple, just beyond the hairline. Where her horns had been. It was comforting. She relaxed instead of cringing in embarrassment like she once would have. "Jere, I... My power is the ability to cause impotence in any male who shares my bed. I got a little carried away with the size of my serviceable harem and Luciefyiore wasn't breeding. There weren't any available males left. The council had to take away my horns to reverse the power."

"Okay, so it can't be undone," he said. "That doesn't mean you can't fix things. Right the wrong. No, it won't be the same as before but it can be better than it is now."

"How can I right the wrongs?"

"Well, you said yourself they dehorned you to fix the, um, male impotence problem, right? Soon Luciefyiore will be breeding again. They sent you here to learn about unselfish love. Sounds to me like you're learning, you just need to prove it. You would have anyway, you just have less time."

"Less time is an understatement. There were so many things I wanted to do that I never had time for. Now there's no time."

"What did you want to do?"

His hand over her sensitive dehorned area was feeling wondrous. Comforting and encouraging, causing her to spill her innermost feelings. Something she never would have done. "I wanted to visit places in this dimension. That gambling place in the heart of Hell."

"Heart of Hell?"

"Where it's so hot and dry? With all the colorful lights? Las Vargas."

"You mean Las Vegas." He said it with a small grin but she didn't even care. As long as he kept rubbing those tender spots on her head, all was good.

"But," she continued, "what do I know? I wasn't even aware of the mess I was making in Luciefyiore. It didn't matter then, now — something's different."

"What's different?"

"I don't know. I think it's this place. I'm out of my element in this dimension. I'm confused and I don't know what the hell I'm doing or where I'm going. I want to go home,

Jere. The original plan, not this new one I was dealt. That's all."

"How do you get home, Talya?"

"I have to give humans unselfish love. But without my powers. It's impossible, I tell you. I've never felt like this, out of control. It's a dizzying, spinning feeling." Distress flooded her voice.

To her surprise, he climbed onto the bed with her, sitting against the headboard. He held her and stroked her shoulder, now kissing her head near the temples where the horns had been. "It'll come. I promise. I have an idea. You have at least a week, right? You can cause true love anywhere. Let's make the most of it. Go see things. Your Vargas."

She almost smiled. "You want to take me to this Vegas? Why?"

"Sin City, baby. You and I, we'll let loose. Have fun. Who knows where we'll end up in a week's time?"

She was missing something. "Where will *you* be in a week's time?"

"I'm not sure. I'm on the run but it's only a matter of time before they catch up with me. Keara thought she could bail me out but the return to Luciefyiore was unexpected. That's why I'm hiding out here until she gets back."

"On the run? What does that mean?"

"From the authorities, baby. I'm a con." His voice was bitter and it tugged unknown feelings from her. It was the strangest dimension, all these odd feelings like aching hearts. Guilt. Acknowledgement.

"My Luciefyiore screw-up affected a lot," she murmured, as if she was just realizing it.

"That's the thing with actions, baby. With every action, there's consequence. Like ripples across water."

"It's not fair that my life affected yours."

"More than you realize," he said with another kiss to her head. "Now we need to get you up and showered and fed so we can start our trip. You want me to watch you shower since the bathroom was the portal to that last incident?"

She knew the council wouldn't be summoning again but hell. The easy human just offered to watch her shower.

With those clear glass doors, polished all sparkly to a high shine.

Temptation was so great in this land. Natalya managed to squeeze a tiny tear from the corner of one eye. "I'd love that. You're so good to me."

He wiped her cheek tenderly where it glistened. "No problem," he muttered in a husky tone.

She strode quickly to the bathroom, glancing back at him to make sure he followed. Her gown she dropped without a second thought as she bent over to adjust the shower spray. Behind her, she heard the sound when he gulped.

Innocently, she glanced at him over her shoulder.

His eyes were glued to the hidden shadows between her legs as she bent over. Her swollen labia, which she knew protruded for his pleasure.

She stepped in and let the water run in rivulets over her body. Across her breasts. Down her nipples, which hardened against the spray.

He stood propped against the wall, arms crossed. Lids heavy while he watched her.

She gathered soap and sudsed her body. Across smooth skin, over sweet spots. Tender, loving.

Still he watched.

She lifted a leg to soap it better.

He licked his lips.

She ran a soapy finger through her slit, watching his face through heavy-lidded eyes.

His breathing had slowed, becoming sure and steady. Aroused. "Are you teasing me?" he asked.

"Yes," she answered, completely honest. "Care to join me? I'm slick inside."

Sure enough, her fingers were deep inside her body, slowly twisting in and out.

Jere stood, methodically stripping his own clothing, exposing his taut skin and a strong cock.

No sooner had he stepped into the glass shower with her than her soft fingers wrapped around his width. He groaned, searching for her mouth with his.

A slender arm pulled him close to her while her other hand stroked him with a rhythm that equaled his own. He ached to be inside her again.

Lifting her body onto his, she wrapped her legs around him. His erection found her opening and they locked.

She exhaled, lowering her forehead onto his shoulder. They paused for a moment, enjoying the sensation of him deep within her.

She began to roll her hips, grinding against him.

"You feel good," he muttered.

"So do you," she agreed as the water pelted his back. She hardly felt the cool of the tiles where her heated back pressed as he fucked her, slowly and surely.

His hands gripped her hips possessively as he inched his cock in and out, ever so slowly, letting her feel every single movement.

When they were breathing heavily, he pulled his body from hers and set her on her feet. He turned her away from him so she faced the built-in seat of the shower. With a hand on her back, he gently pushed her down.

She splayed out both palms on the bench. He caressed the curves of her rounded bottom, then reached up and ran his hand over the indentation of her waist, up along her spine, between her shoulder blades.

Back down he traced down her spine. Slowly, to the cleft of her buttocks. Ever more slowly, he trailed through her cheeks and dipped into her swollen labia while she moaned.

He spread her wide open and slid back inside her hot sheath. Filling her up, moving gently, driving her crazy and forcing her to push back against him, wriggling in circular motions.

She was moving faster, reaching for her climax, driving him insane and never even knowing it.

Deeper and deeper he thrust, also moving faster as she moaned and panted. When she begged for more speed, he fucked her hard, jerking her hips back against him so her breasts jiggled with the effort, until she shattered into a million pieces around his cock.

Only then did he allow himself to come.

Chapter Four
Whispers from the Past

ತಿ

Jere was curled against her, watching her while she slept. Here and there she'd whimper, soft little sounds so unlike her strong character. She amazed him, this gorgeous creature from another dimension. So adaptable, to come to a foreign place determined to fit in. To be stripped of one's defenses and tossed into another land.

What could she be dreaming that distressed her so?

When she was upset earlier, he'd caressed her temples where her horns should be. She'd instantly relaxed, practically purring at his touch. Maybe she needed it again. He reached out but as soon as he connected with her dehorned spots, a spark zipped through his fingertips.

He was drifting in slow motion, moving so carefully he felt drugged. Pulled through a thickness that was a mixture of heavy air and unscented smoke.

Maybe he was dreaming.

The smoke curled into images he could watch. She was having dinner alone at a long table when a gong sounded. She glanced up at the door, keeping her face deliberately blank to mask her concern.

The gong blasted again, echoing throughout her large house. Sounding angry in the somber silence.

Still she sat, chewing her food slowly.

The heavy wooden doors crashed open, smashed by uniformed demons. Splintered wood stuck out at odd angles.

Natalya never moved as the officers drew their weapons and approached her. Something wasn't right.

All the officers were feminine. Not a single man.

"Natalya Hershkle. You are under arrest. You are to come quietly and compliantly at once."

"I get a twenty-four-hour summons," she said calmly.

One of the officers snickered. Another put on gloves. "Who says?" she said rudely.

Natalya leaned back.

The three officers stepped in.

"Whoa, ladies, wait a minute," Jere said.

No one listened to him. Either he was invisible or he was dreaming. If it was a dream, was he invading Natalya's? Still, he had to speak. "You gotta be kidding me. Three against one?"

Natalya stood quickly and two of the officers grabbed her arms. Natalya's horns shimmered, a pearlescent hue almost. And then her eyes glowed, a fluorescent blue that looked as dangerous as hell.

"Bitch," one woman snarled. "You knew I was going with Jessel."

"Not my fault you couldn't keep him."

The officer grabbed her stick and struck. Or tried to but it never connected. Instead, Natalya ducked and took her out with a well-aimed kick to her thigh. The officer dropped like a rock.

Everyone else moved in at once.

Jere grabbed for one of the attacking women but his arms fell right through her, like he was some sort of ghost.

Watch and listen.

See but don't touch.

The message was loud and clear.

But Natalya was The Huntress. Three puny demonettes couldn't take her down. She was holding her own against the trained officers. Despite his fear, he felt a glimmer of pride.

One officer, the first one who struck her, was on the floor, moaning with a broken back. Although he'd obviously missed the action, he was still so proud. The other two were bruised and battered when two more approached through the shattered door.

"What's going on?" someone said, grabbing her stick.

"She resisted arrest."

"You didn't call for backup?"

"It was too fast," the officer tried to explain through a swollen lip. As if she hadn't watched her broken friend throw the first punch.

"We have orders that she'll be dehorned by the council," one of the new officers said, a gleam in her eye.

"No way," Natalya spat.

"Shouldn't be resisting arrest," she laughed while her two partners held Natasha down to her knees. She pulled out a miniature sledgehammer while her two partners wrestled Natasha still.

He was frustrated, unable to help. He grabbed and grabbed the officers, to no avail.

One, two, three cracks with the sledgehammer and a sickening scream tore through his gut, leaving him with the urge to retch while her horns were broken from her head. One heartwrenching scream of fury was all she had time to give before Natalya lay unconscious from the blows.

While she was out, she was dragged into the back of a van. He climbed in, wondering how long he could stay and watch the dream or memory, whatever it was Not even sure he wanted to see but knowing he couldn't leave her alone.

She was locked in solitary confinement. "Protection," the crooked female officers laughed. Jere sat with her in the confinement cell for hours while her face swelled and her body bruised from the beating. She lay unconscious the whole time.

He'd never laid a hand on a female before but he wanted to tear the demon cops apart limb from limb. He could see the pain etched in Natalya's eyes, feel every lump across her beautiful face.

She definitely had twenty-four hours before the hearing. The officers just made sure she was locked up for them.

Hurt. And humiliated. For what reason, he had no idea.

He had no idea how the dream fast forwarded but she was back at home now. He sat on her bed, watching her.

She was to be banished to Earth. Dazed from the hearing outcome, she sat listlessly in her vanity chair before her mirror at bedtime that night. Simple pajamas, white and blue. A silky tank top with pants. The bruises had faded from her face, showing the passing of time, but the shadows in her eyes remained.

And she still stared at her broken horns. The bare spots on her head were a sensitive subject.

She wore her hair in a new style. Straight now, bangs dropping across to cover the missing protrusions. He could kick himself for touching the scars. Massaging her spots, calling attention to what she lacked.

"Your Essence?" A man stood behind her. He was young and buff, a male cover model who wore black leather pants and nothing else. He looked at Natalya longingly, staring at her like he had a right to.

Jere wanted to rip the man's head from his body, demon or not.

"Yes?" she answered.

"May I share your bed tonight?"

Her voice was nonchalant. "You're not next on the list."

She had a list?

"But I love you," he began.

"I know. But you had last night."

"See, that's the thing. Last night was a short night—"

"Short night? What are you talking about? How can one night be shorter than another?"

"Well, you were out late with the trial preparations. I didn't get as long as Tobias did the night before."

"No. You do not get dibs on another night until your name cycles through the list again."

She looked frustrated as she brought her silver hairbrush up to stroke her hair.

"I'll brush it for you."

She sighed, handing the brush to him. As if she gave up.

He ran the brush through her silky strands slowly, like he relished each movement. He took a strand of hair and rubbed it between his fingers. "I'm sorry I wasn't here when the police came for you."

"You couldn't have been."

"It was Hazen, wasn't it?"

Natalya's expression never wavered. Her voice was slightly monotonous. "She was one."

The brush paused in mid-stroke. "One?"

"There were a few others."

He dropped to his knees before her. "Marry me, your Essence. Let me be the one to fertilize your eggs. Make you the permanent ruler of Luciefyiore."

She sighed and looked away from him. "It's too late. I'm banished."

"It can't be permanent! Not when you have so many minions! We'd have to travel with you, we can't live without you."

Natalya was still expressionless. "We'll see," she said noncommittally. The poor bastard never noticed her lack of commitment and focused on what he wanted to hear.

"Shall I concentrate on the travel?"

"Sure," she said and watched as he left the room.

As soon as the door shut, her face fell. She looked exhausted. She rose and headed for the bed, where she crawled across to lie down in a fetal curl. Jere sat next to her, caressing her forehead, brushing her bangs back, trying not to notice they never moved.

"Hang strong," he whispered.

Her door opened behind her and she clenched her eyes shut as a look of disgust crossed her face at the intrusion.

"Your Essence?"

She never answered, feigning sleep until the door shut again.

That was a different man from the one before. Could he also be after a turn with her?

Jere felt white-hot rage. Then surprise. It was pure jealousy.

But she'd turned him away. That meant something. She'd turned the last two away, because she could have had the leather-pants who brushed her hair.

Not many women would turn down a specimen like that.

He ran his hand over her hair, down the side of her cheek. He knew she couldn't feel him but he couldn't resist the sexy blonde in the thin pajamas, which outlined every curve she had.

To his surprise, she turned over onto her back, staring at the ceiling thoughtfully. He trailed a finger from her forehead, down the bridge of her nose and across the pucker of lips.

The pink tip of her tongue licked her lips.

Down her chin he stroked, over her throat, along her collarbone.

She arched her back, the smallest movement. Thrusting her pointed nipples into the air.

Could she feel him?

He cupped one breast fully. She reached out with both hands to finger the lace at the bottom edge of her top.

Surprised, he withdrew his hand and watched as she lifted the silk of her tank top over her head. Nude from the waist up, she lay again, flat on her back.

He touched the peak of her breast. One finger was all he used as he pressed the pink nipple in gently.

She moaned and turned her head to the side, stretching the slim length of neck as if she wanted a love bite.

How he wished to oblige.

Instead, he consoled himself with opening his mouth over her erect nipple, imagining she could feel the heat of his suck.

She made the tiniest little noise. Pleasure.

He flattened his tongue and laved her entire breast, wide fat licks, and watched her hand disappear into her pajama bottoms. How he wished he could see her glistening juices coating her fingers. Gently, he stroked her abdomen. One line, across the area where her waistband sat against her skin. Trying to convey a mental thought to her to pull off the rest of her clothes.

He watched as she lifted her hips and skimmed the waistband over her curves, down her thighs and across sexy pink-polished toes.

She was amazing, glowing polished skin in the height of arousal. Plump lips, above and below.

He leaned down between her long legs. Softly he stroked her inner thighs until she opened wide.

She was hot-blooded, ready for a man to plunge in for the ultimate satisfaction. She was slippery, wet, and when she brought her knees apart and up to her chest, her lips parted.

He blew hot breath over the glistening pussy spread before him.

She moaned loudly and smeared her juice up over her clit.

He was as hard as a rock. He ground his bulge into the mattress as he lay on his stomach between her luscious thighs.

She spread apart her labia with one hand while the other massaged her clitoris. He watched every movement, every expression across her face, watched as she began to sensuously roll her hips to a tune only she could hear.

He couldn't help himself. He released his cock and stroked it with his own hand. He pressed his face against her pussy, imagining he could smell, taste, anything.

He pretended it was her hand bringing his greedy cock pleasure.

He could hear though. He listened to the noises she made, the sounds of gratification, the gasps of enjoyment.

He rose onto his knees and rubbed his cock right above her mons. When he came, he could lose his seed on her body.

Or he could try to fuck her.

He halted mid-stroke when the idea crossed his mind. Was it possible? He grasped his penis at the base and led it to her lips, nudging inside.

He felt warmth.

She halted her movements, an odd wonderment crossing her features.

He pushed inside and felt her grip him welcomingly.

Yes! He could feel her tighten around him.

She shuddered and he just knew it was over the sensation of his cock widening her sheath, stroking gently, in and out.

She began to massage her clit in tune to his thrusts, round and round, as he moved deeper then withdrew. Her eyes were closed when he leaned down in a push-up position and kissed her lips.

They opened and stared right through him to the ceiling above. When they fluttered shut again, he leaned down again.

She kissed back.

He bucked his hips, reaching as far and deep as he could, pushing in a rhythm that moved faster and harder.

She was vocal when she came, clenching her internal muscles and moaning her pleasure while her body rolled through waves of pleasure.

"Fuck," he muttered and reached his own orgasm within her.

To his surprise, he didn't awaken after his climax. He rolled onto the bed next to her, where she curled into a fetal position and slept. Just like in real life, he watched her drift off.

Next came the actual hearing with the council. In the morning she dressed, sending away countless male servants who offered to help her. To his supreme satisfaction.

The councilmembers were glitter and gold, wrapped in white robes like Greek gods. Sitting around a long table with expressionless faces, which made them look even more judgmental.

Natalya wore a bright red strapless gown. Skin tight. Jere took note of the demon audience in the swamp. They were all male, so at least she didn't have to contend with the crooked female cops in any way.

The council was speaking. "You must marry."

"I will not," Natalya returned.

The man blinked, obviously not used to refusal.

"Excuse me?"

"Forcing me to marry sets females back like…like some Earthling. Why not just take away our right to vote along with it?"

"You must head the dimension. Becoming a leader in fertility shows your mistake in causing a halt in reproduction."

"It's my body…my choice. I've not intended to reproduce, or I would have borne Enishka's little lizard-like offspring."

"Unfortunately, when we make mistakes of this magnitude, we don't always have the same choices we had before."

She raised her chin and said, "But I am Natalya Hershkle. I make my own destiny with my choices."

"So you have," the man murmured. "Your punishment is doled out lightly due to Keara Van Trump speaking on your behalf. You are to relinquish all holds on your minions and spend a banishment period on the Earth dimension to live life as a human. Humans are born to learn lessons, which is your own fate. You will learn and cause true love, a selfless love before you can return to Luciefyiore. Do you accept your punishment?"

"I do not."

The head of the council actually sighed. "It's for the best, Natalya. Fighting it is a waste of time and effort."

"Best for whom?"

"Best for the dimension. You are regrettably dehorned, your powers reversed. You have the option of earning your powers back if you can learn the lessons needed. Go to Earth, cause unselfish true love. It is a simple enough banishment."

There was silence at the standoff. Natalya glanced shrewdly at the faces around the table. "I'll accept my banishment on one condition. My minions are to be cared for."

There was a pregnant pause, following by the clicking of someone's fingernail tapping thoughtfully on the table.

"Minions are usually killed or die off when separated from their head demon."

"Yes, they are. They have no protection. But I will willingly accept all punishment should my small request be granted."

There was one small movement of the councilmember's head. A slight acknowledgement. "They will be allowed to return to their previous jobs and relationships."

"No. They will be allowed to return to whatever they wish. They've earned the right. They're set free. That's my only condition."

The council as a whole sat completely still. "You will accept all punishment we dole?"

"As long as my condition is met."

"Done."

Lightning struck across the sky that had darkened within the last few minutes. Storm clouds rolled, threatening to release fat droplets of fresh rain.

One wave of his hand and her dress was replaced with a flowing skirt and loose top. The outfit Jere'd first seen her in at the train station.

"Keara has agreed to rule in your banishment. You will seek her on Earth and remain there until we summon you."

"Agreed."

The white-robed councilman looked off to her side. Stared straight at him, as if he knew he was there. "You have a lot to learn."

An eerie feeling hit the pit of Jere's stomach, remaining with him long after he woke.

But the blonde princess lay in his arms, now sleeping peacefully.

Chapter Five
Entanglements

ৰ্জ

"Come on, Jere," she coaxed, eyes crinkling at the corners. "I'll be returning soon. I'd like to get married once, in the strange Earth custom." She grinned. "We both know I'll never be able to wear white back at home."

Las Vegas was an experience worth attending with this blue-eyed vixen. She'd squealed in delight when the plane hit turbulence, causing several passengers to reach for the barf bags.

Now she'd noticed a wedding in a tiny mock chapel. Performed by Elvis, of all people. To her, marriage was just a ritual. She didn't seem to realize they'd legally become husband and wife.

"Getting married by Elvis is really tacky," he said.

"I think it's fascinating." She leaned in, her eyes aglow with happiness. "To be married by a well-known rock star long dead, reincarnated over and over. He's famous! Wearing white instead of black. All three of us. It's so ridiculous to wear such an atrocious color! And I just love that jumpsuit he wears, with the big collar."

Jere wasn't sure he wanted to share with her that it wasn't really Elvis. She was so excited. Could she really believe he kept showing up in Elvis bodies all over Las Vegas? And did they really dress in black at demon weddings?

"Black is for funerals," he muttered.

"Perhaps why the tradition was started for weddings," she returned impishly before she turned on her heel.

He literally pulled her back from marching into the front doors of the building. "We'd be tied together, princess. Bound to each other and no one else."

"Well, I haven't been with anyone else here on Earth since you. You got any other prospects?"

"Um, no." That wasn't the point, dammit, but her reasoning was exhausting to argue with.

"Then I see no cause why you should not be my Earth husband. My other choice is that old geezer drinking from the paper sack over there. He's been watching me awhile and if he's willing…"

What harm could it do? So they got married, she returned to the Hell dimension, he either became free or was incarcerated, they'd be no different.

Except he could watch the excitement rise in her eyes during the ceremony. See the flush that covered her ivory complexion when the sweep of flaxen hair swished from her face.

The same flush that matched her nipples in the heat of arousal.

She stepped toward him and pulled him to her with her fingers in his front belt loops. She lifted her lips toward him.

"Please? Marry me."

How could any guy refuse? He gave his answer by bending down to touch her lips with his.

And knew everything would be fine when her small fingers entwined with his.

She was like a small child during their ceremony. She ran up to Elvis, eyes large in her face. "We wish to get married," she announced.

"Well now, little lady. It just so happens I got a free slot open." He rolled his hips for effect.

Jere fought the urge to roll his eyes.

Natalya mimicked the hip movement. Although stiff, Jere had to admit it looked a lot better on her than on the unnaturally dyed, black-haired man standing before them.

"Mercy," Elvis said.

"Mercy," she repeated faithfully.

"Will you marry us or not?" Jere grumbled.

"Well now, son, you need a witness. See if there's anyone available outside."

Natalya rushed off to the chapel doors again, dragging the drunk from outside. Her other suitor, who busily complained in a nasal falsetto.

"Hush," she snapped at him. "I'll buy you a new bottle when it's done. But I want you to sniffle and cry a lot."

"That's gonna be easy, considering someone's gonna grab my brand new bottle you left out there."

"There was barely anything in it!" she snapped.

"So? I just bought it. It's still brand new. Empty or full, don't matter."

"You are very obnoxious," she told him. "And I may know of the perfect mate for you. As soon as we get her bladder condition taken care of. Course, you stink too. You may not mind each other."

Jere winced.

"Dearly beloved," Elvis intoned, shaking his leg.

Natalya concentrated on everything Elvis said. As if she memorized the lines, word for word. His movements, everything.

But then she gave Jere her full attention, gazing at him with her beautiful blue eyes, and said, "I do."

He felt a pull somewhere in the vicinity of his chest.

When Elvis performed his rendition of *Love Me Tender*, she swayed in time to the music, closing her eyes for better feeling. Even the drunk swayed and when he began to sing also, Jere knew it was time to leave.

They walked out of the chapel with arms around each other. "Now what?" she said excitedly.

"Kind of hard to top that," he said dryly.

"Ahh but you'll be topping me later, won't you, husband?" she winked.

"Naughty girl."

"I like this husband and wife thing. I like *you* as my husband," she said.

He was too surprised to tell her he liked it too.

"I know what comes next, my bride," he said as he pulled her to him.

She inhaled deeply and he watched her eyes darken with the beginning of arousal. "What?' she asked coquettishly.

"We come together as man and wife."

"You mean—

"Yes."

She was actually quiet. Reserved. This different anticipation was intriguing, to say the least.

They took their time getting back to the room. But before the door was even shut, arms and legs tangled as various clothing was flung from each other. Between kisses and caresses, they managed not to pop buttons or rip material. Barely.

When they were naked, he picked her up and tossed her onto the soft mattress, where he pounced between the thighs she spread eagerly.

"I've been wanting to eat this pussy," he muttered, spreading her lips with his thumbs.

"And I've been wanting you to," she whispered, raising her hips. He looked his fill before dipping his head to lick into the tender pink flesh that opened before him like a wild orchid.

She squirmed.

He used his tongue to find every fold and when she was glistening wet he pointed it and delved inside her entrance.

She arched like a cat. "More," she demanded, making him smile against her intimate parts.

He sucked her swollen clit into his mouth and released it with a pop. She wriggled against the mattress, not sure if she wanted to be up or down.

Somehow her feet had found their way onto his shoulders and her knees dropped wide open. He cupped her sweet ass into his hands and brought her up to his mouth, where she then swung her legs over his shoulders.

"I love that your pussy is bald," he said. He tongued her bare perineum from her clit down but concentrated lower. Gently he sucked her entire swollen labia into his mouth and inserted a finger gently into his lover's sheath.

"Oh," she moaned. "Slow down, Jere. I'll come right in your mouth."

He plunged his finger in and out, stretching the taut rim of her anus.

"Next time you'll take my cock here," he warned.

She convulsed, bearing down on his finger as her orgasm hit in full force.

"Oh, oh, oh," she gasped and her vagina quivered in his mouth. She bucked her hips helplessly.

He moved away to stare at the open treasure before him. Her pussy was wet and glistening, swollen and flushed.

It would grip his cock nicely, a warm velvet glove wrapped around him fully.

"Turn over," he muttered.

She did as he asked and he plunged into her slick sheath. She was so hot internally, she set his dick on fire.

Quickly he plunged in and saw her hand disappear to massage her clitoris.

She was going to give herself a second orgasm immediately following the first.

He nudged her legs wider apart so she was splayed to his view. Her puckered little ass was so much temptation. He gently circled it with the same finger that had plundered it earlier and then delved into the tight little button.

She clenched hard and fingered herself at record speed, pushing back against his hand.

"Deeper," she moaned and he let his finger slide in. All the way.

"Tell me you want me to fuck this sweet ass," he said.

Before she could agree, his world exploded.

He was barely aware of her screaming out her release but was afraid the entire hotel heard. Their breathing was harsh in the silent room and surprisingly the hallway just beyond the door sounded silent also. Unlike earlier when a gaggle of voices could be heard.

She turned onto her back and laughed. "Think they're all listening?"

"I think you stunned them into silence," he said, a grin on his face. He had a sweet breast under his cheek, the scent of satisfied female against his nostril. Life was good.

"I'm wide awake," she announced.

He bit back a groan. "Princess, we flew hundreds of miles. Walked endlessly. Got married. Had incredible sex. I'm exhausted."

She bit back a disgusted, "Humans." Instead, she caressed the back of his head where it lay on her breast. His calm, even breathing told her when he was out.

But she was still wide awake. It was the excitement of the city. Jere slept soundly, she could slide out from beneath him and wander the casinos, looking to accomplish love.

Earth wasn't so bad. Maybe she could get herself banished here permanently. *After* she caused true love and got her horns back, of course.

Carefully she wriggled out from beneath him. He curled against the spot she left on the pillow and she tenderly smoothed out his brow before she kissed it.

She stood in a corner, watching the humans intermix. She was back to the chore of trying to match the unluckies with the uglies.

She'd spotted a man earlier who was missing his front teeth. There was a cross-eyed woman directly ahead of her who might be interested. At least one of her eyes was focused on him. However, how would she get them together?

She tapped her finger on the wall as she thought out a plan.

"Drink, miss?" a waiter asked as he approached her.

"Sure."

"What would you like?"

Did it matter? Human alcohol didn't affect her metabolism one whit. "Whatever. Surprise me."

The waiter turned and then she noticed his odd dress. She called out, "Wait."

He turned back to her.

"What is this Hollowthing?"

The man stared at her incredulously. "You mean Halloween, lady?"

"Yes."

"I guess you're not from around here?"

"No."

"We dress up to celebrate. Lots of costume parties around here tonight. Huge prizes for the most elaborate, the most creative, you get the picture."

"What are you?"

Again, he looked at her as if she had her horns. "Bill. Want to be my Monica?"

"What would that entail?"

He grinned slowly, wriggling a thick brown phallus between his lips. "I have this cigar, see…"

No one noticed when the waiter walked away rather stiffly and missing the *cigar* just a few minutes later.

Jere awoke with a start. She was gone. A dangerous demon on the loose. Oh, not a danger to others of course but to herself. He sprang from the bed and threaded his fingers through his dark hair, mussing it to a carefree look

He had to find her.

He practically ran down to the elevator and tapped his foot impatiently as he waited for it to whisk him to the smoke-filled casino. When the doors at last sprang open, he looked quickly around to see what trouble she could have caused.

A toothless man grinned at a cross-eyed woman who sat in his lap, fingers inching up her leg. She looked familiar. Then it dawned on him. The airport. She'd traveled alone on the plane here. He watched in disgust. Easy targets, if only Talya had noticed them. Obviously there was someone for everyone. His new bride could have brought those two together for a quick and easy love. Instead they found each other on their own. She lost out on an effortless ticket back home.

Where she'd be safe. For what would she do on her own when he was found and carted off to prison?

"Hurry, we have to get to the roof," the woman giggled as his fingers tickled. "That blonde is doing a 'dance naked under the moon' skit."

No way.

It had to be a different blonde. Still, his heart raced as much as his feet pounded as he ran back the elevators and punched the button for the roof.

The roof was quiet with just the breathing of ooh's and aah's muttered every now and then.

"Natalya Hershkle!" His voice sounded harsh and overly loud.

"Rousseau. We are married," she reminded, her voice carrying in the quiet.

He saw red.

His wife created a spectacle on the roof of the hotel. Under the full moon, she danced naked. Not a stitch on...except for a child's demon horn barrettes.

"What the—"

"Shhh," the man next to him said, without removing his eyes from Jere's wife. "Don't make a sound. We don't want to stop the show."

"This isn't a show," Jere growled.

He wanted to throw her over his shoulder and carry her away. Wait, he couldn't. That would expose her entire backside to the voyeuristic world.

He wanted to turn her over his knee and give her the spanking she deserved. Hell, that would probably turn on the perverts who had their eyes glued to her exquisite curves.

There was a whole lot he wanted to do but in the end he chose to just walk over to her.

"Hi, sweetheart," she said brightly. "Want to get naked and dance?"

"No," he said through gritted teeth. "Why would I want to get naked?"

"It's Halloween. It's an Earth tradition," she informed him.

"No, it's not."

"Well, almost Halloween. And I know it's supposed to be witches," she continued as if she didn't hear him. "But witches worship demons and I'm a demon." She twirled leisurely, on her toes. "So I dance."

"You'll walk slowly out of here with me before you attract cops," he snapped.

Alarm filled her eyes as she remembered he was a wanted man. For once his naughty little demon did as he directed and followed him. He grabbed her hand as he led her from the roof, blocking her view as much as he could from the gawking stares.

"Boo!" sounded a voice from one of the crowd.

"Hush," said a female voice. "We might miss the next part of the show. I love Vegas, all the free shows they don't tell you about. I wonder what act comes next?"

"Are we coming up to the roof tomorrow?" asked another voice as they disappeared through the doors

"Where's your clothes?" he hissed as he stripped out of his t-shirt and pulled it quickly over her head.

She had the nerve to look at him like he was ignorant. "Where we had sex. Didn't you see them? We flung them off from one end of the room to the other."

His patience at an end, he grabbed her hand again and hauled her as quickly as he could back to the elevator.

Of course, this was Vegas. There was a crowd of older people in the elevator when the doors opened. The old women fanned themselves as they tutted over the shapely expanse of Talya's lean, bronzed legs poking through the bottom of his shirt.

The old men fanned themselves when they noticed the stiff nipples poking through the cotton fabric.

Jere growled, his eyes felt like they'd pop out of his head. Finally, they reached their floor and he pushed her out first, blocking the view of her shapely ass as he strode behind her.

"Did you see how those old women leered at your naked chest?" she whispered furiously.

He did the only thing he could. Groan.

He pulled her into the room and plopped into the tiny chair, holding her bare ass to his lap. He closed his eyes as he thought about how to burst her bubble without hurting her.

"What's wrong, Jere?"

He sighed. "Here's the thing about being my wife." Tenderly, his finger encircled a nipple through the thin cotton of the shirt. "The only one that sees you naked is me."

She genuinely looked surprised. "Oh. Well, that wasn't in the rule book, was it?"

"Marriage not such a good idea?"

"Not that," she amended hastily. "You did tell me I'd be bound to only you. I just didn't understand all the ramifications. I wander around naked quite a lot. I am beautiful."

"Yes, you are," he agreed solemnly. "So beautiful I get jealous easily when others look at you."

"You do?"

"Uh-huh."

"Oh. Wait. Does this jealousy feel like anger? Crabbiness? Pre-menstrual syndrome?"

"You got it," he muttered.

"Is that how I felt when the old mummified females in the elevator stared at your chest?"

A small bubble of joy threatened to grow and explode in his heart. "Yeah. That's it."

"Oh. That didn't feel good at all."

"Exactly."

She curled her head into the crook of his neck, silently lost in her thoughts. His finger still swirled gently over her nipple.

It was some time before she spoke again. "Jere."

"Mmm?"

"Will you help me find humans? To make them fall in love?"

"I saw a couple earlier. I knew she flew here alone, she was on the plane with us."

Natalya sat up excitedly. "Was she googly-eyed? Like a bug? Her name was Cathy. I remember her telling the airline attendant when she threw up into the bag."

"Yeah. Bug-eyed. She found a balding toothless guy. I saw him with his hand on her thigh. There's someone for everyone."

"Exactly!" she said excitedly. "A lid for every pot."

"Except they did it on their own, princess. You missed out."

"Pooh. What are the chances? I noticed them too but I didn't think the slut would move in on him that quickly. Who else would want him?"

"Never underestimate humans, my dear."

"Apparently." She still sounded crabby. "Have you ever been married before me?"

There was quite a pause before his answer. "No."

"Really?"

"I came close," he admitted.

"You did?" Surprised, she lifted her head to look into his eyes. She couldn't imagine the thought, Jere bound with another woman instead of her.

"She left me. Remember? The fiancée I told you about."

"Why did she leave?"

"I'm headed to prison. When I was convicted, Kelly ran off." His voice was harsh. He still loved this silly human female who smashed his heart.

Idiot woman. How could she toss him aside?

"Hey," Jere said. "Is it getting hot in here?"

The air was thickening, making it harder to breathe.

"Not so soon," Natalya moaned, rising from his lap and making him follow. "They can't want me back already! It hasn't been that long."

Sure enough, a swirling vortex started on the floor before them, air hissing as the suction steadily grew, creating a dark spot in the carpet.

"Don't go," Jere said, pulling her tightly against him.

"I have to. I don't belong in this dimension. If I don't step in willingly when it wants me, it'll grow enough to suck me through. A much more painful way to go. Imagine human abortion, Jere. Sometimes a vortex grows strong enough to suck limbs from a struggling demon."

When the swirling vortex opened, she kissed Jere goodbye. And stepped through.

Chapter Six
Enrichments

&

But before the spinning clouds of thickened air stopped, Jere jumped in after her Air sucked from his lungs and consciousness was nearly yanked from him. When the pain stopped pulling at his limbs, he studied where he was. For the first time ever, he looked around at Luciefyiore.

It was so different from Earth. The horizon wasn't blue but a reddish orange. Up ahead, the sky darkened to the crimson of semi-dried blood.

And then the sulfurous smell hit his senses, an acrid odor that signaled a swampy marsh.

Trees grew close together, obscuring the slight glow from the sky. It screened the view, the slim limbs and vines twisting like overgrown fingers and mixing with shadows for a mysterious effect. Mud thickened the ground beneath his feet, causing each step to sink with his weight.

He must have landed in a different spot from where Natalya had, for she was nowhere to be found. The only place she could be headed for was deeper into the swamp. It seemed to beckon, as if the trees swayed to no breeze.

In the far-off distance he could hear distinct voices, if not conversations, so he followed his natural instincts and tracked them.

Natalya stood on a raised platform before a gold table where white-robed people sat. He remembered this committee of people from her dream before Las Vegas. Caleb and Keara stood on another circle platform near her. A hearing of some sort.

"Natalya Hershkle, Huntress of Luciefyiore, you are on trial for the near downfall of Luciefyiore. How do you plead?"

"I am not guilty. Impotence has been reversed in our dimension, making the 'downfall' non-existent at this point."

"Written arguments against you say it will be quite a while before males are mated, eggs are fertilized and children hatched. Making the near downfall a very real threat."

"The slower timing serves to make the demon seeds we do have more cherished. The way children should be. Now about returning my powers…"

"Not negotiable. You're on trial brought by the ex-ruler of Luciefyiore, Enishka. Not on your own trial regarding your punishment."

Slowly, Keara left Caleb's side. She moved to the platform with Natalya, showing a unique unity between the two women that not only enhanced their differences but pointed to their unusual similarities. She spoke with authority and her voice rang through the swamp. "We all know Enishka is bringing forth charges for his own benefit. It has nothing to do with the welfare of our dimension."

Jere stayed silent, hidden behind a tree. The golden table was quiet, the faces of the white-robed men and women unresponsive. Still, even with their lack of emotion, the council of gods were a blond, beautiful race of people. It was amazing how much Caleb resembled them, now that he was aware of Caleb's lineage. He had learned that much from Demitris.

"Enishka has the right to bring her to trial. We are not here to decide on the fate of her powers," the council reiterated.

Before Jere realized it, he left his hidden spot behind the tree. "How can you point the finger at her without talking directly to the accuser?"

Natalya looked up at the voice she knew so well. Jere. He was here. How had he gotten into Luciefyiore? He must have jumped into the vortex. Insane human, what was he thinking, insisting that Enishka be brought here? This wasn't some sort of macho fist fight, Enishka could turn a human's organs inside out with one look, even from his remote location.

And would if he knew she was the least bit attracted to him.

While there were laws to protect innocent humans, Jere gave up his rights by willingly stepping foot in their dimension. Once Keara had been attacked by Enishka but had been saved by Protection Fairies, for she was human and had been forced into the dimension.

Jere hadn't been forced in.

Although helpless humans had no idea, they were assigned the protection by the ancient Greek council. Jere had unknowingly given up that right.

With one signal of his hand, the head of the council had swamp demons surround Jere. He was bound with his hands behind his back before he was brought forward.

"Enishka is kept banished for a reason, Jere Rousseau." The head of the council's voice rang out. No one bothered to ask how the man knew his name.

"Then how can he be allowed to bring charges against her?"

"His charges are valid."

"How do we know that? We have no choice but to take your word for it."

A silence hushed over the swamp. No one ever questioned them. The head of the council gave one look to a smallish demon with faint skin imprints, like tattoos in diamond shapes. He was a meek and mild creature, only four feet tall. The timid little snake demon's eyes rounded before he closed them and began to chant. It was impossible to make out the hissing sounds he made but they grew louder and more intense. Eventually he raised his arms and one of the three moons—the center one now known as the one that kept Enishka prisoner—slowly began to gravitate across the sky.

The shadows on the surface created by the hills and craters began to swirl, dancing through the smoke as though it were a giant theatrical screen.

Suddenly, the harsh demon face of Enishka appeared, his anger a tangible force that reached through the dimensions. Sweat poured from his brow and his face was red with heat, horns fully extended.

"How dare you?" he screamed. "I am not an underling to be beckoned whenever you wish!"

The white-robed councilmember raised one hand. "Hush."

"I will not!" the demon lord screeched in his grating voice. His small, close-set eyes scanned the perimeter of what used to be his swamp, focusing on Keara and Natalya standing side by side.

Natalya, helpless without her horns.

His eyes glowed red, twin laser beams of light aimed directly at them.

Natalya went down like a flash.

Pain ripped instantly through her midsection, white hot licks of torture, tearing through her organs and knocking the air from her lungs. She screamed long and hard and everyone stared in disbelief at the sight of The Huntress down for the count.

The agony! She twisted on the ground, her insides searing and binding, vaguely aware of another commotion. Jere, at the side of the council's table, raising all kinds of hell while being held back by several robed members. Of Keara, trying desperately to stoop but her hugely swollen belly a hindrance. Of Caleb, pulling Keara out of harm's way of Natalya's wildly spasming arms and legs to avoid accidentally being hit.

And then the pain cooled, as magically as if ice-water washed in and throughout her body. It was wiped away in a frozen swish and the frenzied shouts and noises in the swamp went still as everyone present watched. The lasers of Enishka's red glow were countered by Keara's own blue. Steadily her force pushed against his until her glow pressed right in his face.

His movements jerked, panicked, as if he knew that should he stop her blue light would blast into his eyes. And yet he couldn't keep from directing her away. Her strength far outreached his in her anger.

He tried to raise his palms helplessly in surrender but Keara was too far gone. Rage strode over her features and her eyes glowed electric blue. Then she reached out and took Natalya's hand, clasping their fingers together.

A bright purplish blue slammed into the demon lord's face, shining too brightly for anyone to watch without permanent scarring to their own vision, then exploding like smoke while he screamed piteously.

Ironically, the white-robed councilmember sighed dramatically. "I thought I said to hush." He raised a hand and swept it through the air. The scream was silenced instantaneously. The swamp was deadly quiet as everyone waited for the smoke on the moon to clear enough to see what Keara's unknown power had done.

Enishka's head was down, chin to chest. When he raised his frozen face, the sight was horrific.

His eyes were no longer centered in his face. Raw, reddened skin melted over where the sockets should have been. Now his eyes were on the sides of his face, near his temples, effectively preventing him from focusing his red laser gaze on anyone again.

His breath came in harsh pants and his mouth moved as though speaking until he realized there was no voice emitting from his throat. He closed his lips and felt the smooth section of face where his eyes had been. Eventually his fingers trailed to the sides of his head where he felt his tightly closed eyelids. Removing his hands, he opened his eyes. Slowly he took a step and turned to the right so his left eye focused dead ahead.

He stared at the swamp and everyone looked back at him, some demons in shock, some with horror. The faces of the council were as neutral as always.

The two bitches from hell were cold and unfeeling. One dark and one light but both evil and rotted inside. The way women could be.

One of the councilmembers released the stupid human male who reached Natalya's side, cradling her in his arms and rocking her gently. Idiot man, besotted with her. She'd probably rendered him impotent with anyone else so he'd worship her fully.

The head of the council who had struck him speechless spoke first. "What did you do to Natalya?"

At last. Retaliation.

Despite his pain, Enishka felt a slow grin move across his face, knowing they could only see one side of his mouth curve. His voice was unhurried as he tested it from the release of the power the councilmember used on him. "Burned out her eggs. She'll never be able to breed now. She'll no longer be fit for the throne, no one will marry an infertile demon. It's a fit punishment for the one who caused a halt in the reproduction of our dimension."

"Fool," Natalya hissed. "I've already married."

The smile vanished from Enishka's face. "Who?" he demanded. "Surely not the human with you now? The marriage isn't valid in Luciefyiore, no more than mine and Keara's was when she returned to Hell on Earth."

"On the contrary," the head of the council spoke. "That is why we summoned you. You have some explaining to do."

"I don't have to answer to anyone."

"Oh but you will." Another wave of his hand and Enishka's left eye stared unwaveringly while he was forced to speak.

"Tell me about how you hunted for a human infant to purchase."

Enishka clammed up. It was so long ago, before laws were enacted by the meddling Greek council. But the words were dragged from him. He spoke clearly and succinctly, each word pulled against his will. "I hunted decades to find two human souls that were pure."

"How?"

"Complete purity comes from suffering. I made sure of the suffering of Elizabeth's ancestors. Her grandparents were highly intelligent, very advanced for their time. It took a lot of manipulation but I talked them into treating their daughter Victoria indifferently so her own soul would mature faster and stronger. In the meantime, I found a human male in the same boat and brought the two together. They both needed love and saving and created a baby from that desperation. My Elizabeth."

"How did you obtain her?"

"The grandparents sold her to me. I slaughtered Roman, Victoria's love, while she was pregnant and unmarried. The grandparents had the right to do what they wished with the child. Victoria died from a broken heart during the birthing of Elizabeth."

"Why would her grandparents sell you the infant? What offer did you make?"

Enishka paused as he continued to fight against telling. The councilmember raised his hand slightly and the words poured freely from his mouth like a spew of vomit.

"I gave them royalty. Made them the king and queen of their country. And offered another child. A different child."

Not this part. Never this part. Fight the goddamn power that sucks the truth from my numbing brain.

"What do you mean?" rang the authoritative voice.

The bastard head of the council knew, he just wanted to force him to grovel with the tale. "They were highly intelligent and advanced for humans. They wanted to continue their now royal bloodlines with another species. I replaced their granddaughter with a demon seed."

There were gasps all about Luciefyiore. For once, the monotonous voice of the council was outraged, showing emotion that had never before occurred. "You allowed a demon to be raised on Earth? Do you even know where the child is at this point?"

Did they really believe he never thought it through? "I'm not stupid. I gave them a sickly child who wouldn't live to adulthood."

"You gave them a child who made it through his teens. Who made it until after he bred there."

Enishka felt sick. He knew he looked shocked with his lips hanging open and tongue protruding. Could it be possible?

"You gave them one from Demitris' line."

Enishka didn't answer, for he didn't need to.

"That is why Demitris turned on you. A member was missing from his family line and he knew you had something to do with it. He knew of your plans to spawn with Elizabeth and destroyed them. Enishka, meet Jere Rousseau. Mixed-breed descendant of that infant egg you traded to Elizabeth's grandparents. Keara's blood cousin. Now Natalya's husband. It appears we have found additional rulers of Luciefyiore that rank higher than you."

Heads in the swamp swiveled to the man, to whom they'd all thought was just a human cradling The Huntress. Now that it was pointed out, he did have an amber glow to his eyes. As they watched, his horns slowly protruded in sync with theirs. A common occurrence during stressful situations.

Natalya stared at her human husband with a white face, the blood drained. She stared until the shock became too much for her. Her eyes rolled back into her head as she fainted dead away. Could it be the bitch had no idea?

The councilmember continued on. "You have broken the highest law set upon Luciefyiore. To allow a demon to reside in the Earth realm without knowing of his heritage. If it hadn't been for Demitris finding him, all hell could have broken out in both dimensions from the imbalance of his hormonal rages. While you are already banished from Luciefyiore, I strip from you the title demon lord. You have no further rights to protect the dimension and cannot call charges against future rulers. Keara ruled as your queen and appointed Natalya ruler. Now her husband Jere shall reign as the highest-ranking blood relative."

"Noooo!" Enishka screamed. All the plotting and planning he'd gone through was for naught? The bitches still got their way? Keara would stay on her precious Earth and allow Natalya to rule with her new husband, who conveniently enough was one of them? And a blood relation, which bypassed any power he had left with his damned banishment to a moon dimension?

He was the demon lord. The rightful blood ruler.

"It's not fucking fair!" He screamed again as the moon that held him prisoner moved away.

* * * * *

Natalya Hershkle awoke in her own bed. Slowly she remembered the horrendous scene yesterday.

She wasn't alone. A demon was with her, though without her horns she shouldn't have been able to sense her.

Keara moved into her line of vision. "Feeling okay?" Her voice was neutral, as if she knew any softness would be interpreted as pity.

"Why shouldn't I be?"

Keara shrugged. "You won't be able to breed."

"I'm not the maternal type. Especially to little mixed-breeds. That's your specialty, not mine."

Keara sighed. "Now it comes out. How do you feel about being married to a mixed-breed?"

Talya clenched her fists into the sheets. "I should have been told. He knew, dammit. He tricked me."

"Yes, he knew. But telling you wasn't a choice he had. We can't help the way we were born, Talya."

"So my marriage is legal in both dimensions now, isn't it? In his and in mine. I'm tied to him."

Keara nodded.

"Please leave. I just need to be alone. To think. For a long time."

"Caleb and I are heading back to the material dimension. We'll take Jere with us. Give you some time."

Talya turned her back to her queen. "Please do."

"Just remember one thing, Talya," Keara said softly. "Jere's appointed to the throne. He's the ruler of Luciefyiore, not you. You're still banished to Earth."

The door clicked shut behind her with a finality that rang in Natalya's ears.

There was arguing in the hallway and before she knew it, her husband burst through the door. "I'm not going back without talking to you."

"I don't feel like talking, Jere."

"You're my wife. I'm not leaving you here alone."

"You tricked me, dammit. You should have told me you were a mixed-breed."

"Why would that matter?"

"Our marriage is valid everywhere. Here, there, everywhere."

"It was valid before. You're my wife, Talya."

"It was valid in *your* dimension," she said coldly.

Dead silence met her statement.

"Why was it okay in my dimension but in yours it angers you?"

"That's exactly why. It's *my* dimension. I ruled it. I was going to figure a way to rule again. I need some time to think. Please leave with Keara and Caleb. They'll take you back to Earth."

"Will you come back to me?" Jere asked.

Natalya closed her eyes to the hurt in his voice. "I don't know."

"I thought there was something you felt for me, Talya. Maybe not love, not like I love you, but something was growing. You married me. It was your idea."

He loved her? Her? She hardened her heart. He was a mistake. With both his parentage and with her.

"I married you just to say I did. Just to have the experience. I'll never again be on Earth. I have no love for anyone, much less a mixed-breed."

She barely was aware of his sucked-in breath. While she lied, what choice did she have? She may have had previous experience ruling but no demon powers left.

She was worthless.

Yes, he could protect her but she didn't even have anything to offer in return. No strengths. She couldn't even protect herself. In addition, her eggs had been burnt out.

Yep, she was pretty worthless. He couldn't be allowed to exist on false hope.

She gritted her teeth and struck to hurt. "If I'm with you, it'll simply be to rule Luciefyiore again."

"In that case, I'll have to turn you down, wife. You may be experienced at ruling but I am the rightful heir."

Rage filled Natalya's soul. She wanted to spit, to scratch. To render him impotent. But she had nothing left, no powers. She was helpless as a baby. As a human.

"Get out," she snapped. "I could never love you. You're disgusting, a creature caught between two worlds. The worst characteristics of both."

Jere clenched his jaw, as though he might say something he'd regret. Before he could react further, he spun on his heel and left.

Keara returned.

"What have you done?" she asked.

"Here to defend your blood relation?"

"Have you learned any lessons at all, Talya? I've been patient with you but I'm tired. And you're screwing up everything."

"Lessons? Of course I've learned lessons. But I need time to correct my mistakes and *that* just keeps getting yanked from me."

"You can't do things on your own. You need help."

"I don't need anyone."

"You're the same little girl who swore that all through grade school. Do you really believe it?"

"Where is this going, Jenesi?"

Obviously Natalya was upset, for it wasn't often that she forgot Keara's name change. "Oh wait. I know. It's about everyone trying to get me to accept a mixed-breed husband."

"You accepted him on your own terms, Talya. I didn't ask you to marry my cousin."

"I accepted him under false pretenses."

"Why? Why does it matter?"

"Do you really want to know, dammit? You. You are the only half-breed I ever knew and you scared me shitless. You burned down our school with your rage. Innocents lost their lives."

"What's done is done. I can't undo it but I paid my debt. I was banished to hell."

"We all thought Earth was hell but it isn't really so bad, is it?"

"Depends on who you ask. I think Jere has a different opinion. Do you know anything about his childhood? Your own husband? Are you aware of his mother's desertion because her own child 'scared' her? The old inherited family power, firestarting. I knew about my ability, although I hid it from Enishka. But Jere never knew he was half demon until my father found him recently and explained a lot. Do you know he's been abandoned by every single person he's known?"

Natalya didn't want to appear selfish or callous by not knowing intimate details about her own husband. "I know his fiancée left him when he was convicted."

"After aborting a child they created. She couldn't raise a baby whose father was a prison embarrassment. Never mind she knew he was innocent. She left with the man responsible for sending him to prison."

"Fine. Your cousin had a tough life. You had a tough childhood—"

"But you had an awful time growing up too, didn't you? I didn't understand at the time we were children but your father was third in command. Directly under mine. The half-breed's father. Where does your prejudice stem from? The fact that your father was infatuated with my human mother also? But he was a married man, whereas my father was not?"

A switch deep inside Natalya shut down. This was something no one ever knew before now. "I don't know what you're talking about."

"Yes, you do. I was different from the other demon children. Never tested. I have powers no one ever knew about.

And while my immature mind couldn't comprehend what those thoughts and emotions your parents emitted meant, my adult mind does. Now I understand why your mother allowed and encouraged you to take your anger out on me. In her head, she felt it was revenge against my mother. But my mother never wanted your father's attentions. She was as innocent as yours. As you. As me. We were all just victims of circumstance."

"Quite the philosopher, you've become," Natalya sneered.

"Enough to know how badly you strike when you hurt."

It was getting to be too much. "Go to hell, Keara."

"Been there and back, baby. But you're living through yours and not doing so well at it. So I'm gonna help you."

"I didn't ask for your help."

"You get help before you continue to hurt everyone around you. Before you screw up both worlds, instead of just one."

"Then wipe me out, dammit. I know you can. I'm useless, I can't rule Luciefyiore and I can't get myself out of the damned Earth dimension. Just strike me dead."

Natalya rose from the bed but a sick wave of dizziness swam over her head. She dropped to the ground, spent.

There was a long bout of silence while Keara studied her. An uncanny silence. "That would be too easy, to give up, wouldn't it? I never thought The Huntress would take the easy road."

"Do it, damn you. I know you still have powers inside you that Enishka didn't get. We all saw you rearrange his face."

"I'll show you some power, little sister. But be careful what you wish for."

Chapter Seven
Hints from the Future

⚘

Keara wasn't joking.

The air thickened and began to choke Natalya. More than once while she struggled to breathe, she wondered if Keara was killing her, if at last she faced death. She was barely aware of Keara's disappearance but as the smoky fog cleared she found she was alone, zapped outdoors.

A different outdoors. It was nighttime here. She was on her hands and knees and the ground was sandy beneath her palms.

Damn Keara. What had she done to her? The fog lifted enough for her to see she was in a playground. One lone little boy sat on the merry-go-round.

In the distance, sirens wailed. Natalya rose and made her way toward the boy. He ignored her, so she sat on the still toy beside him.

"What are you doing?"

"Nuthin. I didn't do it." The child's lower lip overlapped his upper, a tiny little pout that tugged strangely at her heart. His light brown hair was tousled, tossed with gold. Surely it would darken as he aged. His amber eyes reminded her of Jere. Of maybe what their child might have looked like.

"What didn't you do, little one?"

"I didn't mean to make the fire."

Fire?

The old fear surfaced, one from ages ago. Keara had set their all-girl school on fire. She'd been teased and tortured all through her childhood and one day she just lost it.

Natalya didn't really know it was her at the time. But through her jealousy, she had pointed the finger at Jenesi, as Keara was called back then, and had her banished to Earth. But the horrors of that fire remained with her still. The screams, the terror, the...smells. Burnt hair, burnt skin, melted plastic.

Still, she tried to make it past her own fears to soothe the sniffling child who tugged at her heart.

"I'm sure you didn't mean to make it. What were you doing? Playing with matches?"

He shook his head emphatically. And then held his eyes downcast.

Talya reached out and placed a hand on his shoulder. The child unexpectedly tossed himself against her, sobbing into her as he clung tightly.

"Shhh," she crooned, smoothing his hair. "It's okay, little guy. Talk to me. Tell me what's wrong."

"I-I wasn't playing with matches, or n-n-nuthin'," he sobbed. "I was just mad and I didn't mean to."

Alarm began to grow in Natalya's midsection. The exact same dread from all those years ago. She had pretended to hate Jenesi back then but the plain truth of the matter was, Jenesi terrified her. It was easier to admit now that she'd voiced it to Keara during their argument but she had never been around a human, they were evil creatures from another dimension. Why one was allowed to live in their realm and attend their school was beyond her. She may be the closest thing she had to a friend now but Keara was hideous as Jenesi when they were children. A bizarre oddity. A scary-looking human, the first she'd ever seen.

"There's something wrong with me," he cried. "I'm not like the other kids. I can't be like them."

"Why not?"

In his distress, his horns were beginning to protrude. She felt an answering call in hers and they slowly rose, inch by inch, in sync with his.

In hers? Her horns should be gone. Obviously she was dreaming.

Oh but it felt so good. She'd missed them dreadfully now that she no longer had them. Hers had been utterly beautiful, shimmery tusks of pearlescent silver that glistened through the platinum crown of her hair. Just as they were now.

This dream had allowed all those feelings to return. She wanted to reach up and run her fingers along the smooth ivory. But she had a child to tend to.

Who the child was and why they were both in this dream was beyond her.

"I don't see any difference between you and the other kids."

He stopped crying long enough to look up. "You don't? Whoa." His eyes grew large at the sight of her extended horns.

"Yes, dumbstruck, aren't you?" Talya smirked. "You aren't the first little man to have that reaction, trust me. I do believe they are the most beautiful in the world."

"I've never seen…"

"Yeah, yeah. I know, little guy. Now tell me about how you started the fire."

His bottom lip quivered again. "I just got hot. A lot. Inside my eyes. And this time it burned."

Those little fingers of fear tingled again. His tiny little face reminded her of Jenesi.

And then realization struck.

This child was Jere. Like his relation Keara, he caused fires.

She wasn't dreaming. *This* wasn't a dream. She was tossed back in time to the Earth dimension. Damn Keara. That original bitch from Hell.

"What, lady?" he asked, his little voice quivering. "Do I scare you too? My mommy left 'cause I scared her. I'm so sorry, I don't mean to be bad. When I grow up, I'm gonna have lots of kids. Good kids. I'll love them. Not kids like me."

Talya gathered the little boy up in her arms, cuddling his adorable innocence and inhaling the silky sweet softness of his hair. This tiny child thought he was pure human and had probably never noticed the extensions when his horns protruded, if they ever had before tonight. Surely it would be hard to control them without any other demon around to transmit pheromones. He hadn't been impressed with the beauty of her horns, he was impressed by the "magic trick".

She was ashamed of her vanity.

"You're pretty," he said shyly.

Talya couldn't resist a small dig. "You'll love me very much in twenty-five years or so. Ask me to marry you, over and over. Don't forget, okay?"

He nodded solemnly.

A niggling thought hit Natalya suddenly. She'd lost everything in her dimension, her leadership, her horns, her life. Her husband.

She'd tossed him aside heartlessly. Stupidly.

But she could do something for Jere. He wouldn't have to grow up a criminal this time, not if she could help him.

"Hey, little guy. Would you like me to visit you? A lot? We could be friends."

He nodded again. Then admitted shyly, "I don't have no friends."

Regret hit Talya. He was so like Keara, it was like reliving their own youth. A child stuck in the wrong dimension, picked on by others. Never belonging, caught between two worlds. Keara had been lucky with her banishment but Jere? He was punished by his own dimension by being labeled a criminal. By becoming a social outcast by time spent in juvenile detentions and jails.

Unless she intervened.

This time around, she could give Jere a better life. A wife who loved him. Maybe even rescue that aborted child. Just because her eggs were destroyed didn't mean Jere shouldn't have children.

"I'll be your friend, okay? And I'll tell you stories, lots of them about my world. My land."

"Are you a fairy princess?"

Talya tried not to grimace. How dreary. "Better. I was the exalted ruler of my entire dimension, Luciefyiore. Come on, say it with me. Lesson number one. Loosh-fee-yor-ee."

The child repeated it slowly and Talya gave him a pat on the head.

"By the way, little guy. Bet I can guess your name."

He giggled. "Nuh-uh. No one has the same name as me."

"Let's see. It rhymes with bear. Are you Jere?"

His eyes widened and his mouth opened. "Whoa."

"Yeah," she agreed. "Whoa, indeed."

"Are you magic, lady?"

"Yes, little guy. By the way, you can call me…Tally. Now, before I tell you a story, I want you to remember something. If policemen come and ask you about the fire, I want you to tell them you *were* playing with a lighter but you got scared and threw it away. You don't remember where."

"But that's lying. I wasn't."

"It's a white lie, Jere. A white lie is something that keeps something worse from happening. Like when a fat lady asks you if she smells and you say no so her feelings won't get hurt. It doesn't hurt you but it makes the fat lady feel better. See?"

The child nodded. "And I just hold my breaths."

"Uh, yeah. So remember, you were playing with a lighter and got scared of the fire, so you ran and threw it away, okay?"

"'Kay."

But Talya was exhausted. Her body began pulling away and she didn't have the strength or energy to fight it

"Tally?" he asked. "You're getting lighter. I can see through you."

"Uh-huh, sweetie. I have to go back to my world. But you remember what I told you."

"Will you come back to me?"

Such a loaded question. Much like the one the adult asked her earlier today. Of course, she couldn't tell the child they were married. "Yes, sweetie. Someday, I don't know when. I'll try hard to make it soon, okay?"

The last image she had was of the child's tear-stained cheeks as he bravely watched her fade away.

To Natalya Hershkle, the child faded to nothing, not her. She was still on the Earthling playground, though it was years and years later.

The equipment had changed. Trees had matured. The weather was warmer. And there was a spot in her heart that changed too.

Also warmer.

A tiny little portion that missed Jere already. The child, the grownup. Just…Jere.

* * * * *

After time skipped ahead on the playground, she made her way to Keara's house. That much didn't change, at least. She'd curled up in her bed, wondering what time or where she would be later. Closing her exhausted eyes, she let herself drift.

It wasn't as hard to wake up this time. She was getting used to this dimension. She lay in bed, wondering what the day would bring.

She woke up in Keara's house. On Earth.

Still missing her husband. That tiniest grain of knowledge hit her suddenly. Acceptance.

She accepted the fact that Jere was her husband instead of resenting that she was tied to him in both dimensions. Too bad she'd accepted it too late. He would never believe that she wasn't just after his throne at this point. It was her own fault.

Unless…maybe Keara and Caleb were here. They'd come back to Earth to keep Jere away from her while she recovered. Maybe since Keara zapped her here instead of leaving her in Luciefyiore, they were still present also.

She sprang from bed and caught herself when she swayed. Still weak. Dots swam before her eyes. As soon as she could walk without keeling over, she made her way to the bedroom door and flung it open.

"Hello?"

The big old house sounded empty. It felt empty.

"Anyone here?"

There was no response. She shuffled her feet slowly, searching every room in the house. There was no sign of anyone.

She made her way back to the master bedroom where she'd awoken. Into the bathroom where a portal had once opened in the mirror and sucked her through.

It felt like so long ago, when it wasn't. Not really.

She stared at her reflection in the mirror. She'd lost weight. Her eyes were too large for her face, as if they silently begged for a portal to open and swallow her. None came.

So how would she re-visit the child she'd promised to watch over?

She took her time showering as she tried to think up a solution to her dilemma. She blow dried her hair and dressed in Keara's clothing before it dawned on her.

She raced to the kitchen where a calendar sat on the fridge. She glanced at the digital kitchen clock that showed the date. Today was it. The day.

All Hallow's Eve.

This day she could access power from her own dimension. Surely Keara would have old texts of human witchcraft in this dimension. Witches worshipped demons and what was she?

Why, she was a demon, dammit. The best of the best. Full-blooded. And she wouldn't allow anyone, not the council, not Enishka, not Keara, no one would keep her from her task.

Fixing Jere's life.

Searching for hours but refusing to give up, she finally found the texts in the most unlikely place. Not the huge library of the house. Not the laptop computer that sat in the office. Not even the office itself.

She found them in Keara's nightstand.

Musty old smelly books, you could almost feel the dampness under your fingers as you thumbed through the pages. There was the information she needed. The midnight hour was the window between portals. She'd have to be up for hours still.

Just as well, it would give her enough time to study the spells and search for the supplies she'd need. She paused, quickly skimming through the listing of ingredients.

Geez. Where the hell would she find demon blood in this dimension?

Oh. Yeah.

The second hardest ingredient. An old woman's urine. Okay, fine. She could prick her own finger for the blood but urine? Eeww, the stench. And what constituted old? She herself was a woman but it definitely said *old* woman.

Briefly she considered Keara.

Scratch that, the pregnancy hormones would probably screw up the delicate spell. If she could even find a way to contact Keara. Natalya clicked her nails against the desk impatiently.

Had she ever had friends? Surely she had an old woman friend. Somewhere.

The answer came to her like a lightbulb switched on in her brain.

She *did* know of an old woman. The old shrew with the weak bladder at the train station.

She didn't have long left. She hurried as quickly as she could to the bench where she'd originally met the old biddy. Surprisingly, the old woman sat in the station just as before. Was she here again, or still? Did the crazy old bat live here, on a bench?

Natalya sat next to her. "I need urine."

"You yearn for what? Speak English, weirdo."

"Urine, old woman. U-R-I-N-E."

"Piss? You want me to pee in a cup? If you don't get outta here, I'm gonna scream for the cops."

Natalya rolled her eyes at the threat. With the way the shrew wheezed, there was no way she could suck in enough air for a belch, much less a scream.

"I don't have a lot of time, old mummy. Pish, or whatever the word was, in a cup for me and I'll grant you a small wish when I use the urine to conjure a spell at midnight."

"Spell, did you say? Witch, are you? That explains a lot."

Natalya raised her nose higher into the air. "Witch? No. I am a demon, not a squirrelly, naked dancer." Forget about that brief moment in Vegas. There was another spell for that—*What happens in Vegas, stays in Vegas.*

"But you can still access a spell, freako?"

"I can. For one cup of pish, I will do one small wish. What do you want?"

"We-ell," she droned, "I have been thinking about some male companionship ever since you came hassling me last. I could probably use a boy-toy or two. Like I said, I don't want no dirty old dough being stuffed into me like a floppy sausage, I want it firm and hard. *Young*."

Ugh. "That's disgusting. How young?"

The old one leaned over and whispered an age into Natalya's ear, blowing a garlicky stench through her soul. She fought the urge to vomit.

"For that, I may need *two* cups of urine, shrew. Want to take a shot at a larger number? Something legal, perhaps?"

The old biddy ended up going into the coffee shop for a cup. Natalya kept looking at Keara's watch on her wrist, a new one since her skirmish with the evil, now-curly-headed Earth child previously. It was getting close. Fifteen minutes to go and still no pish.

She finally arrived.

"It's about time," Natalya snapped.

"Hold onto your panties, tramp, I can't go yet."

"What? How do you know you can't go?"

"I don't feel the need."

"Apparently you go at unexpected times, 'cause you always reek."

"Do not."

"Do too."

"Well, anyways, I ain't got nothin' in me yet."

"Geez, I only have fifteen minutes to do the spell," Talya hissed. "Go drink something and bring me back a warm *full* cup, woman!"

"You're awful uppity, you know that?" the old shrew said. "Give me a dollar to buy a pop." She held her hand out, muttering something about a cheapskate as she walked back into the station.

She finally returned at ten minutes before midnight. With a full cup.

Natalya wanted to grab the cup but thinking about its contents, very slowly reached for it instead.

"It ain't a bomb," the old woman said.

"Oh hush. I need to concentrate and you're driving me nuts."

"Hmmph," the old bag muttered. "Uppity little slut."

Talya rolled her eyes as she centered her ingredients around her. The book open in her lap, she began to chant the strange words on the pages.

"It's a full moon. You're not gonna get weird and dance naked, are ya?"

"No," snapped an exasperated Talya. "Those are witches. I told you, I'm a demon."

She continued to chant until it was time for the blood. She took the sharpened claw of the rabbit's foot and pricked her finger. A drop welled to the surface.

"Hey, your blood is blue. That's nasty."

She tried to tune out the old biddy because, quite frankly, she was getting on her nerves.

"When do I get to make my wish? It's my pee, you know."

Concentrate. Ignore her. Pronounce each syllable directly and succinctly.

She began to feel lightheaded and then the words took on a life of their own, spewing from her lips faster and faster. She was vaguely aware she didn't even have to look at the book anymore.

"Do I wish yet? Do I say it out loud, or in my head?"

She ignored her. The chanting was automatic, vague, whispered words that had no meaning. Exactly like…time.

Things were morphing, images blurring right before her. Scenes all around, like watching a soap opera, bits and pieces being rewound and blended together in spots that shouldn't be.

There she was. Not long ago. Enjoying an oily massage from the last demon she'd added to her harem. At the time she justified she had a busy and stressful job. After all, she was the ruler of Luciefyiore. Adding a massage therapist to her list of minions was completely necessary.

And he had the most amazing *horns*.

More images swirled. But something caught her eye.

Focusing in on the view, she watched as Jere opened his door to a redheaded woman, his face growing hard at something she said.

Wait. This was important.

She focused on ignoring the old, urine-soaked woman who still whined in front of her and tried to be one with the illusion before her. It worked.

Instantly she was right there with them and she could hear the words they spoke.

"I'm so sorry, sweetheart. I just woke up and realized it's not gonna work."

"You don't just wake up one day with that thought in your head, Kelly."

"I did. You're a great man. For someone else. I think I just don't love you anymore. I mean, I love you. But I'm not *in* love with you."

What the hell did that mean?

And by the look on Jere's face, he was just as stumped. He was completely white, his hands clenched into fists as he fought for control.

"Now do I make my wish?" The voice broke in, yanking her concentration, pulling her to where Jere and Kelly became transparent images again.

Natalya opened her eyes to see old stinky about an inch from her face.

"Interrupt me again and I'll curse you with a string of unclean men. Syphilis, gonorrhea, herpes. You name it, you'll have it rotting within you."

"Hmmph!"

Closing her eyes, she watched the dots of lights swirl behind her eyelids. Sure enough, they began to morph into shapes. Faster this time, slide shows being forwarded.

Time forwarded to show him approaching her apartment later, raising his hand to knock and then stopping. He reached for a key in his pocket and used it to unlock the door.

Talya jumped in right along with him.

The living room showed dim lighting. Slight indentations on the sofa. Two glasses of wine on the coffee table.

Jere cut his eyes to a back hallway where the bedroom must have been. Talya's stomach felt sick, wondering if there was some way to avoid what was imminent. He walked steadily down the small hall, to a bedroom door where definite noises were coming from. He reached for the door handle.

Talya reached out to put her hand on top of his. To stop him. He didn't want to do this. She didn't want him to go through this.

Jere paused. His face looked uncertain.

And then Natalya realized it already happened. So instead of stopping him from turning that handle, she kept her hand on his and gave him strength. Helped him turn the knob, push open the door.

Kelly rode.

Long red waves of hair flowed down a shapely, feminine back. His hair-ridden legs stuck out from underneath her.

Shocked at the noise, she turned and looked over her shoulder at the same time her lover looked up.

"Jere," they both said in unison, mutual expressions of shock on their faces.

The scene ended.

But in her time, everything solid around her had faded, the trees, the bench, the old woman. The ammonia stench that wafted from the old bat.

Replacing it was...

Chapter Eight
Learning to Love

ॐ

Jere as a young man. Now as solid as the world once was. Alone and filled with rage. He'd just caught his fiancée, who'd broken things off with him yesterday, in bed with another.

Such a cliché, you wouldn't think it would hurt. But reality bites, sometimes hard enough to draw blood

His voice was bitter and resentful as he stared at her. "You haven't visited me in a long time," he accused. "I thought I was a crazy kid. That I made you up. An imaginary friend who told me lying was okay."

"Visitation is not in my control. I had to find my own way back and I can't control when or where I pop in! Besides, I'm changing the future by visiting you. Originally you didn't meet me until you were an adult, now you remember meeting me when you were seven."

"So why are you changing things? What's happened in the future and how do I know you?"

"I can't share that with you, Jere. I don't know the rules. I don't know how this all works."

"Why are you here this time?"

"To repair some patterns that shouldn't be. Some things I can fix but nature has a way of correcting those changes. Originally your fiancée left you for another reason, I've fixed that and now she's left you anyway. I'm thinking you probably need to accept that it's meant to be. I know it hurts but unanswered prayers are best."

"What do you know?" he sneered. "You don't look like a preacher. Are you even married?"

"Actually, I am."

As soon as she said it, she wanted to take it back. What would she do if he asked her for her husband's name? She withheld too much information and he would get suspicious. She gave too much and it would arouse more future paths criss-crossing.

But how she longed to reach out and hold him. His heart was breaking with the loss of his fiancée. She wanted to embrace him to her breast, to assure him he would find love again someday.

With her.

She wanted to tell him that she hadn't appreciated his love but how she would beg anyone and anything for it now.

"So Kelly's left me in every situation, huh?"

Talya grinned. "Pretty much. And your last one was much worse. Trust me, you were a loser then."

It brought a smile to his lips, if not his eyes. Those remained damaged, hurt by tragedy.

Her smile vanished as she reached out and tentatively stroked his cheek. He looked lost. Much like the child she'd just left behind.

"I miss you so much," she admitted, the gut-wrenching words torn from her.

He looked surprised. Of course, he didn't know the relationship between them was more than what he knew of now, in this time and place.

Slowly she brought his head to hers and touched his lips with her mouth. It felt the same as it had earlier in her own time—a much-missed kiss with her husband.

Familiarity and a rush of heat.

He felt the spark too, he must have. He opened his mouth on his own, deftly met her tongue. Passion flared, grew with each breath, with each swirl of tongues.

The very air around her thickened, rushed at her as though she controlled it. But it was too much, she couldn't manage it, it wasn't the passion erupting through her soul, it was *her* being ripped from time.

Again.

No. She dug in her heels and refused to let go. It wasn't a portal, it couldn't rip her through. She wanted to be here with Jere, she missed him dreadfully.

Her fingers began to unbutton his shirt but they were clumsy and unpracticed. She ripped the two halves apart, buttons scattering everywhere.

It was so worth it. His chest was magnificent. Perfect. She bent to press her lips against it.

He cupped the back of her head, bringing her face back up to his for more kisses. She unsnapped his jeans, hearing the button as it popped free. She was getting better at it. But she couldn't tell him that he chuckled at her first attempt at it, could she? For technically, that hadn't yet happened.

Her kisses became frantic. She was afraid she'd get pulled away. He was sensing her need or dulling the pain of his fiancée, whichever worked. In either case, their tongues twined and she couldn't get close enough to him. He thumbed her hipbones, rubbing erotically through the sundress she wore.

"You always go around without panties?" he asked.

She smiled. "Only when I time travel."

If only he knew he'd seen her more often naked than clothed.

Their lips meshed again and somehow he twisted her skirt up around her waist without her even being aware of it. He cupped her mound with his hand and the heat poured from his palm.

It had been so long. Lightly his touch skimmed along her swollen labia, feeling the smooth skin.

Then his finger parted her nether lips, dipping inside to feel how wet she was. He began to thrust his fingers in and out, stretching her entrance. She was melting inside, she could feel the honey gather just from his kisses alone.

She moaned, a girlish gasp escaping when he reached deep inside.

It was a wordless coming together but yet he magically seemed to know which spots to hit.

He cupped his hands under her buttocks and lifted her body onto him. She wrapped her legs around his hips, dress still pulled up to her waist.

Mouth still locked to hers, he carried her into his bedroom and sat on the bed. She was splayed open to his view and he looked his fill when he leaned back and spread her labia open with his thumbs.

She was squirming against his touch. She popped a breast out of the top of her elastic shirred dress and pulled him down to her nipple. He sucked it eagerly, frantically even, as if they'd run out of time at any given moment. His fingers were continually playing with her swollen lips, spreading slick moisture over and around her clitoris.

She unwrapped her legs and slowly moved from his lap. She tugged a little on his jeans and his heavy cock burst out from the top. She moved in and licked leisurely, long and wide. She nearly swallowed his cock, she was so eager to have it in her mouth. He groaned when he hit the back of her throat, before she pulled up and sank down again. Over and over, while he gripped the sheets and thrust upward with his hips.

Weakly, he pushed her away with a hand to her shoulder. He stood, swinging long legs off the bed, and pushed her face down on the mattress. Her legs were still on the floor, so she leaned over the edge of the bed. He whipped her dress to the middle of her back and caressed the curves of her shapely ass.

Suddenly he spread her cheeks wide and plunged in. Wet slickness slid from her sheath and coated his silky hardness.

He pulled out, leaving just the swollen head of his cock imbedded between her thickened lips, then thrust deeply inside again. His cock was so warm, heated first from her mouth, then by the silky cream of her pussy.

Her nether lips were swallowing him as he plunged in and out. He could feel she was ready to come by the tightening of her sheath, gripping him mercilessly as he fought to pull out.

She moaned long and hard and then came, rippling internal muscles rolling along his stiff cock. She wriggled her ass against him and he couldn't hold out. His cock emptied itself, spurting cum deep inside her.

He collapsed onto her, both of their chests heaving. He curled her onto her side, pulling her into him with a strong muscled arm to her abdomen.

Now it started. The whistling of a breeze, the magnetic pull of invisible air. She wanted to fight it but knew it was wrong.

She didn't belong. She was in a time and place that wasn't real for her form. She needed just a little longer, a little comfort with the man she missed so dreadfully.

She turned to him, wanting to speak.

Wanting to tell him how much she loved him.

But she was pulled from the place where she most wanted to be, her own husband's arms. Double damn, the spell wasn't strong enough. It was the old woman's pee, had to be.

Dimly she was aware of his calling out to her, it was almost enough to make her dig in her heels again and fight to stay.

But the name he called out was Tally. Not Natalya. Not Talya as he had known her. Tally, the name she'd given him this time around when she met him. As a child of seven.

Regretfully, she allowed her soul to slip into the vortex of time and let it yank her away. Because this one couldn't be the right pathway.

It was morning now and she awoke on the park bench. No sign of the stinky old woman.

Now that she was back in the future, she had to find out information about Jere. Was he in prison? Was he ruling Luciefyiore? How would she find out?

That was when it dawned on her. The only person to contact was Demitris.

It was a short walk across the street to find a yellow car to take her there.

As she had less than a week earlier, Natalya knocked and then kneeled at the front door of Demitris' home.

"Master," she said when he opened the door.

"Natalya? Come in, my dear." He stood aside to allow her in, then motioned for her to sit. "What are you doing here on Earth?"

She looked at him blankly for a moment. "Oh, this reality is altered. You don't realize I've been banished here, do you?"

Concern etched across his face. "Altered realities? What have you been playing with, Natalya?"

"Time travel. I don't have a lot of time, I'll give you a quick run-down. I'm here now to find out how the half-breed Jere is."

"Jere Rousseau? The man we discovered was Keara's cousin? How do you know him?"

"It's a long story, one that you used to know before I time-traveled and changed the future. Originally I was banished to Earth and he was here, healthy and fine. We married but he was made ruler of Luciefyiore instead of me and Keara zapped me through time. I decided to fix his life so he wouldn't get dumped by his fiancée when he went to prison and I just got back. I need to know how he is, if she married him, or if he's happy just ruling our dimension."

Demitris was quiet. "You're married to Jere?"

"Yes but I don't know if it's really happened now or not, since I changed things. In any case, I want to find out how he is."

"Talya, he's not ruling Luciefyiore."

"What? Nuts, I screwed things up somehow. What happened? I just explained to him that Kelly kept leaving him and maybe he should leave it at that. That was probably selfish of me, wasn't it? I knew it but I was my usual bitchy self and ignored my own intuition." Okay and maybe she shouldn't have lost control and jumped his bones but hell, she was a naughty demon.

"Talya."

"Yes?"

"Jere's dead."

The world dropped out from beneath her. She gripped the table, afraid to fall. "Ex-excuse me?"

"He was sent to prison. Had a lot of fights and was stabbed. I'm sorry."

Her knees were weak, quivering like gelatin. Surely there was some mistake. Her heart pounding, she asked, "You're sure?"

"Very, my dear."

"Did he know? That he was a half-breed? That was why he started fires and stuff?"

"Yeah, we found him after he was convicted and told him. But it was too late at that point, he was a hard and violent man. Definitely fit for prison. I'm having a hard time imagining you were married."

"He wasn't hard and violent before. Oh, a little bitter maybe but never violent. What did I do? I messed things up worse."

She missed Jere. He couldn't be gone.

She missed her husband, the friends they'd become before the Luciefyiore mess. She wanted to turn to him now, to share her feelings with him. Tell him she didn't know what to do, how she could fix his past without influencing his future.

Didn't even know how she would go back.

She dropped her head onto the table but just as quickly popped up again. "You have to find a way to get me back."

"Me? How can I do it?"

Natalya narrowed her eyes. "Apparently, there's a small bit of time-traveling in your genes. Keara's the one that sent me back the first time."

Demitris knew it was fruitless to deny it. Still, he sighed. "There's huge consequences in time travel."

"Don't I know it? But this isn't right. It wasn't supposed to happen this way. His life isn't supposed to be cut short."

They were at a standstill.

"I can't intervene, my dear."

"Please, master. This is wrong."

She knew he was weakening by the softening around his eyes. "If I do it, I'll only do it once."

"I know. But please, please don't leave him dead because of me."

"Do you love him?"

Natalya thought about it. "Yes. I do."

That was what tipped Demitris' choice. Because finally, The Huntress knew love. And as far as he knew, no matter what time or dimension, she never had. This might be worth the shot. Still, it was dangerous.

"There's always a price, Natalya. You might not return. You might cease to exist. Are you willing to give your life?"

"I would give anything to make things right."

Slowly, he nodded. "Be careful what you wish for."

The last thing Natalya thought of was, those must be the magic words in both he and Keara that unlocked the traveling power within them.

A fresh day, a new place. That was the next thought that hit her mind. A bright summery place on Earth, she came to standing in front of a window, looking out over a courtyard where well-dressed guests were arriving.

Keara had obviously been irritated with her when she'd originally sent her to the past, for the choking smoke was torture. She didn't have that same problem with Demitris and was as surprised as Jere when she morphed into his chambers pain-free.

"You! What are you doing here? Today of all days," he said.

It should have been a happy day. He looked amazing in his wedding clothes. But the bride was all wrong.

The bride was another woman. Jealousy flared but she quickly swallowed it for the greater good. After all, she'd screwed up the last trip. "I guess I finally fixed it, somehow."

"That's what you've been doing by visiting me for years? Fixing my life?"

"Yes. The first time I met you, you had just escaped from prison. Kelly had left you when you were sentenced. I fixed it but she left you again. I fixed that and it looks like the third time's the charm. You'll get married this time. Um, it is Kelly you're marrying, right?"

"Yeah."

She tried not to allow the swoosh of air to escape too loudly. But the relief was great. So far so good.

He would never remember what transpired between them last time. She'd fixed that.

"You'll be happy," she continued. "You deserve happiness."

"Why?"

The question puzzled her. "Why? Because you deserve it. You're an amazing man."

"What if I'm not? What if it's not meant to be?"

"Of course it is. You love Kelly, you always have. You were very bitter over your breakup when I met you."

"I'm not sure."

"What do you mean? Something's not right, you've always loved her."

"I never had doubts?"

Talya thought about it. She wasn't sure but she didn't want to influence him in any way either. Because last time she talked him out of marrying Kelly, she caused his death. "No, Jere. Not that I'm aware of," she said carefully.

"I feel sick."

She forced a laugh. "Pre-wedding jitters. It's nothing. Just nerves." Yet she didn't have them when she married him, did she? Was it a telling sign? A premonition?

"I've had three different people tell me I didn't have to go through with this."

Oh no. Others could see the problem? What was wrong now? Was it something she caused?

"And," he continued, "you have always been in the back of my mind. A childhood crush on a figment of my imagination. Always wondering, are you real or aren't you? Will you be back, or won't you? Should I marry her or wait for you?"

"I'm the reason you're wondering if you should marry? Oh, oh, that's not supposed to happen."

"Why not?"

"Well, you're supposed to get married."

"How do you know?"

Because you can have children with her and you can't with me. And that seven-year-old little boy wanted a child to love and never leave.

"I just do."

"If I'm meant to be with her, why am I unsure?"

"I don't know, Jere. Unless it's something I've done."

"What do you have to do with it?"

"Every time I go back into the past, I warp something new. I don't know how but maybe I've done something this time."

There was a soft knock on the door. Natalya slid stealthily behind the drapes of the window, years of experience as The Huntress taking control. While she couldn't be seen, she also couldn't see. But she could hear everything.

"Hey, man. How ya holding up?" said a male voice.

"I'm good. Why?"

"Just checking up. That's all."

There was quiet for a while before the stranger said, "You know, you don't have to go through with this, right?"

"What do you mean?"

"If you're not sure about things, it's not too late to call them off. It's never too late to call things off."

"Why would you think I'd want to stop the wedding?"

"I'm not saying that, Jere. I'm just saying take your time, be sure about things."

"We talked about this yesterday, Shawn. Everything's set. I can't disappoint her just because I'm unsure."

There was a big sigh. "Okay, fine. We'll be here for you no matter what."

She waited until she heard the door click shut before she emerged from behind the curtains.

When he turned to face her, his eyes were bleak.

Wordlessly, she held out her arms. He was between them in a heartbeat. It felt like she'd never hold him again, so she pressed in tight.

At this moment he was alive. He was well and he was hers. She was desperate, holding her emotions in check but so scared that she'd screw this up and wipe him out with the slightest mistake.

For wasn't she the queen of mistakes? It didn't matter who or what was involved, if there was something to screw up, she'd do it.

"I'm still not so sure I should be with her. She's all I know and something feels off."

"It's because I changed the pattern of things. Nothing that you know right now is as it should be. That's all you're sensing. Nothing else."

"What's my relationship with you?" he asked suddenly.

"I can't share that. The more you know, the more that might change the future. Again."

"You keep fixing it."

"I have to. I keep screwing it up. But, Jere, this is my last chance. I don't have any other options on how to travel, so I'm really worried. Please, trust me. Go through with the marriage."

"If I love her, why am I tempted by you?"

"I'm just new. A mystery. That's all. It's nothing."

"But I should be sure. In either case, I should know what I want."

"Trust me, you want her. You want your marriage to her."

"Then why do I feel like this?" he muttered harshly and ground his lips to hers.

She wasn't ready for it. There was no time to protest, no time to think about not enjoying what was offered to her. She liquefied, from deep in her belly, to trickle between her thighs.

"We shouldn't do this," she protested when she could pull away at last. It was a halfhearted attempt at best and they both knew it.

"If this is the last chance, then why not?" he whispered. "I'll be safely married, you'll go back to the future. All we'll have is our memories. Let's make them good."

He was the most sinful temptation she'd ever known. And she'd caused many to stray. A niggling little doubt still rooted in her brain, however. Was she making the future even worse for him? But what if this was it? Could she return to her own life without this last chance with the love of her life?

The one man she'd once tossed carelessly aside?

He tired of waiting for her to make up her mind. He moved in and kissed her. Long and deep and it made her melt. She felt the liquid gather deep inside her. His tongue swept her mouth, slowly at first and then faster as he sensed her need. He thrust into her, showing her with his mouth what it would be like when he sank into her with his cock.

She was a horny demon. There was no way she had any willpower to preach to him about marrying another within the hour. Her mind justified that Kelly would have him the rest of her life, she just got Jere this last time. One last time.

She broke from the sensuous kiss long enough to mutter, "Please. I'll get undressed, you just unzip and release your cock, okay?"

"Okay," he agreed, before locking his mouth to hers. "You're like a dream come true. You kiss just like I thought you would," he said between kisses. Together their hands worked to pull her clothes off, leaving her bare and tanned and smooth beneath his touch.

He sat her in the armchair, swinging both her legs over the arms. Then he slipped his hands under her butt, pulling her forward to the edge. His mouth dipped, tasting her as she gasped at the first pass of his tongue.

She was delicate and pink and ready for loving. Spread open waiting for his wet suck. He sucked her pussy into his mouth, rolling her swollen lips into his hot warmth as she squirmed, her hands gripping her inner thighs as if she could spread them further. He inserted a finger into her sheath as he sucked, feeling the liquid honey gather to welcome his wide cock.

"Jere," she moaned. "You're so good. You make me want to come so hard."

He looked up at her. "Do you want to come in my mouth, sweet?"

She nodded shakily, afraid to voice the words lest she explode then and there. His tongue playing against her clitoris, flicking over and over, massaging it with velvety softness.

Then he grabbed it between his thumb and forefinger, pinching gently, and pulled it into his mouth for a hard suck.

She exploded into a starburst of light, her entire midsection quaking with the force of her climax.

Her open pussy spasmed when he rose to his knees and inserted his long cock deep into her pussy.

It was an overload of sensation, the wondrous right feeling of him inserted where he should be.

He moved in and out, thrusting as hard as he wanted. She snaked a finger down to her clitoris and began to manipulate it into another orgasm now that she had a thick penis filling her.

Rhythmically she stroked as she thrust her hips to meet his movements, tightening her sheath around him with quick movements as she clenched her inner muscles.

He was breathing hard and she knew he fought his orgasm until she was ready again. So she let loose, pulling his mouth to hers while she climaxed around him.

He groaned, thrusting his own climax into her while he thrust his tongue into her mouth.

She loved this moment, after sex. When her body still had tremors of aftershocks, when his body was still locked deep in hers, slowly softening. He was on his knees, his head resting on her bare breasts.

It felt perfect. So right.

"I can't do it," he said, raising his head. "I can't marry her."

"Listen to me," she said, cupping his cheek. "You have to. This is the last travel I get. I couldn't bear it if I messed up again. You have to go through with the marriage to Kelly."

Because I can never, ever give you the children you crave, my love.

He looked directly at her. Slowly he nodded, before clenching his eyes shut. "Okay."

The door banged open to show the redheaded bride.

"What the hell's the hold-up—" Kelly stopped and her eyes rounded with shock. "Oh you bastard," she screamed.

Oh no. Not yet. Not now. Desperately, Talya tried to hold onto Jere but her body lightened, fading away, lighter and lighter, until she was gone.

Chapter Nine
Living Anew

෨

She faded away, much like she had when Keara's power had worn off. But this time when she returned, it was to watch a scene replay while she stood by, invisible. As she stood there, her body was drawn to the bed, where a version of herself lay, talking to Keara. It was the scene when Enishka had burned out her eggs, before the first time she traveled.

"You get help before you continue to hurt everyone around you. Before you screw up both worlds, instead of just one," the now-Keara said.

"Then wipe me out, dammit. I know you can. I'm useless, I can't rule Luciefyiore and I can't get myself out of the damned Earth dimension. Just strike me dead," she heard herself say.

She'd forgotten how much she meant it at the time. She certainly didn't feel that way anymore and wanted to stop the first time she said it.

Her invisible body and soul were being pulled into the bed, when it wanted to merge with itself. While she was being sucked to the past self, she watched herself rise from the bed. She slammed into herself, present and past colliding, all at once collapsing on weakened knees.

Just like the first time, she fell on the floor.

Although then she had no idea what caused her to weaken so to nearly faint.

There was a long bout of silence while Keara studied her. An uncanny silence. Did this Keara now know what was going on all this time? Both times? "That would be too easy, to give up, wouldn't it? I never thought The Huntress would take the easy road," she said.

"Do it, damn you. I know you still have powers inside you that Enishka didn't get. We all saw you rearrange his face." She fought against the words but apparently, she didn't have control over changing what had been said previously.

"I'll show you some power, little sister. But be careful what you wish for."

She tried again. "Keara, wait!" she shouted, showing more strength than she had. Physically, she was slaughtered. Emotionally, she was exhausted. She'd forgotten how much pain she was in after the burning of her eggs, the brutal surgery and cauterizing she had taken from Enishka.

Keara looked expectantly at her.

Natalya didn't have a clue how she'd explain that this scene already happened. "Jere. I want Jere," she gasped, frustrated tears from the sting in her heart rolling down her cheeks.

She was barely aware of Keara leaving the room and Jere slipping back in but there he was, gathering her up into his arms while she sobbed like a weakling. A baby.

Like a human.

He was actually here. He was actually real. He carried her to a chair and rocked her gently, smoothing her hair, murmuring sweet words she couldn't catch. How could she tell him how badly she missed him? How could she explain how close he was to being dead? She consoled herself with touching him constantly, her fingers on his forearm, his biceps. Her other hand slipped behind him and underneath his shirt to feel his back beneath her fingers.

"I don't care," she hiccupped. "I don't care that you get to rule instead of me. I'm so sorry for the way I hurt you. But I couldn't leave you stuck with me, a worthless demon, for a marriage that was just supposed to be a moment's fun."

"What's this?" he said, brushing fruitlessly at the tears that ran down her cheeks like rivers. "Who would dare call my wife worthless?" His tone was gentle, as if he tried to tease but sensed her honesty. "I'll always protect you, my love. I always have. You know that. You don't need horns."

"I'm worthless, Jere. My horns are gone, my eggs are gone and you know what? You've wanted kids since you were seven."

"Kid," he corrected. "Maybe I sobbed out that I wanted lots of kids when I was young, but as I got older, I just wanted one, someone I could love and who would love me unconditionally. Someone I would never leave, like my mother left me."

"I have nothing to offer you."

He lifted her chin. "Then what do I have to offer you? I'm just a half-breed, remember? Not full-blooded demon."

She looked appalled. "You have so much to offer. You're the rightful ruler of Luciefyiore. You're the biggest catch of the dimension, who cares if you're half demon? You still have demon blood. You're still one of us."

"Then quit crying, princess. You and I are walking through that door, we're having dinner with the Van Trumps and we're sending them back to Earth early so we have time alone together."

"So everything is all right this time?"

"I don't know which time you're talking about," he laughed. "Come on."

Hand in hand, they were out the bedroom door before she even realized it. Noise came from farther down the hallway.

The house looked unfamiliar but oddly familiar too. Was it hers, or Keara's? Had she really realized how similar they were before? It was odd, one on Earth, one on Luciefyiore but the same floor plans. The same color schemes. Who would have guessed it?

And then she caught on to what he said. "We're sending them home early so we can have naked time, right?"

He pulled her into him, bringing her pelvis right up against him. Letting her feel his need. "Yes, princess. You and me."

She met his kiss eagerly. This was it. This was the right path. Demitris did it. He'd corrected the broken trail she'd left in her wake.

She moaned softly when Jere's tongue invaded her mouth. She tasted him, he was exactly the same as she remembered.

"You let me talk you into marriage when you knew you were a mixed-breed," she murmured.

"Yes." His face was hard, showing no remorse.

"Why?"

"I wanted you to be mine in both worlds."

"Back then?"

"Yes, my love."

"I love you, Jere. So much. I didn't tell you before. I want to tell you now."

He smiled, as if he'd always known it. "As I love you. Talya. Just as I always have. It's you and me together forever, my naughty little demoness."

A voice interrupted. "Geez, not again. Mommy, why can't my Aunt Tally and Uncle Jere fight like normal people in Luciefyiore instead of kissing all the time?"

Natalya almost fainted from the shock. There between Keara and Caleb stood a small child dressed in ruffles and lace. Blond and angelic with her blue eyes.

Wearing reddish horns the exact color of Jere's.

"Talya?" Jere asked, staring at her reaction. "You okay?"

But Talya was stuck staring at the child's features, the combination of genes between her husband and Keara and

Caleb. The gene pool was a funny thing, toss in a relative and watch the sparks fly.

In any case, it was the child she could never have. The child who had none of her features whatsoever.

"Your aunt's not feeling well, sugar. Go get her a glass of water, will you?" Keara said softly.

"Come with daddy, babydoll," Caleb said, scooping the child into his arms.

As soon as they left, Talya voiced what was stuck on her brain. "H-how? My eggs were still burned out by Enishka. Right? I can never rule again because I am infertile? Yet you have borne a child? My niece who looks remarkably like Jere?"

"Yes," Keara said. "She does look like her uncle. She's too young to rule Luciefyiore, but someday she may choose to. You and Jere are her guardians here. She lives on Earth with Caleb and me, but she comes to you for her demonic training. No demon should ever have to deny their heritage."

Jere pulled her back into his arms, resting his chin on her head. "You and I still rule Luciefyiore as guardians for Randi."

Natalya looked over at Keara, still slightly unsure. "What's happening now? At this time?"

"Where were you left last, Talya?"

"The last thing I remember, I was banished to Earth. Couldn't return to Luciefyiore until I caused true love. But then I was to be returned to Luciefyiore without my powers, dead meat."

"I'm going to leave you two to catch up," Jere murmured. "But everything will be fine, my love. Your memories of the last few years will return," he said, kissing her forehead.

Both women watched him leave before Keara continued. "Okay. So you're in Luciefyiore now."

"What?" Natalya scrambled to a window and threw open the curtains. Sure enough, the sky was overcast with a reddish hue so unlike the strange blue of the Earth dimension. "I'm back? How is that possible? And why do our houses look the same?"

Keara smiled. "We redecorated, you and I." Then she grew serious. "You fulfilled your sentencing, Talya. You were to cause unselfish love without your powers. You were stripped of your horns to make sure you didn't use them."

"The love?"

"You corrected Jere's life over and over. Until you gave him the happiness you thought he deserved. Even with Kelly."

"He loved her."

"He loved you, silly."

"Later, maybe. But I didn't deserve it, Keara. That's why I fixed it with Kelly."

"It wasn't meant to be. But you unselfishly tried to give him what you thought he wanted. Who you thought he loved. It still wasn't meant to be, Talya. Kelly left him the third time when he called out your name on their wedding night. He missed you and knew it was wrong. She ran sobbing to the arms of a man she was having an affair with the whole time."

"So I'm still married to Jere?"

"Yes. And together you rule Luciefyiore. Although you can't have any children, you never seemed like you wanted any. I'm actually envious of the freedom you and Jere enjoy." She sighed. "Caleb and Miranda and I visit here often, when she's not staying with you."

"Miranda?" Talya hadn't remembered the child's name.

"Auntie Tally!"

The miniature five-year-old Keara re-entered the room, riding piggyback on Jere's back. "I lost to the little monster," teased Jere. "Now Randi and I have to play Barbies. And some of them are missing their horns."

"They got losted," she said, giggling as he bounced her down the hallway. "Broken off, like my Auntie Tally's."

Natalya still stared after the two.

"I take it you've never seen Randi?" Keara asked gently.

"You were pregnant the last time I was here. So much is different now."

"You'll get used to it. It's as it should be." Keara leaned in. "You know, your husband fought for your memories to be returned within a night of your return time travel, don't you? That's why he promised you everything would be fine."

Natalya turned her full attention to her. "Why? What did he trade?"

"You'll have to ask him."

Natalya nodded, distracted by the image Jere made with Randi. He was so handsome, the man she loved. Even now, he would take care of her. She began to walk away. "Keara!" Natalya called out, turning suddenly. "Thank you for that last fix. That bit of information."

"Thank you for the last fix you gave me once." Keara winked. "Dean's impotence."

Natalya laughed. She'd never realized that Keara knew she'd gone after the human who had treated Keara so poorly. He'd been the first one in her Luciefyiore harem.

"You girls are dangerous when you get together," murmured a now familiar voice at her ear.

Her husband.

The strangeness wasn't as shocking as it was earlier. But the butterflies floated deliciously in her belly. He cuddled her, an arm wrapped around her waist. His lips nibbled at her earlobe.

"Later. When everyone's in bed," he whispered, his palm splayed on her abdomen. Heat from the open palm radiated throughout her midsection.

Her husband.

The man she loved. The other half of her soul. No matter which race he was born, demon or human or mixed. The man meant for her.

Her husband.

She was starting to remember.

Memories were hitting her, like the snippets of a five-year dream. She kept calm, letting them wash through her as she stared out the picture window of her living room at the sundown.

The Earthlings called it a sunset.

At this time of the day, you could watch the changes in her dimension. Landmarks shifted and shadow creatures walked. No wonder the humans thought this dimension was hell.

While she watched, a tree morphed into a creature with the roughened features of a wooden man. He pulled his outstretched limbs from the sky and used his finger-leaves to help yank new legs from the suddenly soft, spongy ground. Slowly he walked from the yard, touching objects in wonderment, a trailing path of leaves falling behind him.

Talya almost laughed when she remembered how the humans spent countless, back-breaking hours in their yards. They'd die the first time a plant transformed into a creature and walked away.

Her husband appeared behind her. Warm hands wrapped her in his strength, pulling her back into him to whisper in her ear. "And you thought it was weird that we eat the ugly little pink creatures."

"I still think that's weird," she laughed, but stopped when a warm breath rolled across the side of her neck. He nibbled on her earlobe until she moaned, then slipped his hands under her shirt to feel her flat stomach. "Your hand's warm," she said, and caught her breath when he plunged it into the waistband of her pants. He cupped her mound, letting her feel the warmth of his palm there.

He let his middle finger dance against her clitoris, making the sensitive organ swell delightfully with his ministrations. She sighed.

"I love when you do that," he said.

"Do what?"

"Sigh, like I'm the only one in your world."

"You are. I don't need anyone but you."

"Exactly how I feel, princess. Now let's get to bed so I can take your clothes off one by one."

Talya pouted. "I wanted it with me sitting on the kitchen counter tonight."

"Tomorrow night," he promised. "Everyone's gone tomorrow, we'll have it on the stairs if we want."

It was more of a race to their bedroom. No sooner had they shut the door when clothes were flung off. His finger was deep inside her, twisting wonderfully when she said, "Jere?"

"Hm?" he asked, her stiff nipple in his mouth.

"Lean back," she whispered.

As always, he complied with her wishes.

Bending at the waist, she licked a trail from his bellybutton to where the head of his hard cock protruded upward. It was flushed with passion, veins trailing over the smooth surface. She heard his gasp as she engulfed the mushroom shape into the wetness of her mouth.

Jere reciprocated by licking his finger and reinserting it deep into her pussy.

She cupped his balls with her hand, massaging them gently as she moved her head up and down on his slick shaft. He mimicked her movements as he finger-fucked her.

"Oh Tally," he groaned. "Sit on my face before you make me come."

She released his rock-hard cock from her mouth, turned herself around and straddled his body. She watched his face as she moved up farther onto his chest. He was staring at the hidden delights of her cunt.

She decided to help him enjoy the view.

She spread the lips of her pussy so he would have a better glimpse inside, and he dug his fingers into her hips in his haste to scoot her closer to his mouth. She lowered her open sex onto his waiting mouth.

"Oh," she muttered at the first sensation of his suck. "Yes, Jere. That's it."

He was sucking hard, as if he couldn't get enough of the wet, juicy pussy over his face. Her slick juice flowed over his chin.

She was too close to coming, heat washed over the exposed, sensitive clitoris that he flicked with his tongue. She ground herself against him when he reached up to pull and twist her nipples. Suddenly, her climax ripped through her body.

She was so limp and quivery, she was scarcely aware of him laying her on her back and spreading her thighs. He plunged into her flooded pussy full-force, myriad expressions crossing his face as he entered.

Talya lifted her legs up over his shoulders and he began to fuck her fiercely, reaching deep inside as if they could become one. He was triggering another explosion within her, one that caught her breath in wonder.

"I'm coming again," she breathed. "Faster, Jere. Fuck me harder."

With her legs up like that, he looked down into her eyes. He fingered the rim of her ass before he dipped deliberately into the tiny hole.

"Ahh," she screamed and watched the corded tendons pop out on his neck as his face contorted before his own orgasm exploded within her passage, flooding her with his cum.

Epilogue
October 30

๛

The Rousseau family always spent the holidays on the Earth dimension with the Van Trumps. It was more fun there, especially with the wacky humans celebrating Halloween.

Together, they made their way up the well-worn path. Talya's feet slowed as they passed the train station.

"What is it?" Jere asked.

"So many memories here. It's where I first saw you, you know. Before I time-traveled the first time when you were seven."

An elderly woman wrapped in furs and dripping with diamonds pranced by in six-inch fuck-me pumps, her hand held tightly onto the leash of a full-sized white poodle.

"Is that...yes, it is!" Natalya said in wonderment as a man half her plastic-enhanced age strode up and caressed her derriere through the spandex. The old woman giggled as she puckered her shiny, glittered red lips and batted her mascara-thickened lashes.

A female tarantula.

"I missed my calling," Talya murmured. "I should have been a witch. That was one doozy of a spell. I even got rid of the urine stench."

Also by Rena Marks

☙

Born Again
Boy Toy
Forgotten Kisses
Man Candy
Plaything
Shared by Wolves

About the Author

ℵ

During my daytime job, I explore people of all types. At night, I love to read.

Why did I start writing? My favorite authors were all between books and I twiddled my thumbs until deciding, "Hey, I can do this for someone else out there who's waiting for a new release too!" My favorite authors in no particular order include: Kim Harrison, Laurell K Hamilton, Jim Butcher, Charlaine Harris and Kelley Armstrong. So obviously, I cling to urban fantasy type work with one difference—I'm a romance author at heart. I must have my happy ending with Prince Charming. And no, it doesn't matter if he has fangs. Or fur. As long as he's naked, we'll be just fine! Therefore, Ellora's Cave seems a perfect fit for my work.

Join me for a few hours and get lost in my worlds! For now at night, I love to write!

Rena welcomes comments from readers. You can find her website and email address on her author bio page at www.ellorascave.com.

Tell Us What You Think

We appreciate hearing reader opinions about our books. You can email us at Comments@EllorasCave.com.

Why an electronic book?

We live in the Information Age — an exciting time in the history of human civilization, in which technology rules supreme and continues to progress in leaps and bounds every minute of every day. For a multitude of reasons, more and more avid literary fans are opting to purchase e-books instead of paper books. The question from those not yet initiated into the world of electronic reading is simply: *Why?*

1. *Price.* An electronic title at Ellora's Cave Publishing and Cerridwen Press runs anywhere from 40% to 75% less than the cover price of the exact same title in paperback format. Why? Basic mathematics and cost. It is less expensive to publish an e-book (no paper and printing, no warehousing and shipping) than it is to publish a paperback, so the savings are passed along to the consumer.

2. *Space.* Running out of room in your house for your books? That is one worry you will never have with electronic books. For a low one-time cost, you can purchase a handheld device specifically designed for e-reading. Many e-readers have large, convenient screens for viewing. Better yet, hundreds of titles can be stored within your new library — on a single microchip. There are a variety of e-readers from different manufacturers. You can also read e-books on your PC or laptop computer. (Please note that Ellora's Cave does not endorse any specific brands.

You can check our websites at www.ellorascave.com or www.cerridwenpress.com for information we make available to new consumers.)

3. *Mobility.* Because your new e-library consists of only a microchip within a small, easily transportable e-reader, your entire cache of books can be taken with you wherever you go.

4. *Personal Viewing Preferences.* Are the words you are currently reading too small? Too large? Too... ANNOYING? Paperback books cannot be modified according to personal preferences, but e-books can.

5. *Instant Gratification.* Is it the middle of the night and all the bookstores near you are closed? Are you tired of waiting days, sometimes weeks, for bookstores to ship the novels you bought? Ellora's Cave Publishing sells instantaneous downloads twenty-four hours a day, seven days a week, every day of the year. Our webstore is never closed. Our e-book delivery system is 100% automated, meaning your order is filled as soon as you pay for it.

Those are a few of the top reasons why electronic books are replacing paperbacks for many avid readers.

As always, Ellora's Cave and Cerridwen Press welcome your questions and comments. We invite you to email us at Comments@ellorascave.com or write to us directly at Ellora's Cave Publishing Inc., 1056 Home Avenue, Akron, OH 44310-3502.

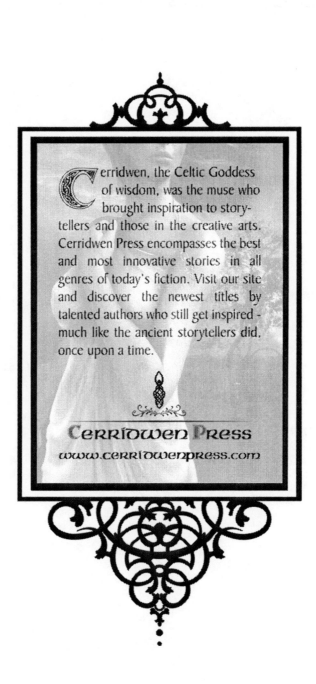

erridwen, the Celtic Goddess of wisdom, was the muse who brought inspiration to storytellers and those in the creative arts. Cerridwen Press encompasses the best and most innovative stories in all genres of today's fiction. Visit our site and discover the newest titles by talented authors who still get inspired - much like the ancient storytellers did, once upon a time.